ULTIMATE ENTROPY

"I wonder if the Timekeepers realize the damage," said Lucas.

"I wonder if they care?" said Forrester. "Their so-called movement has been effectively destroyed. There can only be a handful of them left. Can you think of a better way to go out than having brought about *ultimate entropy*?"

"Is that actually a possibility?" said Andre.

"Delaney seems to think so," Forrester said.

"But that would mean . . ." Andre's voice trailed off.

"The end of time," said Lucas softly.

4 TIMEWARS

THE ZENDA VENDETTA

BY
SIMON HAWKE

HEADLINE

ISBN 0 7472 3087 0

Printed and bound in Great Britain by
Collins, Glasgow

HEADLINE BOOK PUBLISHING PLC
Headline House
79 Great Titchfield Street
London W1P 7FN

For Robert M. Powers
with friendship and respect

"Illegitimati non carborundum"

A CHRONOLOGICAL HISTORY OF THE TIME WARS

April 1, 2425:   Dr. Wolfgang Mensinger invents the chronoplate at the age of 115, discovering time travel. Later he would construct a small scale working prototype for use in laboratory experiments specially designed to avoid any possible creation of a temporal paradox. He is hailed as the "Father of Temporal Physics."

July 14, 2430:   Mensinger publishes "There Is No Future," in which he redefines relativity, proving that there is no such thing as *the* future, but an infinite number of potential future scenarios which are absolute relative only to their present. He also announces the discovery of "nonspecific time" or temporal limbo, later known as "the dead zone."

October 21, 2440:   Wolfgang Mensinger dies. His son, Albrecht, perfects the chronoplate and carries on the work, but loses control of the discovery to political interests.

June 15, 2460:	Formation of the international Committee for Temporal Intelligence, with Albrecht Mensinger as director. Specially trained and conditioned "agents" of the committee begin to travel back through time in order to conduct research and field test the chronoplate apparatus. Many become lost in transition, trapped in the limbo of nonspecific time known as "the dead zone." Those who return from successful temporal voyages often bring back startling information necessitating the revision of historical records.
March 22, 2461:	*The Consorti Affair*—Cardinal Lodovico Consorti is excommunicated from the Roman Catholic Church for proposing that agents travel back through time to obtain empirical evidence that Christ arose following His crucifixion. The Consorti Affair sparks extensive international negotiations amidst a volatile climate of public opinion concerning the proper uses for the new technology. Temporal excursions are severely curtailed. Concurrently, espionage operatives of several nations infiltrate the Committee for Temporal Intelligence.
May 1, 2461	Dr. Albrecht Mensinger appears before a special international conference in Geneva, composed of political leaders and members of the scientific community. He attempts to alleviate fears about the possible misuses of time travel. He further refuses to cooperate with any attempts at militarizing his father's discovery.

February 3, 2485:	The research facilities of the Committee for Temporal Intelligence are seized by troops of the Trans-Atlantic Treaty Organization.
January 25, 2492:	The Council of Nations meets in Buenos Aires, capitol of the United Socialist States of South America, to discuss increasing international tensions and economic instability. A proposal for "an end to war in our time" is put forth by the chairman of the Nippon Conglomerate Empire. Dr. Albrecht Mensinger, appearing before the body as nominal director of the Committee for Temporal Intelligence, argues passionately against using temporal technology to resolve international conflicts, but cannot present proof that the past can be affected by temporal voyagers. Prevailing scientific testimony reinforces the conventional wisdom that the past is an immutable absolute.
December 24, 2492:	Formation of the Referee Corps, brought into being by the Council of Nations as an extranational arbitrating body with sole control over temporal technology and authority to stage temporal conflicts as "limited warfare" to resolve international disputes.
April 21, 2493:	On the recommendation of the Referee Corps, a subordinate body named the Observer Corps is formed, taking over most of the functions of the Committee for Temporal Intelligence, which is redesignated as the Temporal Intelligence Agency. Under the aegis of the Council

of Nations and the Referee Corps, the TIA absorbs the intelligence agencies of the world's governments and is made solely answerable to the Referee Corps. Dr. Mensinger resigns his post to found the Temporal Preservation League, a group dedicated to the abolition of temporal conflict.

June, 2497– March, 2502: Referee Corps presides over initial temporal confrontation campaigns, accepting "grievances" from disputing nations, selecting historical conflicts of the past as "staging grounds" and supervising the infiltration of modern troops into the so-called "cannon fodder" ranks of ancient warring armies. Initial numbers of temporal combatants are kept small, with infiltration facilitated by cosmetic surgery and implant conditioning of soldiers. The results are calculated based upon successful return rate and a complicated "point spread." Soldiers are monitored via cerebral implants, enabling Search & Retrieve teams to follow their movements and monitor mortality rate. The media dubs temporal conflicts the "Time Wars."

2500–2510: Extremely rapid growth of massive support industry catering to the exacting art and science of temporal conflict. Rapid improvement in international economic climate follows, with significant growth in productivity and rapid decline in unemployment and inflation rate. There is a gradual escalation of the Time Wars with the majority of the world's armed services converting to temporal duty status.

Growth of the Temporal Preservation League as a peace movement with an intensive lobby effort and mass demonstrations against the Time Wars. Mensinger cautions against an imbalance in temporal continuity due to the increasing activity of the Time Wars.

September 2, 2514: Mensinger publishes his "Theories of Temporal Relativity," incorporating his solution to the Grandfather Paradox and calling once again for a ceasefire in the Time Wars. The result is an upheaval in the scientific community and a hastily reconvened Council of Nations to discuss his findings, leading to the Temporal Strategic Arms Limitations Talks of 2515.

March 15, 2515–
June 1, 2515: T-SALT held in New York City. Mensinger appears before the representatives at the sessions and petitions for an end to the Time Wars. A ceasefire resolution is framed, but tabled due to lack of agreement among the members of the Council of Nations. Mensinger leaves the T-SALT a broken man.

November 18, 2516: Dr. Albrecht Mensinger experiences total nervous collapse shortly after being awarded the Benford Prize.

December 25, 2516: Dr. Albrecht Mensinger commits suicide. Violent demonstrations by members of the Temporal Preservation League.

January 1, 2517: Militant members of the Temporal

Preservation League band together to form the Timekeepers, a terrorist offshoot of the League, dedicated to the complete destruction of the war machine. They announce their presence to the world by assassinating three members of the Referee Corps and bombing the Council of Nations meeting in Buenos Aires, killing several heads of state and injuring many others.

September 17, 2613: Formation of the First Division of the U.S. Army Temporal Corps as a crack commando unit following the successful completion of a "temporal adjustment" involving the first serious threat of a timestream split. The First Division, assigned exclusively to deal with threats to temporal continuity, is designated as "the Time Commandos."

MENSINGER'S THEORIES OF TEMPORAL RELATIVITY___

1. *The Theory of Temporal Inertia.* The "current" of the timestream tends to resist the disruptive influence of temporal discontinuities. The degree of this resistance is dependent upon the coefficient of the magnitude of the disruption and the Uncertainty Principle.

2. *The Principle of Temporal Uncertainty.* The element of uncertainty expressed as a coefficient of temporal inertia represents the "X factor" in temporal continuity. Absolute determination of the degree of deviation from the original, undisrupted scenario is rendered impossible by the lack of total accuracy in historical documentation and research (see Heisenberg's Principle of Uncertainty) and by the presence of historical anomalies as a result either of temporal discontinuities or adjustments thereof.

3. *The Fate Factor.* In the event of a disruption of a magnitude sufficient to affect temporal inertia and create a discontinuity, the Fate Factor, working as a coefficient of temporal inertia, and the element of uncertainty both already present and brought about by the disruption, determine the degree of relative continuity to which the timestream can be restored, contingent upon the effects of the disruption and its adjustment.

4. *The Timestream Split.* In the event of a disruption of a magnitude sufficient to overcome temporal inertia, the effects of the Fate Factor would be canceled out by the overwhelming influence of the resulting discontinuity. The displaced energy of temporal inertia would create a parallel timeline in which the Uncertainty Principle would be the chief governing factor.

PROLOGUE ═══════════

It was a room where time did not exist. Whenever Moses Forrester entered it, he left the 27th century behind and stepped into the limbo of his memories. Here, in his private den, the world of 2619 did not intrude. Outside the door of his small sanctum were his quarters in the section of the TAC-HQ building housing bachelor officers on command staff. From the massive window in his living room that took up one whole wall, Forrester could look out over all of Pendleton Base spread out far below him. At night, the garish glow of the urban blight that was Los Angeles could be seen in the distance. Behind the door, however, there was just one small room with no windows out of which to gaze. There were other things to look at here, all of which called forth panoramic visions of their own.

The door slid aside into a recess as he approached it, the lock responding to his voice speaking the code phrase, "old time not forgotten," and he took two steps inside, the door sliding shut behind him. With a somber expression, he gazed at the many incongruous items displayed about the room which, at first glance, gave it the aspect of a storage place for worthless junk. However, the like of this agglomeration could not be found in any museum.

One wall was floor-to-ceiling bookshelves. Arranged upon

1

the shelves were priceless first editions, ancient tomes, yet all in absolutely mint condition as if they had just come off the presses. The rarity of the titles was matched only by their diversity. It was the library of a scholar with quite eclectic tastes, many titles autographed—*Honoré de Balzac, Sigmund Freud, Fyodor Dostoevski, Mickey Spillane, Barbara Tuchman, Isaac Asimov.*

Hanging upon one wall was a sword, a heavy weapon with an ornately jeweled hilt inlaid with solid gold. It had been taken from the scabbard of a dead knight named Rodrigo Diaz, better known to history as El Cid. Beneath this beautiful broadsword hung a far more plebian-looking weapon, an old and somewhat rusty rapier, a gift to Forrester from one of the officers under his command. It had been discarded by its owner when he had received a better one from George Villiers, the Duke of Buckingham. Major Lucas Priest had known how greatly Forrester would value a blade that had belonged to a Gascon swordsman named D'Artagnan.

Next to the two swords hung a badly weathered powder horn, which had once been the property of an American frontiersman by the name of Daniel Boone. Above it was displayed a long flintlock rifle named "Old Betsy." It had been found near the body of Colonel David Crockett at the Battle of the Alamo. Close by the rifle hung a wicked-looking knife that was only slightly smaller than a Roman short sword. There were many imitations of it throughout later years, but this was the original Bowie knife, rumored to have been forged from a piece of a star.

Displayed in a velvet-lined case was the black powder pistol that had slain Alexander Hamilton in a duel with Aaron Burr. Encased in a small frame upon the wall was a cloth mask once worn by a famous black-clad avenger in the days of Spanish California and, beside it, another pistol, a pearl-handled .45, which had been stolen from the most famous tank commander of them all. On the small writing table, next to a framed letter written to Forrester (though the name by which the author of the letter addressed him was "Murray"), a small block of lucite stood about six inches high. Inside it was a misshapen piece of metal, about the size of a man's thumbnail. It was a jezail bullet which had been removed from the shoulder of an army surgeon attached to the Berkshires (66th Foot) on July 27, 1880. The letter was from the same surgeon, whose life "Murray" had saved at the Battle of Maiwand during the Second Afghan War. The return address was 221B Baker Street.

These and other, less celebrated mementos comprised what was referred to by the soldiers under Forrester's command as "the old man's collection"; to smuggle back an item that was deemed worthy of inclusion was considered a great coup. It was all very much against regulations, but the soldiers of the First Division were given the greater leeway in such things, and rank had its privileges. In the case of Colonel Forrester, those privileges were considerable.

He was the only colonel in the service whom a general would salute. Those who did not know him by sight needed only to glance at his golden division insignia to recognize him. There was only one full bird colonel who wore the number one bisected by the symbol of infinity and that was Moses Forrester, commander of the First Division of the U.S. Army Temporal Corps, leader of the Time Commandos. He owned a chestful of decorations, though he never wore them, preferring the clean and uncluttered uniform of crisp black base fatigues. This rather austere look was more than compensated for by the appearance of the man himself. Tall, barrel-chested, broad-shouldered and completely bald, Forrester looked like nothing less than a tank made of flesh and blood. The only evidence of his great age were his wrinkled, craggy features. His face looked as though it had been sewn from well-worn leather. His hands were huge and gnarled, but the power in his arms was considerable. He could curl an eighty-pound dumbbell easily with just one hand. Everything about him, from his erect carriage to the direct gaze of his deep-set eyes, to the sharp crease in his immaculate fatigues bespoke a soldier. In the Temporal Army Corps, Forrester was the most widely respected soldier of them all.

The men and women under his command performed the most unenviable job a soldier could be called upon to do. They were the guardians of history, assigned exclusively to deal with temporal disruptions created by the actions of the Time Wars. Forrester was proud of his command and of the work they did. His one great regret was that he no longer accompanied

them on their hazardous missions to Minus Time. His days in
the field were now over. After a lifetime spent fighting on the
battlegrounds of history, he was now firmly stuck in time, in
the 27th century, on a large military base in Southern California. He lived in luxurious quarters located in the heights of the
Temporal Army Command Headquarters; he ate and drank
nothing but the best; he had orderlies to see to his needs and he
lived the full if regimented life of an officer and a gentleman.
Yet it was not enough, far from it.

He longed for the old days. During the quiet times, a great
wistfulness would sometimes come upon him. At such times,
he would enter his den, light up a pipe, pour himself a glass of
wine, and toast his memories. He would gaze at the collected
artifacts and books, select one item or another, run his fingers
over it, and smile as the memories flooded back to him.

Here was the pith helmet he had worn when he served under
"Chinese" Gordon at Khartoum. Here was the iron cross
which Otto Skorzeny himself had pinned on him for saving the
German commando leader's life during the raid to free Il
Duce. Here was the cutlass he had carried when he sailed
under the freebooter, Sir Henry Morgan. And here was the
most significant memento of them all—a lock of raven black
hair kept in a tiny enameled box.

It was the one item not prominently displayed. He kept it in
the left-hand drawer of the ancient rosewood writing table at
which Lord Byron penned his poems. He never took it out.
Now, for the first time in many years, he took out the tiny
box, holding it in his hand as if it were a sacred object. His
eyes softened as he thought of the woman it betokened. She
was long dead, her dust stirred by the passage of some eight
hundred years. It had been one of only two times in an incredibly long life, even by the life-extended standards of the
27th century, that he had ever been in love. Both loves had
been ill-fated. Both were part of a past he had tried hard to
forget, never with complete success. Those memories were
very fresh now. Painfully so. He held the tiny box in one hand
and a letter in the other. Each represented one of those two
loves. One woman was long dead; the other, whom he had
thought dead, was still very much alive. She had reached out
across the centuries to unite them all and twist the knife.

He had received the letter earlier that evening, delivered by a bonded courier from New York. However, it had been written in another city, in another country, in another time. He sat down at the rosewood writing table, placing his elbows on it, pressing the letter in one hand and the enameled box in the other against his temples. He sat that way for a long, long time, his eyes shut, his breathing laborious. The past had finally caught up to him and this time, there was no escape.

1

As the train pulled out of the Dresden station in a cloud of steam and early morning mist, Rudolf Rassendyll sat in the dining car over a light breakfast, trying to recall where he had seen the scar-faced man before. The object of his ruminations sat several tables away from him, drinking coffee. They had exchanged several glances and Rassendyll found the situation somewhat embarrassing. Clearly, the man remembered him from somewhere and was awaiting some sign of recognition. With none forthcoming, he must have thought that Rassendyll was slighting him. To stall for time while he racked his brain for some clue as to the man's identity, Rassendyll hid behind his copy of *The Strand Magazine*, pretending to read while he kept glancing furtively at the scar-faced man, hoping to jog his memory into remembering where they had met.

He was an unusually large man with the broad shoulders of a laborer and big, muscular arms. However, he was quite obviously not of the working class. The large ruby ring he wore on his left hand indicated that he was a gentleman of some means, as did the diamond stickpin, the gold watch chain, and the elegant, gold-headed ebony walking stick he carried. His suit was the height of Parisian fashion, but the man did not look French. His dark complexion and curly black hair gave him a Slavic aspect that was further borne out by the high forehead, the strong nose, the prominent jawline, and the square chin. His eyes, which one might have expected to be dark, were a surprisingly brilliant shade of emerald green. Their bright hue, combined with his dark complexion, gave his gaze a piercing, magnetic quality. His striking good looks were marred only by the scar that ran from beneath his left eye, across the high cheekbone to just above the corner of his mouth. It was arrow-straight, quite likely a dueling scar. Hardly anyone dueled anymore, especially with sabres, except for the young Prussians and the Central Europeans, who were known to drop a glove at the slightest provocation.

The man's posture, the quality of his dress, and his impeccable grooming all spoke of wealth and breeding. Taking into account his Slavic features, the dueling scar, the expensive clothing and the man's carriage, Rassendyll deduced that he was probably a Balkan, a nobleman from one of the small mountain principalities perhaps. This deduction was facilitated by the fact that they were aboard a train that was heading for the Balkan frontier, but Rassendyll decided that not even Sherlock Holmes himself could have done better under the circumstances. Unfortunately, he was still no closer to recalling the man's name, although he seemed to remember now that they had met in London fairly recently, at some sort of function. In another moment, surely, he would have him placed.

The scar-faced man glanced up and saw Rassendyll staring at him intently. Immediately, Rassendyll averted his gaze, but he was too late. The scar-faced man stood up and approached his table.

"I beg your pardon," he said in a startlingly deep and resonant voice. "Forgive me for intruding, but I seem to have the strongest feeling that we have met somewhere before."

"You're English?" Rassendyll said with surprise. The man spoke in English, without a trace of an accent, which made Rassendyll disappointed at having guessed so far off the mark regarding his nationality.

"I have spent a great deal of time in England," the man said, "but I am not a native. Permit me to introduce myself.

The name is Drakov. Nikolai Drakov.''

"Rudolf Rassendyll, at your service." They shook hands and Rassendyll felt slightly vindicated.

"Rassendyll?" said Drakov, frowning slightly. "By any chance, would you be a relation of Lord Burlesdon's?"

"Robert is my brother," said Rassendyll. Suddenly, it came to him and he struck his forehead with the palm of his hand. "But of course! I saw you at a party hosted by my brother several weeks ago in London, in honor of the new Serbian ambassador. You were the chap escorting that dazzling Countess Sophia! Forgive me, my dear fellow, for having such an abominable memory. Won't you join me?"

They sat down opposite each other at the table. "No need for apologies," said Drakov. "As I recall now, we were never formally introduced."

"Yes, well, Robert's parties do tend to be somewhat informal, despite their size," said Rassendyll.

"Still, I can hardly blame you for having failed to place me at once," said Drakov, with a smile. "Next to the countess, I must have been quite invisible."

Rassendyll laughed. "Hardly, old chap! It would take quite a bit of doing to render a man of your formidable dimensions invisible! How is the lovely countess?"

"As lovely as ever," Drakov said. "As it happens, I am just now on my way to join her in Strelsau."

"What a coincidence!" said Rassendyll. "I, too, am traveling to Strelsau! Doubtless, you are going there to attend the coronation of Rudolf Elphberg?"

"I am to escort the countess to the coronation," Drakov said.

"Perhaps, then, you will introduce me," Rassendyll said. "I did not have the opportunity to meet the countess in London. I could not seem to break through the throng of admirers she was surrounded by. To tell the truth, I felt myself at a bit of a disadvantage in that witty crowd. Though I'm ordinarily a garrulous fellow, I tend to stammer like a schoolboy in the presence of a beautiful woman."

Drakov smiled. "I doubt you would have had that problem with the countess. She has quite a way about her. You should have asked Lady Burlesdon to introduce you. The two of them seemed quite taken with each other."

"Yes, that's just like Rose," said Rassendyll. "Lady Burlesdon takes her position in society quite seriously. She has a knack for insinuating herself into the center of attention, or as close to it as possible."

Drakov raised his eyebrows. "I seem to sense a note of disapproval."

Rassendyll grimaced. "The disapproval is more Lady Burlesdon's than mine. Rose considers me the bane of her existence. Not only does she find my lack of industry appalling, but it is a source of constant irritation to her that my features bring to mind the family scandal."

"Scandal?"

"You mean you haven't heard the story? I would have thought that someone would have brought it up that night, at least once."

Drakov frowned. "No, I must confess to ignorance. If it is an awkward topic, perhaps we should—"

"No, no, dear fellow, not a bit of it," said Rassendyll with a wave of his hand. "Frankly, I'm surprised that you've been spared. The so-called skeleton in our family closet sees such frequent display in London society that it is something of an open secret. Since Lady Burlesdon blushes so prettily, some wag always brings it up whenever someone comments on the difference in the coloring between my brother Robert and myself. Though it's something of an embarrassment to the sensitivities of my sister-in-law, I find it somewhat amusing. My father did, as well. He gave me the name of Rudolf because it is an old and common Elphberg name and I was born with what my family refers to as the 'Elphberg Curse'—I mean this rather aristocratic nose of mine and my red hair. I suppose I should explain. As you are on your way to Rudolf Elphberg's coronation, you might find it diverting to hear the story."

"I must admit to being intrigued," said Drakov.

Rassendyll leaned back in his chair and tucked his thumbs into his waistcoat. An inveterate gossip, he delighted in telling the tale afresh to a new listener.

"It happened in 1733," he said, "when George II was sitting on the throne of England. A prince who was later known to history as King Rudolf the Third of Ruritania came on a visit to the English court. He was a tall and handsome fellow marked by a somewhat unusually straight and sharp nose and a mass of dark red hair—in fact, the same nose and hair that have stamped the Elphbergs time out of mind. The prince stayed some months in England, where he was most courteously received, but in the end, he left rather under a cloud. He fought a duel with an English nobleman well known in the society of his day not only for his own merits, but as the husband of an exceedingly beautiful wife."

"Ah," said Drakov, with a knowing grin.

"Yes, quite," said Rassendyll. "In that duel, Prince Rudolf was severely wounded and, recovering therefrom, was adroitly smuggled off by the Ruritanian ambassador, who found him a pretty handful by all accounts. The nobleman in question was not wounded in the duel, but the morning being raw and damp on the occasion of the meeting, he contracted a severe chill. Failing to throw it off, he died some six months after the departure of Prince Rudolf. I should add that he passed on without having found the leisure to adjust his relations with his wife, who after another two months bore an heir to the title and estates of the family of Burlesdon. This lady was the Countess Amelia and her husband was James, fifth Earl of Burlesdon and twenty-second Baron Rassendyll, in both the peerages of England and a Knight of the Garter.

"As for Rudolf, he went back to Ruritania, married and ascended to the throne, whereon his progeny in the direct line have sat from then till this very hour. The results of this episode can be seen today if one were to walk through the picture galleries at Burlesdon. Among the fifty or so portraits of the last century and half, you would find five or six, including that of the sixth earl, distinguished by sharp noses and a quantity of dark red hair. These five or six also have blue eyes, whereas among the Rassendylls, dark eyes are the commoner. So now, the occasional appearance among the dark-haired Rassendylls of a red head such as mine brings to mind Countess Amelia's indiscretion. Some might consider it Fate's way

of smirking at my cuckolded ancestor, but I see it as a romantic reminder of a refreshing episode in an otherwise crashingly
dull family history. I fear that Lady Burlesdon does not share
my view of it, however, which would account for her having
neglected to introduce me to the charming countess and yourself. Actually, it would please her no end if I were to make my
residence in Ireland or someplace equally far removed from
her social circle."

Drakov chuckled. "I see no reason why she should concern
herself. Even the finest of bloodlines have less than noble
tributaries, though that would hardly be the case in your situation. Your Countess Amelia might have done far worse than
to dally with an Elphberg, and a prince, at that. So you and
Rudolf the Fifth are cousins, then! How extraordinary! I take
it that you are enroute to the coronation as a representative of
the English branch of the family, so to speak?"

"Dear me, no!" said Rassendyll. "That would be highly in-
delicate of me, I should think. No, I have received no formal
invitation and I go as a representative of no one save myself.
In fact, if Robert knew that I were going he would not ap-
prove, and poor Rose would be absolutely beside herself with
shock at my impropriety. Lady Burlesdon is very proper in all
things, you see. She is determined to do something about me
and her latest scheme is to saddle old Sir Jacob Borrodaile
with my humble self as an attaché. He's to be posted to an em-
bassy somewhere. Frankly, I haven't the foggiest notion of
what it is that an attaché is supposed to do. If it isn't very
much, who knows? I may even find it to my liking."

Both men laughed.

"So you see," continued Rassendyll, "with the imminence
of this attaché business, it would appear that my days of
leisure are numbered. Therefore, I decided upon a holiday to
celebrate the final days of my indolence. Upon reading in *The
Times* of the impending coronation in Ruritania, I became
seized with a sudden desire to see how the other half lives. In
order to spare my sister-in-law any anxiety, I put it about that
I was off on a hunting trip to the Tyrol. Not a soul knows that
I am on my way to Strelsau save yourself. It may sound a bit
clandestine, but I merely intend to observe the proceedings

from a quite respectful distance, do a little fishing and shooting in the countryside, and then depart for home and a life of depressing diplomatic drudgery.''

"I commend you on your discretion, Mr. Rassendyll," said Drakov. He reached into the pocket of his coat and withdrew a slender flask. "Some brandy for your coffee, perhaps?"

"The very thing!" said Rassendyll. He held out his cup and Drakov poured a small amount into the coffee, whereupon the flask trickled dry.

"Oh, dear," said Rassendyll. "It appears that I have taken your last."

"Think nothing of it," Drakov said. "I have another bottle in my compartment. In fact, perhaps you'd care to join me there for brandy and a cigar or two?"

"A capital idea!" said Rassendyll. "I must say, this promises to be a most pleasant journey."

They adjourned to Drakov's compartment after a few moments, where they opened a bottle of Napoleon brandy. From an elegantly finished gentleman's necessary case lined with plush red velvet, Drakov removed two small glass snifters and poured for them both. Then he offered Rassendyll a handsomely crafted cigar case with the name Alfred Dunhill, Ltd. engraved upon it. Rassendyll paused for a moment to admire it before selecting one of the excellent Havanas it contained, an exquisitely mild leaf in a maduro wrapper. Drakov handed him a tiny silver cutter with which to snip the end off. Before lighting it, Rassendyll removed the band.

"My father always used to say that one should never smoke a fine cigar with the band still on it, just as one would not make love to a beautiful woman without first removing all her clothing."

"Most amusing," Drakov said, turning his cigar slowly as he held a match to it.

Rassendyll shifted a bit uncomfortably in his seat, feeling a slight numbness in his lower region. "You know I really must compliment you, old chap," he said. "You certainly travel with all of the most modern conveniences."

Drakov smiled. "Interesting that you should say that. Since you appear to have an appreciation for such things, perhaps you will be intrigued by this."

He reached beneath his seat and pulled out a small black case. At first, Rassendyll thought that it was covered with a finely grained black leather, then he realized that it was not a covering at all, but some sort of curious material that he could not identify. He noted that the case had extremely unusual-looking fastenings. He watched with interest as Drakov opened it, holding it upon his lap.

"You know, Rudolf, if I may call you that," said Drakov, "I have a confession I must make to you. This meeting of ours was not entirely accidental."

"Oh?" said Rassendyll, watching with growing fascination as Drakov removed a series of curiously shaped strips from the case. They were translucent and appeared to have very intricate workings within them. He had never seen anything quite like them before.

"I arranged this encounter," Drakov said. "I also arranged to be present at your brother's party, so that we might see each other. That way, when we ran into each other on this journey, I could more easily approach you in a familiar manner."

"I say," said Rassendyll, "this all sounds like quite the plot." He frowned. There was a peculiar tingling sensation in his legs. Was it possible that so small an amount of brandy could be affecting him?

"But wait a moment. How could you possibly have known that I would be aboard this train? I only decided to take the journey several days ago!"

"As you say, it's quite the plot," said Drakov. "I wish I had the time to explain it to you fully. However, I fear that it would prove to be quite beyond your comprehension."

Rassendyll looked puzzled. Was the man insulting him? "I'm afraid I don't quite follow you," he said, uncertainly. The tingling sensation had now spread to his chest, and his legs felt numb. "By the way, what *are* those things?"

Drakov was bent over, connecting the strange-looking strips together in a circular pattern on the floor of the compartment. Though Rassendyll watched closely, he could not make out just how they were connected.

"They're called border circuits," Drakov said, finishing his task and straightening. "I'm afraid the term will not mean anything to you, but you should find their operation fascinating, just the same."

He reached for the case once more, this time opening it so that Rassendyll could see inside it. What he saw baffled him completely. It looked like a device out of one of those fantastic novels by that imaginative Frenchman, Verne. Rassendyll had no idea what it was. It seemed quite complicated, what with controls of some sort, reflective surfaces upon which numerals appeared as if by magic and tiny, winking, glowing lights.

"See here, Drakov, what manner of contraption *is* that?"

"It's called a chronoplate."

"A chronoplate? What does it do?"

"It is a device for traveling through time."

"For—" Rassendyll looked astonished, then realized that the man was having him on. He laughed. "Traveling through time, eh? Jolly good! What say we voyage to tomorrow and see what the weather will be like, what? Come now, really, what does it actually. . . ."

Rassendyll's voice suddenly trailed off and he turned pale.

"Is something wrong?" said Drakov.

"I do believe I'm feeling a bit ill, old chap. Perhaps a little air—" He attemped to stand, only to discover that he was unable to move from the waist down. "What the devil? I seem to have lost all feeling in my legs!"

"That's because the poison is taking effect," said Drakov.

"*What did you say?*"

"That brandy I poured into your coffee," Drakov said, making some adjustments inside the case. "It was laced with an interesting concoction that would totally baffle your present-day chemists. By now, the numbness you've been feeling should be spreading very rapidly. In another few seconds, you will be completely paralyzed and dead moments after that."

Rassendyll's eyes grew very wide. "*Dead*? You cannot be serious!" He abruptly realized that he could not move his arms. Realization of his situation plunged him into abject terror. "*My God! Poisoned! No! No, please, in Heaven's name, man, help me!*"

"I'm afraid that you're quite beyond help," said Drakov. "I'm sorry."

Rassendyll now found it difficult to speak. He wanted to scream, but he could not. The most he could manage was a croaking whisper.

"*Why?*" he said, forcing the words out. "What have I ever done to you?"

"Nothing," Drakov said. "There is nothing personal in this, Rudolf. That is the main reason I have made it as physically painless as I knew how. It's slower this way, but at least it doesn't hurt. In a way, I'm even doing you a favor. You would have died within another year of tuberculosis—what you call consumption. Not an easy death, by any means, what with fever, chills, internal lesions causing you to cough up blood; this will be far less unpleasant. Soon, you will simply lose consciousness, almost like falling asleep. When your body is discovered, it will appear as though you had suffered a stroke."

Rassendyll could no longer move at all. He could not speak; he could not feel a thing. Large tears made wet tracks down his cheeks. Drakov wiped them away gently with a silk handkerchief. While he spoke, he reached into Rudolf's coat and removed his billfold, replacing it with one of his own. Then he systematically searched his other pockets.

"I knew all about your trip," he said. "In fact, I know all there is to know about you, such as your relationship to Rudolf Elphberg. However, there are always slight historical discrepancies that one cannot account for and I had to engage you in conversation to make certain of a few things. You were very helpful, telling me all I needed to know with almost no prompting on my part. If it's any consolation to you, you're dying in a good cause. Your death is something that I find regrettable, but necessary."

He did something inside the case and the border circuits on the floor began to glow. He shut the case; then, holding the walking stick in one hand and the case in the other, he stepped into the glowing circle.

"I'm afraid that Lord and Lady Burlesdon will believe that you must have had some sort of accident upon your hunting trip," he said. "The papers you are now carrying identify you

as Peter Andersen, the name under which I booked passage.
Rudolf Rassendyll will simple disappear, as shall I. I'm sorry
that it had to be this way. I truly am. You will be missing the
adventure of a lifetime. However, we have someone else in
mind to play your part. Goodbye, Rudolf. Better luck in the
next life."

The glowing circle flared and vanished, taking Drakov with
it.

2

"Ruritania?" Lucas Priest frowned. "I've never even heard of a country called Ruritania. Which time period are we talking about, sir?"

"The late 19th century, Major," said Forrester. He stood behind the podium in the small briefing room on the sixty-third floor of the TAC-HQ building. Major Lucas Priest, Master Sergeant Finn Delaney and Corporal Andre Cross sat before him in the first row of seats. They were dressed in green transit fatigues, form-fitting and lightweight, with their division pins attached to their collars and their insignia of rank on narrow black armbands.

Though Lucas Priest was the ranking officer on the commando team, Finn Delaney had the most seniority in terms of service. The antiaging drugs gave him a deceptively youthful appearance, despite the fact that he was already a veteran of the Temporal Corps when Lucas Priest was still a boy. He owed his lowly rank, out of all proportion to his length of service, to the fact that he had the worst disciplinary record in the entire corps. His most frequent offenses were insubordination and striking superior officers. Each offense, without exception, had been committed in Plus Time. On the other hand, he also held the record for the most promotions for outstanding performance in the field in Minus Time, with the result that he went up and down in rank like a yo-yo. He had only made officer once, for a very brief period of time. The irrepressible, burly, redheaded lifer was a sharp contrast to the slender, brown-haired Priest, a model officer who had quit his job as a well-paid lab technician and joined the Temporal Army on a whim, only to find his true vocation. He had been assigned to Forrester's division after several tours of duty in the regular corps, and he had risen in rank steadily and rapidly until he was now Forrester's second-in-command. Though quite different by nature, the two men complemented each other perfectly and, as frequently occurs with close friends, some of their traits had rubbed off on each other. Finn had learned to control his wild temper at least occasionally and Lucas had developed the ability if not to break regulations, then at least to bend them every now and then.

Biologically, Finn Delaney was the oldest of the three at the age of one hundred and twelve, senior to Lucas by almost fifty years. However, if their ages were to be reckoned chronologically, that distinction would have gone to Andre Cross. Though biologically only in her late twenties, a child by the standards of the 27th century, Andre had been born over a thousand years earlier in the mountainous Basque country of the 12th century. Hers was a case of temporal displacement. She had been taken from her own time and transplanted to the 27th century, an act facilitated by computer implant education and her own unique abilities. Tall, broad-shouldered and unusually muscular for a woman of her time, she felt much more comfortable in the 27th century than she had in 12th-century England, where she had found it necessary to wear her straw-blonde hair like a man's and conceal her gender so that she could become a mercenary knight and live life on her own terms.

Together, the three of them made up a crack commando team. The most difficult and hazardous historical adjustment missions were usually assigned to them, a fact that they were well aware of as they sat and listened to Forrester conduct the briefing. It did not escape their notice that Forrester seemed unusually preoccupied and uncharacteristically tense. It wasn't like him. It did not bode well for the upcoming mission.

"Ruritania was a tiny sovereign state," said Forrester, "a vestpocket kingdom in Central Europe located in the Balkans. It was annexed by Austria-Hungary shortly prior to the First World War. Historically, it was a nation of no great significance in and of itself; however, certain recent events have given it a great deal of significance from the temporal standpoint."

He punched a button on the podium console, activating the computer. "Forrester, code 321-G, clearance blue."

"Clearance confirmed," said the computer. "How may I assist you, Colonel Forrester?"

"Request general background on the conspiracy to depose King Rudolf the Fifth of Ruritania in the year 1891," said Forrester. "Proceed when ready."

"Working," said the computer. "Will you require visuals, Colonel?"

"I'll specify them as the need arises," Forrester said.

"The file on the requested data is incomplete," said the computer. "Available data is unsubstantiated; repeat, unsubstantiated."

"Wonderful," said Finn, wryly.

"Shut up, Delaney. Proceed, computer."

"Available data is derived from a single source," said the computer, "that source being a novel—"

"*A novel!*" said Finn.

Forrester gave him an irate look.

"Repeat, a novel," said the computer, "specifically, an historical romance titled *The Prisoner of Zenda*, written by Sir Anthony Hope Hawkins, also known as Anthony Hope, a London solicitor (modern equivalent: attorney) and published in England in the year 1894. The work was reportedly based on the personal diaries of Rudolf Rassendyll, born August 21, 1862 in London, England; died of tuberculosis on April 14, 1892—"

"Visual on Rudolf Rassendyll," said Forrester.

The holographic image of a tall, well-built man dressed in formal evening clothes circa the late 19th century appeared standing in the staging area before them. The image of Rassendyll stood slightly in profile with his head held erect and his chin held high. He had a thick shock of dark red hair, bright blue eyes, and a sharp, regal-looking nose. The effect of the projection on the three commandos was instantaneous and pronounced.

"What the hell?" said Finn Delaney, leaning forward and staring at the hologram intently. "*That's me!*"

"Maintain present projection and let me have a visual on King Rudolf the Fifth of Ruritania," said Forrester.

A second holographic image appeared standing beside the first. King Rudolf was dressed in a resplendent white military tunic festooned with medals and gold braid, with large, fringed epaulets upon his shoulders and a bright red sash across his chest. He wore white riding breeches and highly polished black riding boots. One arm hung relaxed at his side while the other was bent at the elbow, the hand resting on the pommel of his dress sabre. In all save the clothing, King Rudolf was the identical twin of Rudolf Rassendyll—and of Finn Delaney.

Finn glanced wide-eyed from one projection to the other. He stood up slowly and approached them, examining them from all angles. With the sole exception of the fact that he stood slightly taller than both images, though not so much so that anyone would notice unless he was standing close beside them, there was no discernible difference among the three of them.

"God damn!" he said, taking several steps backward and shaking his head slowly. "I have a very nasty feeling that I'm just going to hate whatever's coming next."

"If you'll resume your seat, Delaney, then we'll get on with it," snapped Forrester, a bit more sharply than was necessary. Lucas wondered what was bothering the old man. Forrester was normally imperturbable, yet now the tension was apparent in his stance and in his voice. There was a grim tightness to the set of his mouth, a stiffness to his posture, an abruptness to his movements. Forrester appeared to be under a great strain and that was a bad sign, a very bad sign, indeed.

"Both of these projections are part of the data fed to us by Temporal Intelligence earlier this afternoon," he said. "They were derived from old photographs. For your general information, Mr. Delaney, I ran a thorough check on your background when I saw these and to the best of my knowledge, neither of these men were ancestors of yours. Your resemblance to them is a remarkable coincidence. Proceed, computer.''

"Hawkins's novel had as its theme a plot to seize the throne of Ruritania in the year 1891," said the computer. "The plot was engineered by Michael Elphberg, Duke of Strelsau, half-brother to the king by a morganatic marriage—"

"Visual on Michael Elphberg," said Forrester.

The two holograms winked out, to be replaced by the image of Michael Elphberg, a saturnine man of average height, gaunt, with deeply-set, hooded brown eyes, and raven-black hair. Despite his dazzling military uniform, Michael Elphberg had the look of a character out of a Dostoevsky novel, one of those dark and brooding young men, like Raskolnikov, driven by an anarchistic soul and deep frustration that the world had not seen fit to recognize his natural superiority.

"Cheerful-looking chap, isn't he?" said Finn.

"What is a morganatic marriage?" said Lucas.

"Computer," said Forrester, "define—"

"That won't be necessary, Colonel," Andre said. "It's a term which has its origins in the time from which I came. It pertains to a marriage between a titled male and an untitled female. In this case, it would mean that the old king had married twice, once to a titled female—Rudolf's mother—and again to an untitled female, who would have been Michael's mother. In a morganatic union, neither the mother nor the offspring would have any rights to rank or property."

"Why would Michael be a duke, then?" said Lucas.

"His father must have granted him a dukedom," Andre said. "However, that still wouldn't change the fact that he had no right to succession."

"Which would explain why he wanted to seize the throne," said Finn.

"Thank you, Corporal," Forrester said. "Proceed, computer."

"At the time of the plot," said the computer, "there were two strong political factions in Ruritania, the Red faction and the Black faction. The Red faction supported Rudolf's rightful claim to the throne of Ruritania. The Black faction was in favor of Michael Elphberg ascending to the throne. The

groups were so identified owing to the dark red color of
Rudolf Elphberg's hair and the black color of Michael Elphberg's hair.''

"Question," said Lucas. "If Michael had no legal right to
succession, what were the reasons for there being public sentiment in favor of his becoming king?''

"Repeat," said the computer, "this is unsubstantiated data.
Rudolf Elphberg was not a popular figure in Ruritania. He
was weak-willed and self-indulgent and he spent a great deal
of time abroad, never bothering to curry favor with the
Ruritanian people. Michael Elphberg took a great deal of interest in the government of Ruritania and maintained a high
public visibility, keeping residences in the capitol city of
Strelsau and in the province of Zenda, where he entertained
influential citizens lavishly. He was also popular with the
Ruritanian army and despite his having no legal right to succession, there was a large segment of the population that
would have preferred to see Michael on the throne.''

"And Michael was not averse to this idea," said Finn.

"Prince Rudolf was engaged to be married to the Princess
Flavia," continued the computer.

"Visual, please," said Forrester and, a second later, the
hologram of Michael was replaced by an image of a red-haired
woman in her late teens or early twenties with bright blue eyes
and a pleasingly heart-shaped face. She had a doll-like pret-
tiness which she wore indifferently and her facial expression
suggested shyness or a natural reserve.

"Flavia was Rudolf's third cousin," continued the computer, "and the marriage was politically motivated to unite the
two strongest families in Ruritania under one house. The
popularity of Princess Flavia and Prince Rudolf's apparent indifference to her contributed to public sentiment against him.

"Michael had Rudolf drugged so that he would miss his coronation, the intent being to make it appear that Rudolf was
unable to be crowned because he had been intoxicated. The
plan was facilitated by the fact that Prince Rudolf had appeared in public in a state of intoxication on numerous occa-
sions. The ensuing scandal would have been to Michael's
advantage, but no scandal occurred due to the fact that two of
Prince Rudolf's followers, an officer in the Ruritanian army

named Colonel Sapt and a nobleman named von Tarlenheim, intervened by engineering a plot of their own. They enlisted the aid of Rudolf Rassendyll, who had come to Ruritania to see the coronation. Rassendyll was distantly related to Rudolf Elphberg and was his physical double. Sapt and von Tarlenheim convinced him to attend the coronation in Rudolf Elphberg's place. Their plan was to have Rassendyll impersonate the king until the drugs wore off and they could make the substitution, at which point Rassendyll would have been quietly smuggled out of the country."

"Visuals on Sapt and von Tarlenheim," said Forrester, "are unavailable. We only have what the TIA provided us with and they haven't had very much time to put all this together. You will, however, get physical descriptions, based on what Hawkins wrote, during your mission programming. Proceed, computer."

"With the aid of Sapt and von Tarlenheim, Rassendyll successfully impersonated the king during the coronation. They were unable to complete their plan because Michael discovered the deception and imprisoned his half-brother in Zenda Castle, causing a stalemate between the two parties. If Michael killed the real king, he could have made Rassendyll's impersonation permanent, with no way of exposing him as a fraud without exposing his own crime. If the marriage to Princess Flavia took place as planned, Flavia would have wedded an imposter. Sapt and von Tarlenheim could not accuse Michael of having kidnapped the real king, since doing so would have revealed the fraud that they had perpetrated. In order for Michael to prevail, he had to find a way to dispose of Rassendyll before he could dispose of his half-brother. In order for Sapt and von Tarlenheim to prevail, they had to find a way to rescue the king from Zenda Castle. The castle was a strong medieval fortification. If any attempt were made to storm it in force, Michael would have had enough time to kill the king and dispose of his body. Sapt and von Tarlenheim could not then accuse him of murder without proof. There was also the difficulty of the fact that Michael was popular with the army, who would have required strong justification for assaulting the home of the king's own brother."

"Sounds like one hell of a mess," said Finn. "They

couldn't exactly tell the army that Michael was holding the king prisoner when the king was installed in the palace. It's a lousy scenario for an adjustment.''

"It's much worse than you think," said Forrester. "Early this morning, Lieutenant Colonel Jack Carnehan—code name: Mongoose—was found murdered in his apartment in New York. Burned into his forehead with a laser were the words, 'Paris 5.' Temporal Intelligence contacted me as soon as they realized that it was a reference to the terrorists you and agent Mongoose went up against in the 17th-century Paris adjustment. Apparently, the Timekeepers have embarked upon a vendetta and the TIA believes that we—or at least you three— will be their next targets.''

Mention of the Timekeepers and of Mongoose's murder had an electric effect upon the soldiers.

"Good Christ," said Lucas. "How did it happen? I thought the Timekeepers were finished.''

"So did I," said Forrester. "However, Temporal Intelligence is now reluctantly admitting that they didn't get them all. I'm told that the leadership of the Timekeepers was composed of a small number of individuals acting as a secret cell within that organization. One of them was Adrian Taylor, whom the three of you brought down on that Paris mission. The TIA knows of at least three others, all of whom managed to escape their dragnet.''

"How in hell did they manage to kill Mongoose?" Finn said. "Not even we knew what he really looked like.''

"Chances are we'll probably never know," said Lucas.

"As a matter of fact, we *do* know," said Forrester. "The TIA has a visual record of the assassination.''

"*What?*" said Finn.

Forrester's mouth turned down slightly at the corners. "It seems that Mongoose had holographic equipment installed in concealed locations inside his apartment, ostensibly for surveillance purposes. The TIA has seen fit to deny me access to the complete recording, for reasons which will momentarily become obvious, I think, but they did send me this still projection from the graph.''

There was a long pause and Lucas noticed that Forrester's hands were white-knuckled on the podium. "Computer, visual on Sophia Falco," he said.

The holographic image of a breathtakingly beautiful young woman appeared standing in the staging area. She had ash-blond hair, blue-grey eyes, and a lush body that was clearly kept in peak physical condition. She was completely nude. There was a catlike sleekness to her, and even though she stood in a relaxed posture, her muscular development was evident and quite impressive. There was a pristine loveliness to her face that would have been icy were it not for the searing heat generated by her gaze. Though it was only a hologram, the image exuded a bestial vitality. She had a charged sexuality so potent that it hit both Finn and Lucas like a blast of hot desert wind. She was holding a laser in her hand and smiling in a bemused fashion. Finn Delaney gave a low whistle.

"Oh," said Andre, dryly. "I see. *Those* kind of surveillance purposes."

"Yes," said Forrester, "the killing took place in the bedroom."

"I can't believe it," Lucas said. "Mongoose would never be taken like that."

"He's right," said Finn. "Mongoose was too good an agent to succumb to a sexual lure. Besides, he was as paranoid as they come. He'd probably test the food his own mother cooked for him. There's got to be more to it."

"There is," said Forrester, tensely. "This is a woman I once knew as Elaine Cantrell. We served together in the Airborne Pathfinders a long time ago. She obviously takes more trouble to look youthful than do I and she's changed her appearance somewhat since we knew each other, but I still recognized her. If you'll look closely at her left hand, you will see that she's wearing an unusual-looking ring." He paused for a long moment. "I gave her that ring. It belonged to my father."

The three commandos exchanged astonished glances. In all the years that they had known the old man, they had never heard him mention having any women in his life. And hard as it was to picture their crusty old commander in a romantic liaison, it was impossible to imagine him being involved with *that* woman.

"The TIA knew her as Sophia Falco—code name: Falcon," said Forrester.

"She's a temporal agent?" Lucas said, with disbelief. "*The Timekeepers infiltrated Temporal Intelligence?*"

"*How?*" said Andre. "Even their clerical personnel have to undergo high-level clearance scanning."

"It would explain a few things, though," said Finn, "like why the TIA could never crack them. Difficult to do if you've got a mole from the opposition in your organization. If you're surprised, imagine how they must feel. It would have been extremely difficult, but not at all impossible. I can think of one way they could have done it offhand, but it would mean that the Timekeepers had far greater resources and imagination than we ever gave them credit for. They could have used reeducation conditioning."

"That means they would have had to subvert someone in the penal system," Andre said. "I should think that would have been impossible. They're constantly monitored."

"Difficult, but not impossible," said Finn. "Hell, nothing is impossible. Besides, they might have been able to get their hands on the necessary equipment. It still would have been very risky. A reeducation procedure that isn't conducted by an expert could easily result in a total mind wipe."

"I still don't see how reeducation conditioning would help them plant a spy," said Lucas.

"I think it's the only answer under the circumstances," Finn said. He glanced at Forrester. "Sir?"

"Go ahead, Delaney. Let's hear it."

Of the four of them, Finn had the most extensive scientific background, having attended Referee Corps School as a young man, though he had washed out of RCS due to his undisciplined personality. The referees' loss was the First Division's gain.

"They probably used a variation on the hypnotic mole conditioning first developed by the Soviets in the late 20th century," said Finn. "The Russians developed the technique of infiltrating agents into key positions—or positions that would *become* key positions—and leaving them 'dormant' for years, capable of being triggered by a key word or spoken code phrase. These agents were frequently preconditioned to perform certain specific missions, based upon long-range projections. Quite often, they were ignorant of the fact that they were agents until the time that they were triggered."

"You're to be congratulated, Mr. Delaney," said Forrester. "Your analysis of the situation and the TIA's coincide exactly, except for one small point. There is one possibility for gaining access to the right equipment and the necessary expertise that you've overlooked. Subverting someone in TAMAC."

"Hell, that's right," said Finn. "That never even occurred to me!"

"The TIA put it all together," said Forrester, "but then, they had all the facts. When they moved to make mass arrests of the members of the Temporal Preservation League based on the results of your Paris mission, one of the people they apprehended was Captain Lachman Singh of the Temporal Army Medical Corps—a psychiatric specialist. He committed suicide before he could be interrogated and we now know why. Once Falcon's identity was discovered to be false, the TIA began to backtrack. It turns out that the woman I knew as Elaine Cantrell was a complete fabrication, in a manner of speaking. Whoever she is, she seems to have no history. She must have had herself imprinted with a personality to match her cover identity as Elaine Cantrell prior to joining the service. A check of her service record reveals that she enlisted in Colorado Springs, which means that she would have been processed at TAMAC, where Captain Singh was in an excellent position to find some 'inconsistency' in her psych profile and put her through a scanning procedure for verification purposes. That would have given him all the cover he needed to put her through a modified reeducation program, imprinting her with a bogus personality and some sort of trigger, as Delaney puts it, to reawaken her true identity. Then he cleared her, as the records show, and she went on to Pathfinder training and eventual assignment to my unit."

Forrester winced slightly as he said that. He swallowed hard, then continued.

"Temporal Intelligence confirms that she applied to the agency while still under my command. She passed their scanning procedures—thanks to Captain Singh—and was accepted for training as a field agent. At that point, Elaine Cantrell disappeared in Minus Time. I believed her to be dead, but now

I've learned that the TIA arranged for her to be MIA so that Elaine Cantrell could 'die' and begin a new career with a new identity, as Sophia Falco—code name: Falcon. She became one of their top field agents.''

"And since Mongoose was the senior field agent, they obviously got to know each other pretty well," said Lucas.

Andre grimaced. "Yes, but unfortunately for Mongoose, not well enough."

"The ironic part," said Forrester, "is that the TIA assigned her to infiltrate the Temporal Preservation League with an aim to making contact with the terrorists and infiltrating them. When she succeeded, the Timekeepers knew that *they* had succeeded, at which point they must have triggered her."

"It's almost funny," said Finn. "It's as though the Timekeepers gave the TIA the ingredients to make a bomb. The TIA assembled it for them, then gave it back so they could push the button. The scary thing is that Falcon might not have been the only one."

"That's precisely what they're worried about," said Forrester. "This has thrown the TIA into an absolute panic. They've recalled every single one of their field agents in order to put them through a series of exhaustive scanning procedures designed to check for the possibility of imprintation."

"*All* of them?" said Lucas. "That could take months!"

"At the very least," said Forrester. "What that means is that you won't have any intelligence support upon this mission. Which brings us full circle. Falcon purposely left behind some personal effects belonging to Rudolf Rassendyll at the scene of Mongoose's murder. Temporal Intelligence has authenticated them. I think that we can safely assume that they're not trying to bluff us. The Timekeepers have clocked back to the 19th century and eliminated Rassendyll."

"But why tell us about it?" Andre said.

"I should think that would be obvious," said Forrester. "They want revenge for what you did in 17th-century Paris. As a result of that mission, their organization was virtually wiped out. They've already killed Mongoose. That leaves just the three of you."

"If they're trying to make certain that we're the team sent out on the adjustment," Andre said, "why play into their hands? Why not simply send in another team?''

"You're not thinking, Corporal," said Forrester. "Sending you three in is our best chance to stop them. They know that. They also know that *we* know that they have already created their disruption. They've made a point of telling us about it. There's nothing preventing them from merely clocking out to another time period except the fact that they want you dead. So long as you're available, they'll stick around and try to get the job done.''

Finn Delaney was shaking his head.

"What is it, Delaney?"

"There are entirely too many coincidences here," he said. "I can't believe that the Timekeepers arranged them all."

Forrester frowned. "What are you getting at?"

"Just this. The whole thing is beginning to shape up as the sort of nightmares we used to construct as theoretical problem modules back in RCS when we were studying the effects of the Fate Factor on temporal inertia. We used to call it 'zen physics,' because it bends your brain around just thinking about it, like one of those old Japanese koans, you know, 'What is the sound of one hand clapping?' Only this is even worse."

"How so?"

"Because trying to figure it out logically will make you crazy," said Finn. "More cadets washed out on zen physics than in any other course. Temporal inertia works in ways that not even Mensinger fully understood. Look at the complete picture here. Everything that's gone down so far bears directly on our actions in 17th-century Paris during that adjustment mission involving the three musketeers. The adjustment was successful and it enabled the TIA to arrest most of the Timekeepers, but we have no way of knowing just how much temporal inertia was affected. Remember that the Fate Factor works as a coefficient of temporal inertia, determining the degree of *relative* continuity to which the timestream can be restored. That depends on the effects of the disruption itself in the first place and the manner in which it was adjusted in the second place.''

"In other words," said Andre, " 'relative' is the operative term. Temporal inertia can still be affected in some way that might show up at some later point in time."

"Exactly. Coincidences are a natural part of a random world, but too many coincidences indicates that there has to be more than randomness at work. That's what we've got here. Too damn many coincidences. One: what the Time-keepers have done in disrupting 19th-century Ruritania is directly related to what we did to them in 17th-century France. Cause and effect. Two: Falcon appears to have been very high up in the terrorist organization, perhaps one of their leaders, which connects her to what we did in 17th-century France. Three: as Elaine Cantrell, she was involved with Colonel Forrester and now, as Falcon, their paths have intersected once again. Four: as Elaine Cantrell and later as Sophia Falco, she was involved with the TIA and with Mongoose, who's been involved with us on more than one occasion in the past, specifically on that 17th-century adjustment. Five: I happen, just 'coincidentally,' to resemble both Rudolf Rassendyll and King Rudolf of Ruritania, who are principal parties in the historical scenario the Timekeepers have disrupted. Possibly, they discovered this resemblance by accident and acted because of it, but there are *still* too many coincidences interrelating here to be dismissed as a random progression of events."

"So you're suggesting that it's the Fate Factor at work?" said Forrester.

"It has to be. Remember that old story about how a kingdom was lost for want of a horseshoe nail? All it takes is one seemingly insignificant action to set in motion a cause-and-effect chain that will eventually lead to one significant event. Trying to analyze such a situation in terms of temporal inertia practically erases the line between physics and metaphysics. It's what finally drove Mensinger to kill himself. He realized that the whole thing is like a house of cards. Sooner or later, it's bound to collapse under its own weight and all it takes is just one card to start the whole thing falling."

"But none of our actions have ever been temporally insignificant," said Lucas. "We've even faced a timestream split before and managed to adjust for it successfully."

"Yeah, so far as we know," said Finn. "The point I'm trying to make is that Mensinger's theories refer to Fate in a literal fashion only obliquely. That's because complete objectivity is impossible under any circumstances. It goes back to Heisenberg's Principle. An observer of any phenomenon can't get away from his subjective relationship to it merely by being there to observe it. Any action we take in Plus or Minus Time is a causal manifestation of our subjective relationship to the timestream.''

"You've lost me," said Andre.

"Let me attempt to translate Delaney's verbosity into layman's terms," said Forrester. "What he's saying is that the Fate Factor governs not only the end result of any adjustment to the timestream, but it also governs the actions of those effecting the adjustment."

"Only in this case," said Finn, "we seem to be confronted with a situation that's eschatological in its implications. We may have adjusted for a split before, but now we've got the potential for a massive rupture on our hands. And what makes matters even worse is that all we've got to work from in terms of intelligence is some sort of drawingroom novel written in the 19th century. Without access to those diaries that Hawkins allegedly worked from, we have no way of knowing what really happened. The TIA is in no position to give us any help. Besides, even if they managed to get their hands on those diaries in time, we'd still only have Rassendyll's word for what actually happened. He could easily have embellished the story for his own sake.''

. "I'll agree that the element of uncertainty in this scenario is very large," said Lucas, "but at least we know what the result was. History records a King Rudolf the Fifth on the throne of Ruritania, and Rassendyll obviously managed to get back to London in one piece to write about it in his diaries. Whatever it was he did, he was successful."

"Not any more he wasn't," said Finn. "I trust we have access to this novel Hawkins wrote?"

"It will be included in the mission programming," said Forrester.

"Good. We'll need all the help that we can get. We're looking destiny squarely in the face here. The Fate Factor is trying to compensate and *we're* a part of it!"

"I wonder if the Timekeepers realize that?" said Lucas.

"I wonder if they care?" said Forrester. "Their so-called

movement has been effectively destroyed. There can only be a handful of them left. Can you think of a better note to go out on than having brought about ultimate entropy?"

"Is that actually a possibility?" said Andre.

"Delaney seems to think so," Forrester said.

"But that would mean. . . ." Andre's voice trailed off.

"The end of time," said Lucas, softly.

3

Drakov was impatient. He kept pacing back and forth in the small turret atop the keep of Zenda Castle, rolling his massive shoulders and stretching to get the kinks out of his muscles.

"Sit down, Nikolai," said Falcon. "Your constant pacing back and forth is distracting me."

Drakov gave her a look of mild irritation. She was reclining on one of two small cots in the tiny room that was otherwise bare except for some equipment and supplies piled in a corner. Her ash-blond hair was pulled back in a pony tail, and she was dressed in low black boots and black fatigues. Drakov was similarly attired, though he added a sheepskin vest to his army-surplus clothing.

"You may find it distracting," he said, "but I find it necessary to move about. The chill and dampness of this place is making my bones ache. While you've been out there socializing as the Countess Sophia, I've been cooped up here for days with nothing but rats and silverfish for company. I don't know how people ever managed to live in such places."

"It may be uncomfortable, but it's an ideal base of operations," she said, still intent upon the screen of the small computer she held in her right hand. "No one's set foot in this part of the castle for years and even if the adjustment team suspected that we were holed up in here, they'd have a hell of a time trying to get at us."

"Unless they decided to try clocking in here," said Drakov.

"The risk factor would be far too great," she said. "They would never attempt it without transition coordinates. They could wind up inside a wall that's eight feet thick. However, it's possible that they could try an assault with floater-paks, which is why I've moved us up here to this turret. It might be colder and windier up here, but we can see out over the entire castle. Once I've got the tracking system set up in those embrasures, there's no way they'll be able to drop in here without setting off a laser."

"What is to prevent them from obtaining their coordinates the same way we did?" Drakov said.

Falcon raised her eyebrows. "By seducing Rupert Hentzau in the dungeon?"

"Don't be crude," said Drakov. "You know very well what I mean. One of them might arrange a visit with Black Michael and ask to see the castle. You might have done the same when you attended the ball in his chateau, only you chose to appeal to Hentzau's prurient sensibilities, instead."

Falcon smiled slyly. "That's true, but I'd never done it on a rack before. There are all sorts of interesting devices down there. You should go down with me and take a look. You never know, it might help take the chill out of your bones."

"Thank you, but no," said Drakov.

"You know, you really are a very pretty boy, Nikolai, but you've got the mind of a neanderthal. That's the trouble with implant programming. It can teach you things, but it can't make you unlearn a lifetime of social conditioning. Perhaps I should have had you totally reeducated, but I liked your personality the way it was when I first found you. It has its own charm and appeal, despite your Victorian attitudes. But for God's sake, you've lived in the 27th century! Haven't you learned anything?"

"I have learned a great deal," Drakov said. "I have learned that your 'modern era' is degenerate and decadent, and not in ways that pertain just to sexual morality. You have replaced quality with quantity, substance with artifice and principles with expediency. Forgive me, but I find little in your time to admire except your technological achievements, and even those you use irresponsibly."

"You're a fine one to take such a lofty moral tone," she said. "When I found you, you were a jaded playboy who could buy everything except the things you really wanted. Your money couldn't buy you peace and it couldn't buy you a sense of purpose. I gave you both."

"I will admit that for a brief time, I found a sense of peace with you," said Drakov, "but that was nothing more than self-delusion. You used me, but I'm not complaining. We used each other and we continue to do so, like a pair of parasites. And where has it brought us? Here we are, the last remaining members of the Timekeepers' vaunted inner circle, sitting in a cold, gray room like a pair of deluded anarchists, plotting our revenge."

"It's what you wanted, Nikolai."

"What I wanted? No, it isn't what I wanted. If I could have had what I wanted, mine would have been a different life entirely. It is, however regrettably, what I need. When this is over, if things should go our way, I can think of nothing that would please me more than to part from you and never see you or your 27th century again."

"Poor Nicky," she said. "What would you rather do?"

"I don't know," he said. "I do know that I can never go back to being what I was. Making war on war has changed me. Whether for the better or for the worse, I cannot tell. I do know that it is a thing that needs doing."

"I see," she said. "You just don't want to continue doing it with me, is that it?"

"If I remained with you, I would become like you," said Drakov, "and that is what I do not want. The end result of fanaticism such as yours is that everything becomes subordinated to the cause. After a time, you perpetuate the cause for its own sake, not for the sake of whatever it was you started out to achieve. Look at what's happened to us. Taylor killed in 17th-century Paris, Singh captured to die a suicide, Tremain trapped forever in the dead zone when he tried to follow us, Benedetto escaped to God knows where in abject panic, and all of those who were arrested, all of those who died trying to escape, yet you feel nothing, do you? To you, it's merely a setback."

"Sacrifices must be made, Nikolai," said Falcon, putting the computer down and looking at him thoughtfully. "I thought you understood that."

"Oh, I understand," he said. "What troubles me is that I'm beginning to accept it so easily. I said much the same thing to Rassendyll when I killed him. I sat there, trying to explain things to him like a fool, watching his uncomprehending eyes staring at me as he slipped away, and I felt no remorse. None whatsoever."

"What do you want, Nikolai, to cry over everyone who has to die so that the Time Wars can be stopped?"

"Someone should, don't you think?"

"Well, you go ahead and grieve for all the poor souls who fall by wayside," she said, flatly. "I've got more important things to do. You want to go your own way when this is over, fine with me. I don't need you. But meanwhile, there's work to be done. Just in case the adjustment team manages to get someone inside here, I've prepared some surprises for them. If staying inside this castle hasn't turned you into an impotent Prince Hamlet, you can help me set them up. Otherwise, you can stay here and muse on the pathos of it all." She got up from the cot. "Priest, Cross, and Delaney are undoubtedly here by now and things will start to happen very soon."

"How can you be so certain that they're the ones Forrester will send?" said Drakov.

"Because those three are the First Division's best," she said. "And because Moses Forrester will realize that he has no choice but to send them, just as he will have no choice but to come to us when we're ready for him. Then you can have your own personal revenge. After that, I really don't care what you do."

Drakov glanced out of the small embrasure in the turret. "Have you ever cared for anything or anyone at all?" he said.

She was silent for a moment. "Yes, once."

"Only once?"

"There was a very special man once. It was another life, but I remember it quite vividly." She smiled. "Ironically, it was the same man you want to kill.''

Drakov looked at her with surprise. "*Moses Forrester?*"

"Hard to believe, isn't it?" she said. She held up her hand. "I still wear his ring. Here," she said, pulling it off and tossing it to him, "maybe you should have it. After all, it was your father's.''

From where they stood, the three commandos had a spectacular view of the Duke of Strelsau's residence. They had clocked in at a point several miles away from the village of Zenda. The province was mostly heavily forested hill country, wild and teeming with game. The village was tiny and bucolic, made up of small, picturesque cottages, an inn, a blacksmith shop, a church and several farms that dotted the hillsides around it. The flavor of the place was decidedly medieval, but the duke's estate was a palatial mixture of the old and new.

They had been met at their transition point by Captain Robert Derringer, the Observer assigned to their mission. He seemed very young for an Observer, despite the fact that the antiaging drugs made appearances deceptive. Derringer didn't look much older than a recruit fresh out of boot camp. He was dressed in period, in a lightweight dark brown jacket, riding britches, high brown boots, and a blue silk shirt. He was sharp-featured with large brown eyes and a thick, unruly mop of dark brown hair. There was a coltish look about him, an energetic restlessness in his speech and demeanor. He had led them a short distance to the top of the hill, from where they were able to take their first look at Michael Elphberg's home.

The long, wide, tree-lined avenue that ran straight for a distance of about two miles to "Black Michael's" chateau was immaculately maintained. It led up to a large courtyard in front of the chateau, then curled around the east side of the estate, making a wide loop around Zenda Castle, following the moat which was as wide as a medium-sized river. Having rounded half the castle, the road then ran south, away from the estate and into the forest, through a small pass and to the village of Zenda. The avenue that led to the chateau's front entrance ran in the opposite direction to the road that led from Zenda to the capital city of Strelsau.

Though it was dwarfed by the castle situated directly behind

it, the chateau was nevertheless quite large. Built in the French
style, it was five stories high with an elaborate, columned portico and a steeply gabled roof. Its gleaming whiteness was
a stark contrast to the murky gray stone of the castle that
loomed over it.

"It's a rather curious architectural mixture," said Derringer. "The chateau was built by the last king as a country
residence, because he evidently liked the castle a great deal but
felt it too uncomfortable to live in. Only that one small drawbridge you see connects the castle to the chateau. It spans the
moat about twenty feet above it and it's wide enough for three
or four men to cross it abreast. It won't accommodate a carriage. With the construction of the chateau, the only way to
get into the castle now is to go through the chateau. The back
door is flush with the wall and it opens directly out onto the
drawbridge or the moat if the drawbridge has been raised. The
castle itself seems to have been constructed in stages. The oldest part is the central portion. You'll notice that there are no
baillies. Apparently, there were at one time, but at some point,
perhaps during the construction of the chateau, the outer walls
were torn down and the moat was widened."

"It does look larger than any I've ever seen before," said
Andre.

"That's right," said Derringer, with a grin. "You're our
resident knight errant, aren't you?"

"I've seen many castles in my day," she said. "This one appears to be old, but quite impregnable. I can see where the
weak point in the fortifications was reinforced by building
that embrasured keep on the southwest corner, but I am puzzled by that addition with the two small towers there, jutting
out over the moat. It seems to serve no useful defensive purpose."

"I think I can explain that," Derringer said. "That was
done most recently. I haven't been inside, but judging by appearances, I'd guess that much of the old castle is in a state of
disrepair. The squared-off section sticking out into the moat
was probably added as a sort of guesthouse, so that people can
move back and forth between the castle and the chateau. It's
the only part of the castle where I've seen lights burning."

"That would explain it, then," she said. "It's a strange arrangement, but an effective one. Though the placement of the cheateau directly in front of the castle limits visibility somewhat, it also renders a frontal attack in force almost impossible. The chateau might be taken without much difficulty, but then there would only be the one narrow access point to the portcullis to be defended."

"How would you take it if you had to?" said Derringer.

Andre shrugged. "I would lay seige."

Finn grimaced sourly. "That would be a bit hard to do with just four people," he said. "Especially since we can't use much in the way of modern ordnance. We're supposed to believe that a pampered Englishman like Rassendyll managed to break in there and get the king out?"

"Perhaps he wasn't all that pampered," Derringer said. "Supposedly, he had been a military officer."

"Just the same," said Finn, "I'm not anxious to try rescuing anyone from that place."

"Maybe our best bet would be to prevent the duke from kidnapping the king in the first place," said Andre.

Derringer smiled. "You're assuming that you can. I'm afraid that option isn't open to you. You're in the curious position of having to effect an adjustment in which there's such a strong manifestation of the Fate Factor in evidence that it makes me wonder at the possibility for any independent action on your part. Any deviation from the original scenario beyond what has already happened is simply unthinkable. You can't adjust a disruption with another disruption, Corporal Cross. Unfortunately, your options are limited, whereas the Timekeepers are free to attempt whatever they please. I don't envy you your task in preserving the original scenario."

"There's just one little problem," Lucas said. "If we don't know for sure what the original scenario was, how can we help but deviate from it?"

Derringer shrugged. "You can't, I'm afraid. The best you can do is to follow the original scenario as closely as you can within the limits of what we know about it and hope like hell that temporal inertia compensates. Sergeant Delaney's going to have to take his lead from Colonel Sapt and Fritz von Tarlenheim. I'll admit that it would be very tempting to foil Michael Elphberg's plot before it ever gets off the ground, but although that might restore the status quo in the long run, it would still alter the original sequence of events as we know them. I could almost guarantee you that you wouldn't get away with it. Apparently, the Fate Factor is attempting to compensate for something that happened back in the 17th century or maybe earlier. None of us knows what that is, but it makes no difference. With all of these coincidences cropping up like temporal 'tilt' signals in some sort of cosmic pinball game, do you really want to take the chance that two wrongs will make a right? From a purely academic standpoint, I must admit to a certain morbid fascination. I'd be curious to see what would happen if you failed. Do we get a massive timestream split that branches off into all sorts of alternate timelines or does time bend back in upon itself and start going round in ever decreasing circles 'til it stops? I've always been fascinated by zen physics, but I never thought I'd actually be confronting it in a field exer—sorry, a mission. it makes me feel as though the Sword of Damocles were hanging over all our heads, suspended by a spider web.''

''Don't take this the wrong way, Captain,'' Finn said, ''but how old are you?''

''Twenty-nine,'' said Derringer. ''You're wondering how a baby like me managed to get through RCS?''

''Well . . . frankly, yes,'' said Finn.

Derringer grinned. ''I cut my teeth on temporal physics,'' he said. ''Albrecht Mensinger was my grandfather.''

''I'll be damned,'' said Finn. ''Small wonder they assigned you to this mission.''

''That may have had something to do with it,'' said Derringer. ''On the other hand, perhaps it's another one of these coincidences we're swimming in. Maybe it's karma. Do you believe in karma, Sergeant?''

''Only when it's bad,'' said Finn.

Derringer chuckled. ''An answer worthy of Lenny Bruce.''

''I'm afraid I miss the reference,'' said Finn.

''Ah. Well, he was a sort of 20th-century philosopher who refined bad karma to an art. Sorry, I tend to be a bit obscure at times. I understand my work well enough to realize that I really don't understand it at all. To paraphrase, there is more to heaven and earth than is dreamed of in our philosophy.''

"Well, that one, at least, I know," said Finn. "William Shakespeare, right?"

Derringer raised his eyebrows. "Really? I thought it was Albert Einstein. It's the sort of thing he would have said, at any rate. Oh, and speaking of bad karma, there's yet another piece of unpleasant news I have for you. The coronation has been moved up to the day after tomorrow."

Lucas stared at Derringer. "How can that be? According to history, we're supposed to have five days!"

"Yes, I know. It's our first evident historical anomaly. I estimate that we have at most until tomorrow before Michael executes his plan. That's always assuming that things haven't become completely skewed."

"Then what the hell are we doing jawing like this?" Finn said.

"Relax, Sergeant," said Derringer. "I may have only been here a few days, but I've been very, very busy. I know what I'm doing. At this very moment, the king is not two miles away from here, in Michael's hunting lodge. Sapt and von Tarlenheim are both with him. Michael is conspicuously absent. I don't think he'd risk having Rudolf drugged before tomorrow night. That gives you all day tomorrow. I've been keeping them under close surveillance. Rudolf has picked himself a hunting stand from which he has a good view of the stream down in that little valley there, where the deer come to drink. I've picked out a spot where you are certain to encounter them. The king has been staying up quite late, getting plastered every night. He goes out to his stand just before sundown. So far, he hasn't killed anything and I don't think he's likely to. Even when he's sober, he's a miserable shot. If it wasn't for Sapt, they'd have nothing to eat. And speaking of food, since it's been several hundred years since you folks have eaten, I suggest that we make our way down to the village and grab ourselves a bite of supper. The inn has very nice accommodations and the food is really quite good. I can recommend either the venison or the trout. The wine stinks, but their beer is first rate. Besides, one should never save the future of the world on an empty stomach."

The timing worked out just right. Not five minutes after

Finn had taken up position beneath a large oak tree on the
wooded trail, he heard men approaching, coming up the rise
toward him. He leaned his head back against the tree and
pretended to be dozing. A couple of minutes more passed by
and then he heard them stop in front of him.

"Why, the devil's in it!" he heard a young man's voice ex-
claim. "Shave him and he'd be the king!"

He opened his eyes and saw two men standing on the trail
several feet in front of him, staring in astonishment. Both men
carried guns and both were dressed in shooting costumes. One
of them was short and heavily built. He had a large head
crowned with thick gray-white hair; a huge cavalry moustache; muttonchops and bloodshot eyes. He was smoking a
very large-bowled pipe with a deep curve to it, a Turkish meer-
schaum that had colored unevenly due to his apparent lack of
concern in handling it. He appeared to be in his sixties or early
seventies, but he was fit and straight-backed with a manner
that clearly labeled him a military man. The other man was tall
and slender, dark-haired with a small, neatly trimmed moustache and rounded, delicate features that gave his face an
insouciant air. He looked to be in his late twenties or early
thirties. He was the one who had spoken. As they came closer
and Delaney stood up, the older man backed off a pace and
raised his bushy eyebrows.

"He's the same height, too!" he said. "My word! May I ask
your name, sir?"

"The name is Rassendyll," Finn said. "Rudolf Rassendyll.
Am I unintentionally trespassing? I'm a traveler from England, you see, and I have come here on a holiday. If I've
ignorantly strayed onto your land, I offer my apologies,
gentlemen."

"No, no, you are welcome, sir," said the younger man. "It
was merely your appearance that took us by surprise. Allow
me to introduce ourselves. This is Colonel Sapt, and my name
is Fritz von Tarlenheim. We are in the service of the King of
Ruritania."

Finn took their hands in turn and while he was shaking the
old man's hand, Sapt exclaimed, "*Rassendyll!* By heaven,
you're of the Burlesdons?"

"Why, yes," said Finn. "My brother Robert is now Lord Burlesdon."

"By God," said Sapt, "your hair and features betray you, sir." He chuckled. "Remarkable! You know the story, Fritz?"

From the look on von Tarlenheim's face, it was clear that he knew the story of Countess Amelia's indiscretion, but was loath to admit to it for fear of bringing up an awkward subject. Finn took him off the hook.

"It seems the story of Countess Amelia and Prince Rudolf is as well known here as it is in London," he said, smiling.

"Not only is the story well known," said Sapt, "but if you stay here, sir, not a man or woman in all of Ruritania will doubt it!"

At that moment, another voice cried out from lower on the trail, "Fritz! Sapt! Where the devil have you two disappeared to?"

"It's the king!" said von Tarlenheim.

"He's in for a bit of a surprise," said Sapt.

As Rudolf Elphberg came into view, Finn could not help staring at him. Though he had seen the hologram, it was still a shock. It was like looking in a mirror. Elphberg was his exact double down to the last dimple, save for the absence of a beard. He saw Finn and froze, staring at him open-mouthed. Finn had been prepared to feign a look of surprise, but found that in spite of being prepared, he didn't have to fake it. After a moment, it occurred to him that protocol demanded a respectful bow.

"Good Lord!" said Elphberg. "Colonel, Fritz, who *is* this gentleman?"

Finn was about to answer when Colonel Sapt moved over to speak softly to the king. As Sapt whispered to him, Elphberg's eyes grew even wider, then he burst out laughing.

"Strike me dead!" he said, still laughing as he came up to take Finn's hand and slap him on the back. "Well met, cousin! For a moment, I thought that the effects of last night's merriment had not quite worn off and I was seeing visions! Hah! Fritz, I'll give a thousand crowns for a sight of Michael's face when he sees the pair of us! You *must* come to Strelsau with me, Cousin Rudolf! Seeing one of me upsets my brother's stomach, but seeing two would give him a stroke, for certain!''

"With all due respect to both Your Majesty and Mr. Rassendyll,'' said Fritz von Tarlenheim, cautiously, "I question the wisdom in your cousin visiting Strelsau at the moment.''

"Oh, balderdash,'' the king said. "Where's the harm?''

"No, Fritz is right, Your Majesty,'' said Sapt. "He mustn't go.''

"I wish to cause no one embarrassment,'' Finn said, feeling that he had to say it and hoping like hell they wouldn't take him up on it. "I'll leave Ruritania at once.''

"By thunder, you will do no such thing!'' the king said. "Pay no mind to these two old women. At any rate, I insist that you dine with me tonight, happen what will afterward. Come, man, you don't meet a new relation every day!''

"We dine sparingly tonight, Your Majesty,'' Fritz said, a bit awkwardly.

"Not we!'' the king said. "Not with our new cousin as our guest! Don't look so alarmed, Fritz, you old stick in the mud. I'll remember our early start tomorrow.''

"So shall I,'' said Sapt, puffing out clouds of heavy Latakia smoke and frowning.

"Well then, I can count on you to roust my royal carcass out of bed, then,'' said the king. "Come, Cousin Rudolf, the devil with the shooting for tonight. The deer avoid me like the plague. Besides, the two of us have much to talk about. I've no house of my own here, but my brother Michael lends us a place of his and we'll make shift to entertain you there.''

They started back down the hill and walked for half an hour down the trail until they came to a wooden hunting lodge, a large, one-story building with a steep roof and a small, railed porch. Elphberg peppered Finn with countless questions about himself and his family, to which Finn responded cautiously, drawing on the subknowledge of his implant programming. Fortunately, Finn didn't have to do much talking, as Rudolf practically never shut up. He was having a high old time while Sapt and von Tarlenheim walked behind them, clearly apprehensive about this sudden turn of events. For his part, Finn found the king to be a pleasant enough fellow, but completely wrapped up in himself. No sooner would he ask Finn a question than he would interrupt his answer to provide some anecdote about himself, his ancestors or somebody at court. He was not rude, exactly, just uncontrollably ebullient and lacking in any sort of concentration. His voice even sounded similar to Finn's, although it had a pomposity to it and a slightly higher pitch.

There were only two servants at the lodge, an old man and an old woman, both as rustic as the cabin. They evinced considerable surprise at seeing two of their king, but they knew their place well enough not to question this amazing occurrence and to speak only when spoken to; Rudolf spoke to them only to give orders.

Dinner, apparently, was already being prepared, giving the impression that during his stay at the hunting lodge, the king had been as impatient a hunter as he was a conversationalist. They did not have to wait too long until it was ready, and then they sat down to a sumptuous feast of venison steak which had been smoked, potatoes roasted in an open fire, fresh baked bread and blackberry jam, baked beans, and Yorkshire pudding. Finn laid to with a hearty appetite, to the king's obvious approval.

"We're all good trenchermen, we Elphbergs, what? But wait, we're eating dry! Wine, Josef! Wine, man! Are we beasts to eat without drinking? Break into that blackguard Michael's cellar and bring us forth some bottles before I die of thirst!"

"Remember tomorrow, Your Majesty," said Fritz. "The coronation."

"Damn it, Fritz, you remember tomorrow," the king said, irately. "You start before I do, you must be more sparing by two hours than I. And I'll have Cousin Rudolf to attend me."

"We really cannot afford to overindulge tonight," said Fritz to Finn, as if seeking his aid in calming down the king's boisterous spirit. "The colonel and I leave here sharply at six tomorrow. We must ride down to Zenda and return with the guard of honor to fetch the king at eight, and then we all ride together to the station, where we take the train to Strelsau."

"Hang that guard," said Sapt, sourly.

"Now, now, it's very civil of my brother to ask the honor for his regiment, wherever their sympathies may lie. I'll not discuss politics tonight, Sapt. At any rate, Cousin Rudolf, you have no need of starting early, so you can join me while these two temperate chaps abstain. What, only two bottles, Josef? Out with you, fetch us two bottles more. Michael can't drink all of it, you know."

It was late when the king pushed back from the table with a belch to announce that he had drunk enough. The wine had been excellent, indeed, a welcome change from the poor claret at the inn. Finn had matched Rudolf glass for glass, so that he now felt relaxed, full, and pleasantly diverted. While the old woman, whose name Finn never learned, cleared away the table, Josef brought in a wicker-covered bottle that looked as though it had been aging in Michael's cellar for quite some time.

"His Highness, the Duke of Strelsau, bade me to set this wine before the king when the king was weary of all other wines," he said, as though he had rehearsed the speech, which undoubtedly he had. "He asked that you drink for the love that he bears his brother."

"Well done, Black Michael!" said the king. "Hang him, he thinks to save the best for last, when my thirst has been abated. Well, out with the cork, Josef, my man."

As Finn watched with disbelief, the king took the bottle, put it to his mouth and drained it without pausing for breath. Then he flung it into a corner of the room, winked at them, put his head down on the table and was snoring within seconds.

As easy as that, thought Finn. All through the meal and well into the night, he had wondered nervously which bottle or which dish had contained the drug that Michael was supposed to dope his brother with, never dreaming that it would be done in so obvious a manner. Obvious to someone who expected it, at any rate. He sighed with relief, grateful for the fact that now he would not have to inject himself with the adrenergen that would have kept him up all night, clawing at the ceiling, regardless of which drug Michael had used or how potent a dose he had selected. He could now enjoy his buzz and get a good night's sleep without having to worry about that frightful nitro hammering through his brain or terrorists sneaking up on him in the middle of the night. The others were keeping watch outside with night scopes. It really wasn't fair. He'd had a great meal and fine wine to drink and he'd be sleeping soundly in a warm bed while they shivered in the cold night air outside, staying awake to protect him.

Ah, well, life's a bitch, he thought. He sincerely hoped it wouldn't rain.

So much time spent in the bowels of Zenda Castle had made Drakov accustomed to darkness, so he was easily able to make out the shape of the Observer. He was so intent upon watching the hunting lodge that he was completely ignorant of Drakov's presence a mere several yards away. Death stood right behind him, Drakov thought, almost within reach, and he didn't even know it. He didn't sense a thing. No subconscious realization made the hairs prickle on the back of his neck, no sensation as though someone had walked across his grave made him apprehensive, no sudden intuition made him spin around to face the danger.

They were all wrong, thought Drakov, all the poets and the storytellers who ever dwelt upon the darker side of human nature in their art. Death is not a melodrama. If anything, it is a pathetic one-act comedy that had been poorly written. The audience never laughs and by the time they realize that the play simply isn't funny, it is already over.

Drakov felt a touch of sadness as he saw that the Observer was little more than a boy. The miracle drug treatments of Falcon's time made physical appearances deceptive, as in his own case, but there were other indicators of the fellow's youthfulness—the tension in his bearing, the restlessness which made him shift position constantly, the subtle yet telling sounds he made despite his efforts at not making any noise. He was like a small boy out on his first hunting trip with an old veteran, spending his first night in a hunting stand. The old hunter, experienced and calm, knew to blend in with the silence of the forest; he knew how to relax into complete motionlessness. The small boy was too excited, too inexperienced to appreciate such subtleties. Despite all his best efforts, he moved too much, unable to synchronize his heartbeat with the gentle sighing of the wind. He would think that he was being quiet, but the tiny sounds he made, almost inaudible to him, would be like claps of thunder to the forest animals. The old hunter, of course, would know this, but he would say nothing. He would know that there would be no game on such a night, with such a green companion. The object of the lesson would be to give the boy an opportunity to learn to wait. In time, the boy would learn. But this boy would never have the time.

Drakov, the old hunter, wondered why it was that artists always attempted to poeticize death and violence. Death was merely final, finality in itself, and real violence was sudden, terrible, and often totally incomprehensible. It wasn't death that was poetic, he thought as he watched his young victim with a mournful gaze, it was survival. That was something few artists ever understood. The Russians understood it. Pushkin, Lermontov, Dostoevsky, Tolstoy, especially Tolstoy. The Russian loves to suffer, Drakov thought, because he has never known another state, and so he has embraced the only state he knows. Wistfully, he thought that the soul of a Russian peasant was a lovely thing, simple and innocent and pure.

"It is from the soil of Russia," his mother had once told him in Siberia, "watered by the tears of all of those who've suffered, that the flower of the new world will one day spring."

"And what if that flower turns out to be a weed?" he had asked her, already a cynic at the age of fourteen, never imagining just how prophetic his words would turn out to be.

"Then that weed will be watered by those self-same tears of suffering," his mother said. "One must suffer before one can know redemption."

If that was true, thought Drakov, then his mother had been redeemed many times over. But he was not certain it was true. He was not certain that one could be redeemed. Another writer, an American—who else?—had written that Byronic melancholy was the opium of the intellectuals and the last refuge of little minds. No doubt Falcon would agree. She never had the time to grieve, as she had so simply and mercilessly put it, for all the souls who fell by the wayside. Reluctantly, he took out his laser and aimed it at his victim's head. He hesitated.

The beam flash would undoubtedly alert the others, who were neither as young nor as inexperienced as this one. He transferred the laser to his left hand and moved forward slowly, silently, closing the distance between them. He raised his right arm and brought the edge of his right hand down hard on the back of the young man's neck, just below the point at which the spine met the base of the skull.

He heard a voice cry out as he struck and he spun instinctively, firing blindly with his left hand and hitting the chronoplate remote with his right. Even as he fired, he felt a searing pain lance along his side and the next thing he knew, he was back in the turret atop the keep of Zenda Castle, collapsing to the floor and grimacing with pain. He had not been the only hunter on the stalk. Just before he had clocked out, he had caught a brief glimpse of a dark shape silhouetted against the moonlight. And, irrationally, in that brief instant he had known exactly who it was.

4

A bucketful of stinging cold water brought Finn sputtering to his feet, ready to commit murder. "God *damn* it!" he shouted, but Sapt pushed him back down onto the bed, ducking under his wild punch easily.

"Stay yourself, man," the old officer said, sharply. "I tried every other means of waking you and you would not budge. It's five o'clock."

"*Five o'clock!*" said Finn, still not fully cognizant.

"Rassendyll," said Fritz von Tarlenheim, taking him by the arm. "Look here."

Rudolf Elphberg was stretched out full length upon the floor, completely drenched. It appeared that they had thrown at least four times as much water on him as they had on Finn and still he slept. Sapt moved over to him and gave him a sharp slap in the face, hard enough to make Finn wince.

"Wake up, Your damned useless Majesty!" he said. "Hang him, he drank three times what either of you did," Sapt said, eyeing both Finn and von Tarlenheim with fury. "And damn me all to hell for sitting there and letting him! This is a fine muddle!"

"We've spent half an hour on him," von Tarlenheim said with exasperation.

Finn knelt down and felt the king's pulse. It was quite slow.

"What, Rassendyll, are you a doctor?" von Tarlenheim said, hopefully.

"I've studied medicine," Finn said, improvising. "However, a thousand doctors wouldn't do him any good right now."

"What!" cried Sapt, with a look of horror on his face. "What are you saying? He's not dead!"

"No, he's not dead," said Finn, "but he has every appearance of having been drugged."

"Drugged!" said Fritz. Understanding dawned on him. *"Michael! Damn the bastard!* It was that last bottle, for a fact! Sapt, we have been taken for a pair of mighty fools! How on earth will we get him to the coronation now?"

"He won't be crowned today," said Finn. "My guess is that he won't come around for at least eight or ten hours."

Von Tarlenheim licked his lips. "This is a disaster," he said. "We shall have to send word that he's ill."

"We are ruined," said Sapt. "If he's not crowned today, I'll lay a crown he's never crowned."

"But why?" said Finn. "Surely, it can't be so serious?"

"Serious?" said Sapt. "The whole nation will be there to meet him and half the army with Black Michael at its head. Shall we send word that the king is drunk?"

"That he's ill," said Finn.

"Ill!" said Sapt. "His 'illnesses' are only too well known. Rudolf's been 'ill' before."

"There's nothing to be done," said von Tarlenheim. "We shall simply have to put on a sober face and make the best of it. I say," he paused, "that was a poor choice of words, under the circumstances."

"I should have known," said Sapt. "I should have known that he would try something of this sort, but I did not give him enough credit. He's let Rudolf be hoist with his own petard!" He slapped the king again. "The drunken dog! Still, I'll rot in hell before I see Black Michael sit on the throne in his place!"

Sapt chewed furiously on one end of his moustache, his brow deeply furrowed.

"Surely, something can be done!" said von Tarlenheim, though his tone of voice did not hold forth much hope.

Suddenly, Sapt looked up, staring at Delaney. Finn played

dumb and simply stood there, looking bewildered, as did von Tarlenheim for a moment or two, until he realized what Sapt was thinking.

"No!" he whispered softly, looking from Sapt to Finn and back again.

"Yes, by God!" said Sapt. "It just might work!"

Finn gauged the moment right to "realize" what they intended, but he had to play it well. "Oh, no," he said, stepping back from them and shaking his head.

"Rassendyll, do you believe in Fate?" said Sapt.

You don't want to know, thought Finn.

"It was Fate that sent you here, man, and now it's Fate that beckons you to Strelsau."

"It would never work," said Finn. "They'd know that I was not the king!"

"If you shave?" said Sapt. "Who would ever expect it? You'd be his spitting image."

"I'd be bound to make some blunder," Finn said.

"We shall be beside you every moment," Sapt said. "Granted, it's a risk. Are you afraid, lad?"

"Sir!" said Finn, in mock outrage at the suggestion.

"Don't take offense," said Sapt, "it's your life that will be on the line, and ours as well if we are caught. But if we do not make the attempt, it is a certain thing that Black Michael will be the one sitting on the throne tonight and the king in prison or even in his grave. You do not know Black Michael. Fritz will bear me out that I do not overstate the danger."

"But what will the king say when he finds out?" said Finn.

"Who cares what he says?" said Sapt. "It's his own worthless hide that we'll be saving. I daresay that he might even learn from this, though I hold out no great hope. What do you say, man? In truth, you owe us nothing and not a man on earth could blame you if you were to refuse, but you're the one chance that we have; you see that, don't you?"

Finn decided that he made enough protestations for the sake of appearances. He looked down at the unconscious form of Rudolf Elphberg, wondering if perhaps Ruritania would not be better served by having his brother on the throne.

"Yes, of course, I see," he said.

"You'll do it, then?" said Sapt, eagerly.

Finn took a deep breath and let it out slowly. "It's insane," he said, "but yes, I'll do it."

"Good man!" said Sapt, relieved. "Listen, then, this is how we must bring it off. Fritz and I will prepare you to the best of our abilities. The ceremony itself is simple enough; an idiot could get through it. We'll hide the king here. We shall be staying in the palace at Strelsau tonight. The very moment we are left alone after the coronation, you and I will mount and ride here at the gallop. Fritz will stay behind at the palace to make certain that no one enters the royal bedchambers. When the king awakens here, Josef will tell him what has transpired. We may depend on him, he has served the king since boyhood. The king will then ride back with me to Strelsau and you must make all speed to the frontier."

"There's a chance," said Fritz, nodding. "Yes, it could work!"

Sapt went to the door and called for Josef, who paled when he saw the king lying on the floor. As quickly as he could, Sapt filled the old man in and sent him for a razor. Josef moved quickly and returned in moments with hot water, soap, and several razors. Finn was not encouraged when he saw how badly the old man's hand was shaking, but he sat down in a chair and submitted to the barbering.

"Christ!" von Tarlenheim said, jumping to his feet. "We forgot about the guard!"

"We won't wait for the guard," said Sapt. "We shall take the train from Hofban. We'll be long gone by the time they come."

"But what of the king?" said Fritz.

"I'll carry him down to the wine cellar. Josef will stay wtih him."

"But suppose they find him?"

"They won't. Why should they bother looking? They don't know about Cousin Rudolf, here. I'll take His Drunken Majesty down there right now."

Sapt bent down and picked the king up easily, throwing his body over his shoulders as if it were a sack of flour. He moved quickly to the door and opened it, revealing the old woman who had served them the previous night standing in the doorway. She immediately spun around and went off without a word.

"You think she heard?" said Fritz. "Heaven help us if she did; she's Michael's servant."

"Leave her to me," said Sapt. He went out with the king, shutting the door behind him. Fritz von Tarlenheim watched as Delaney's beard was shaved. When Josef was done, having managed to avoid shedding any of Finn's blood, Fritz stood back and examined the results.

"I really do believe we'll pull it off!" he said. "I don't think I'd know you from the king myself!"

Sapt returned in a short while, having taken the king down to the cellar. He told them that he had taken the old woman there as well and left her bound and gagged beside the king, where Josef could watch them both.

"By the time she tells anything she heard to Michael," Sapt said, "the coronation will be over, the king will be in the palace, and Cousin Rudolf will be on his way to London. Let Black Michael try to prove that anything untoward happened. He will have been beaten. When the old woman tells him about Cousin Rudolf here, he'll know just how we did it. He can stew till hell freezes over and be powerless to change a thing!"

They brought the king's uniform and helped Finn put it on; then they dressed in their own. Finn was given the king's helmet and sword and with two hours to spare before the guard was due, they mounted up and rode at a breakneck pace to the village of Hofban, where they took the first train to Strelsau. On the way, both Sapt and von Tarlenheim briefed Finn as to what he could expect, what to look out for, whom to know and how, and what the proper etiquette was for all that he could be expected to go through.

From the time that they had left the lodge to the time they boarded the train, Finn had seen no sign of Andre, Derringer, or Lucas. He hoped that they were keeping on top of things. Sapt and von Tarlenheim both drilled him ceaselessly, making him mimic the king's voice until he had the pitch and intonation down. Both men seemed as delighted with his per-

formance as two schoolboys in the midst of planning a great
prank. However, as the train drew closer to Strelsau, they
both began to show their nervousness. Finn was nervous, too,
but not so much because of his impersonation as because he
did not know where the others were and he had no idea what
he could expect from Falcon. Soon, the towers of the palace
were visible from the windows of the train and then the city of
Strelsau came into view.

"Your capital, my liege," said Sapt. He looked at Finn intently. "How do you feel?"

"Positively regal," Finn said.

Sapt chuckled. "You'll do. Fritz, you look white as a sheet.
Drain your flask, for God's sake, and put some color in your
cheeks."

As the train pulled up to the platform, Sapt glanced outside
and nodded to himself. "Things look well," he said. "We are
early and no one expects us on this train. No one's here to
meet us yet. We'll send word of Your Majesty's arrival, meanwhile—"

"Meanwhile, His Majesty is starving," Finn said, "and
he'll be hanged if he doesn't have some breakfast."

Von Tarlenheim hiccoughed and Sapt grinned. "You're an
Elphberg, all right," he said. "Every inch of you. Well, with
God's help, we'll all still be alive when this is over."

"Amen," said Fritz.

You can say that again, thought Finn.

The train came to a stop and Sapt and von Tarlenheim went
out first. Finn put on his helmet and stepped out onto the platform, trying to walk with the same sauntering strut as Rudolf.
He was recognized in no time at all and the entire area around
the train station became a flurry of activity, a helter-skelter in
which he was the center of attention. Sapt and von Tarlenheim
stayed close by him every second, running interference for him
as they took him through the quickly gathering crowd to
breakfast. Finn ate with a hearty appetite, Sapt ate sparingly
and drank lots of coffee, while Fritz von Tarlenheim merely
sat there looking ill and chewing on his fingernails. As Finn
finished his breakfast of shirred eggs and sausage with biscuits
and gravy, the bells of the city began to ring in a cacophony of

clanging and people in the street outside were shouting, "God save the king!"

Sapt smiled. "God save 'em both," he said. "Courage, lad."

"Lad," thought Finn, I'm old enough to be your father. Here's hoping I live to be a little older. He raised his coffee cup to Sapt in a silent toast and drained it. If you think this is bad, he wanted to tell him, wait'll you see what's coming next.

Von Tarlenheim and Sapt never left Finn's side as the dignitaries arrived and paid their respects prior to forming the procession. Whispered promptings from Sapt identified to Finn people who had already been described to him during the train ride or, in the event of an omission in the hurried briefing, the old man would give quick thumbnail sketches, such as, "Marshal Strakencz, Ruritania's most famous veteran, a trusted ally, but not an intimate friend." Then, a quick bit of stage direction to guide Finn's manner. "Warmly, but speak loudly. Strakencz is hard of hearing."

Things flowed smoothly and the procession formed, with Finn, Sapt, and von Tarlenheim taking up position in the center of the parade that wound through the streets of Strelsau's New Town and into the old quarter, where the avenues narrowed and the three- and four-story houses showed signs of age. Many of these houses also showed signs of Ruritania's political polarity, differing from those around them in the conspicuous lack of red flags or red bunting being displayed. Some of them were not decorated at all, while others showed a touch of black. Others still, more boldly, displayed Black Michael's portrait in their windows. Invariably, the people who stood upon the balconies of these houses did not wave or cheer, but stared sullenly and silently at Finn as he rode by on his horse with Sapt and von Tarlenheim flanking him on theirs.

Sapt kept his eyes on Finn, like a coach critically watching the performance of a favored athlete, while von Tarlenheim all but shook with nervousness, sweating rivers in his white regimental uniform and darting glances all around as if expecting at any moment someone to call out, like the young boy who cried that the emperor wore no clothes, "That's not the king!" But no such cry came and Finn played his part by waving to the crowd and removing his helmet to display "the Elphberg red" whenever they passed a group of houses adorned with Michael's raven-headed likeness. Finn found himself rather enjoying the whole thing, catching bouquets of red roses and then tossing them back into the crowd, smiling at the flirtatious glances of young women who leaned down from their balconies to watch him pass, and returning the salutes of old men who stiffened to arthritic attention as he rode by. Then, when the procession approached the palatial Grand Hotel on the Grand Boulevard of Strelsau, the grim reality of his situation was driven home to him. As they rode up to the balcony of the Grand Hotel, Finn spotted one woman who neither waved nor cheered, standing out from those who surrounded her by virtue of the daring dress she wore, scandalous by the standards of the time, jet black and form-fitting with a deeply plunging neckline. Long and lovely ash-blond hair framed her striking face. His stomach muscles tensed as their eyes met and she gave him a small half-smile.

After that, the approach to the cathedral, the greeting of the archbishop, the shocked and furious stare of Black Michael, and the ceremony itself were all anticlimactic. Finn went through it all like an automaton, kneeling before the altar and being anointed, accepting the crown, swearing the oath, receiving the Holy Sacrament, and being proclaimed Rudolf the Fifth of Ruritania, all the while seeing her standing there upon the balcony as if to mock him, remembering that moment when their eyes met. She knew that he knew her. There had been no effort at pretense, no surreptitiousness, no subtlety. She simply stood there in plain sight, gazing at him as if he were her next meal. In that one instant, Finn had understood the fatal attraction that she had for Mongoose. The woman projected an aura of carnal hunger, as though the blueprint for her design had been drawn by Grigori Rasputin and the Marquis de Sade. She had a savage beauty that somehow managed to both attract and repel at the same time. It was a presence that was instantly recognizable to anyone who had come across that particularly rare and deadly species before.

Few people had it and those who did always seemed to stare at you with little crosshairs in their eyes. Finn could not imagine her and Forrester together. For Mongoose, the pairing would have been completely natural, like the mating of two were-wolves. Falcon had played the first move and she at once controlled the board. The woman had thoroughly unnerved him.

It was with an effort that he finally managed to wrench his concentration back to the matters at hand. With some dismay, he greeted his future queen, the Princess Flavia, for in their eagerness to prepare him for the ceremony and for every official he was bound to meet, Sapt and von Tarlenheim had neglected to tell him—or had forgotten—that he would be riding in a coach alone with her to the palace.

They greeted each other in a warm yet formal manner and Finn noticed right away that she was distant. Not quite aloof, but very cautious and reserved. They took their place together in the coach that was to take them to the banquet at the palace, and Finn caught von Tarlenheim's look of total panic. Sapt was trying to give him little signals, a slow nodding of the head and languid palm down gestures as if to say, "You're doing fine, keep playing it the same way. Formal. Polite. Regally detached." However, his furrowed brow clearly spoke of his concern.

Finn felt a little ill at ease, not quite knowing what to say to her, so he occupied himself instead with looking out the window and waving to the crowd. He was aware of her gaze upon him and, after a little while, it began to feel uncomfortable. He turned to look at her and smiled, waiting for her to say something. What she said was not encouraging.

"Somehow, Rudolf, you look a little different today."

"Oh?" said Finn, hoping she would respond with something that would give him a bit more to work with.

"You appear somehow more sober, more sedate," she said. She smiled, disarmingly. "Almost as if you actually had serious matters on your mind."

Tell me about it, Finn thought. "Is that so unlike me, then?" he said, still smiling.

"If it is not, it is a side of you I have not seen before," she said. Then, changing tack abruptly, she pursed her lips and narrowed her eyes. "Did you see Michael's face?"

"That must have been what sobered me," said Finn.

"I think you take him far too lightly, Rudolf. Did you see how he looked at you?"

"He didn't seem to be enjoying himself," said Finn.

"You should be more careful of him," Flavia said. "You don't know— You don't keep enough watch on him. You know how he feels."

"I know he wants what I've got," said Finn. "But then, can you really blame him?"

"If you cannot, I can," she said. "You should see the way he watches me when you are not looking."

Finn grinned. "No doubt, the way that any other man would—when I was not looking."

She drew her lips together tightly and shook her head. "No, not that way at all," she said. "It makes me think of a wicked little boy watching someone playing with a toy that he regards as being his."

"Somehow I've never thought of you as being a toy," said Finn. "Nor of Michael as being very playful."

"Oh, you're insufferable!" she said, looking away from him. "I thought perhaps the coronation would make you realize your responsibilities, but I see that nothing's changed!"

And with any luck, thought Finn, things will remain that way. They finished out the remainder of the ride in silence, with frozen smiles on their faces as they waved to the crowd.

Finn was exhausted by the time he reached Rudolf's rooms inside the palace. He took off his helmet and threw it on the bed, unbuckled his sword, and simply let it drop onto the floor, then collapsed into a chair. He unfastened the high collar of his uniform blouse and gave a great sigh of relief.

"What a day for you to remember!" said von Tarlenheim, ebullient now that it was over. "King for a day, what? Imagine what your friends in London would make of it, though of course, you must never tell them! Did you see Michael? He looked positively green! We've done it! We've actually done it! You were magnificent!"

"We haven't done it yet," said Sapt, puffing on his ever-present pipe. "Don't get too comfortable, Cousin Rudolf." He handed Finn a flask. "Here, have some brandy. Rest a moment, but rest briefly. We have a hard ride ahead of us." He reached into his pocket, pulled out a gold watch and consulted it. "It is now five o'clock. By twelve, if all goes well, you should be Rudolf Rassendyll once more and safely on your way to England. I've brought a change of clothing for you. The fit may not be exact, but it should do. I've stolen it from my orderly, who is about your size. The quicker you can change, the sooner we can be on our way and the more secure my old head will feel on these weary shoulders."

Finn got up and started changing. Sapt turned to Fritz von Tarlenheim.

"Once more, Fritz," he said, "the king is weary and has retired for the night. He has given you strict orders that no one is to disturb his rest till nine o'clock tomorrow morning. Michael may come and demand an audience. You are to refuse him. Say anything, tell him that only princes of the blood are entitled to it."

"I say," said von Tarlenheim, "that's pushing it a bit, don't you think? If I goad him in that manner, he's liable to draw steel on me!"

"Even if he does, you are to remain unmoved," said Sapt. "You are acting on orders of the king. That should be clear enough, even to Black Michael. If this door is opened while we are away, you're not to be alive to tell us about it. You understand?"

"You can rely on me," said Fritz.

Sapt then led Finn through a secret panel and into a passage that he said the old king had had cause to use upon occasion to slip in and out of the palace unobserved. It led to a quiet street behind the palace gardens, where Sapt had two horses waiting. He dismissed the man who held them, then beckoned Finn forward, and they mounted and rode through back streets at full gallop, scattering those whom they encountered. Finn was wrapped in a long riding cloak and he wore a hat pulled low over his eyes, so that no one could get a clear glimpse of his face. He crouched low like a jockey and kept his head down until they were well out of the city.

They had ridden hard for twenty-five miles when they stopped to rest their horses and wash some of the dust out of their throats with whiskey. Finn felt totally exposed. They rested by the side of the road for a few minutes, then were about to proceed when Sapt grabbed Finn's arm and said, "Listen!"

Finn had already heard it. "Horses," he said.

Sapt swung up into the saddle. "It could be a pursuit," he said. "It sounds like they're riding hard. Quickly, man, set spur!"

The growing dark and the curving road sheltered them from their pursuers as they worked their horses to a lather once again. After a half an hour's ride, they came to a division in the road and Sapt reined in.

"Our way is to the right," he said. "The left road leads to Zenda Castle. Get down and muzzle your horse. I want to see who rides behind us and which way they are headed."

They took their horses into the trees at the side of the road and held them on short rein with their hands covering their muzzles. They had a clear view of the road. Before very long, two horsemen rode into view, one leading the other by about three lengths. The first rider reached the division of the road and reined in.

"Which way?" he said.

"*Hentzau!*" Sapt said softly.

"To the castle," said the other loudly, having pulled even with Hentzau. "We'll learn the truth of the matter there. I'll know why Detchard sends word that all is well when they have bungled it! They'll have much to answer for!"

As he watched them ride off at full gallop down the road to Zenda Castle, Sapt swore. "Hentzau and Black Michael! This bodes ill, indeed!"

"Who's Hentzau?" Finn said. Though it was a name he knew from his mission programming, Rassendyll would not have heard it.

"Rupert Hentzau," Sapt said. "A young gamecock soldier of fortune Michael found somewhere. Of the six throat-cutters he has retained of late, Hentzau is the worst. He'll be at Michael's own throat if Michael doesn't watch him. I don't like the looks of this at all. Come, full speed to the lodge!"

Sapt leaped into the saddle with a spryness that belied his years and took off down the road leading to the lodge. Finn had to ride hard to stay with the old man and both horses were about done in. When they reached the hunting lodge, there was no sign of life anywhere about. The horses were still out in the paddock when they should have long since been taken back into their stalls. Although it was dark and the night was chill, there were no lights burning in the lodge; there was no smoke curling from the chimney.

"Something's gone wrong," said Sapt, drawing his revolver. "Watch yourself, Rassendyll."

Finn had a revolver of his own that Sapt had given him, a top-break British Webley, but he felt much more secure knowing that he had a small laser tucked into his boot.

The lodge was empty. Sapt made his way directly to the wine cellar, reaching it just ahead of Finn. Finn heard him cry out as he came through the door. There was no sign of the old woman whom Sapt had tied up. More importantly, there was no sign of the king. There was only old Josef, lying on the floor of the cellar with his throat cut.

Sapt was bent over the table, sitting on the edge of his chair, his hands clenched into fists and gouging at his temples. "I've got to think!" he kept saying in a low, savage voice, over and over again.

The shock of seeing Josef dead and the king gone had thrown the old soldier. He was trying to wrench himself out of it, not quite knowing how.

"The old woman must have gotten loose somehow," said Finn, trying to prompt him, to get his motor started.

"No, no," said Sapt, "I tied her up myself, I tell you. She could barely move!"

"Then it must have been Josef," Finn said. "They would have been alone for some time before the guard came to escort the king, right?"

Sapt looked at him, puzzled, still not quite recovered.

"She's lying there, a poor, harmless old woman, somebody's grandmother, for Christ's sake, bound hand and foot and gagged. Josef sits there watching her, waiting for the guard to come so that he can go upstairs and tell them that the king has departed early without waiting for them. She stares up at him with wide, frightened eyes. Perhaps she's crying, maybe she is having trouble breathing. She moans patheti-

cally. The ropes are cutting into her skin, stopping the circulation. Poor old Josef wrestles with his conscience, then gives in.
He'll loosen her bonds just a bit, perhaps adjust her gag, make
it easier for the poor old girl to breathe. The guard of honor
arrives and Josef goes upstairs to greet them."

"And she gets loose somehow or cries out!" said Sapt,
snapping out of it at last. "Yes, it must have been something
like that. Damn it, I should have killed her to begin with!"

"Could you have?" said Finn, gently. "She was just an old
woman after all, being loyal to her master."

"Yes, you're right, of course," said Sapt. "Thank you,
Rassendyll. I imagine that it must have happened almost
exactly as you say. Detchard would have been with the guard,
of course. Michael's given the blackguard a commission. Possibly Bersonin, as well, maybe one or two of the others. The
Six, that's how they're known. Black Michael's private squad
of bodyguards. A killer, each and every one of them. I see
what must have happened now. The old woman somehow
managed to alert them and Detchard and several of the others
stayed behind while they sent the guard on ahead. They found
the king, much as they expected to, killed poor Josef, and sent
word on ahead to Michael that all was well. Only, having seen
you, Michael knew that all was far from well. The moment he
sees the real king, he'll realize what we have done. And the old
woman, of course, can tell him who you are. We are undone.
We are completely undone. All is lost."

"Where will they have taken the king?" said Finn.

"To Zenda Castle, undoubtedly," said Sapt. "No hope of
freeing him from there. The place is a fortress."

"We must do something, Sapt," Finn said. "We must get
back and rouse every soldier in Strelsau."

"And tell them what?" said Sapt. "That we had arranged
for an imposter to be crowned while the real king lay drunk in
Zenda? You forget, Rassendyll, that much of the army sides
with Michael. How can we tell them what Michael has done
without revealing our deception?"

"But the king may be murdered even as we sit here!" Finn
said, trusting to the old soldier's quick thinking to leap to the
logical conclusion. Sapt did not disappoint him.

"No, by God!" he said, rising to his feet with a wild gleam

in his eyes. "No, they can't. They will not dare!"

Finn looked at him with feigned uncomprehension.

"We've shaken up Black Michael, by the Saints," he said, "and we'll shake him some more! Aye, we'll go back to Strelsau, lad. The king shall be in his capitol again tomorrow!"

"The king?" said Finn, still playing dumb.

"The crowned king!" Sapt said.

"You're mad!" said Finn. "We'd never get away with it."

"If we go back now and tell them what we've done," said Sapt, "what would you give for our lives?"

"Just what they're worth," said Finn.

"And for the king's throne? Do you think for one moment that the nobles and the army and the people will sit still for being fooled the way we've fooled them? Will they love a king who was too drunk to be crowned and sent a servant to impersonate him?"

"He was drugged," said Finn, "and I'm not his servant."

"Mine will be Black Michael's version," Sapt said. "Can you disprove it?"

Finn chewed on his lower lip. "No," he said. "You're right, Sapt, that would be playing right into Michael's hands."

"So we do the one thing left for us to do! You must return with me and continue playing the king. Michael will know the truth, as will those who are in on his plot with him, but don't you see, Rassendyll? They cannot speak! Just as we cannot speak for fear of revealing what we have done, so they are in the same predicament! Do they denounce you as a fraud, thereby revealing that they have kidnapped the king and killed his servant? No, they cannot. Michael has the king in his power now, true, and in that his plot has succeeded better than he had hoped. Your playing Rudolf enables him to keep the king a prisoner, but he cannot murder him, for that could make your impersonation a lifelong one. Nor can he produce the king to unmask you without unmasking himself, as well. It is a stalemate. A stalemate works in our favor. We need time to plan and you can buy us that time!"

"But suppose you're wrong, Sapt," Finn said. "Suppose they kill the king?"

"If you do not carry on with the charade, my friend, I can assure you that the king is as good as dead. We have slipped away from the palace like thieves in the night, leaving poor Fritz to guard the royal bedchamber with orders to admit no one. Suppose Michael, having realized our plan, returns posthaste to Strelsau with Hentzau and some of the others in tow? Suppose he confronts Fritz and demands entrance to the royal bedchamber?''

"Von Tarlenheim will stand firm," said Finn.

"Aye, that he will and against Michael alone he could hold the doors, but against Michael and Hentzau together? Hentzau by himself would not be deterred by Fritz. The man is the very devil of a swordsman and an expert marksman. So they kill Fritz, storm the royal bedchamber and the king is nowhere in evidence. The secret passageway will be discovered and it will be clear to all what has occurred. Having attended his coronation and quaffed wine at the banquet, the king slipped out the secret passage for some clandestine assignation. That is how Michael would construe it! And he would have the devil's own confederates to back him up."

"What do you mean?"

"I have lived as long as I have because as a soldier, I always asked myself, what strategy would I employ if I were in my enemy's position? With no king in the palace, a frenzied search is made for him and as the search progresses, Michael moves to assure himself the throne. He has the king. He murders him. And then the king is 'found' in the bedchamber of some woman, killed by a jealous lover who recognized the man that he had slain and fled. If I were Michael, I would no doubt enlist the aid of the Countess Sophia, that woman you were staring at so fixedly when we passed the Grand Hotel. She has scarcely been in Strelsau for a month and already her reputation as a libertine is notorious. In any case, with the king in his power, Michael can murder him at will and dispose of the body in some such fashion and who will be able to gainsay him?''

"But so long as I'm alive and playing the king . . ." said Finn.

"Exactly."

"Which means that Michael would have to dispose of me, first," Finn said.

Sapt looked grim. "I will not try to deceive you, Rassendyll.

There will be great risk, even greater than before. But without your help—"

"We'd best get going, then," said Finn."I saw fresh horses in the paddock. If we ride hard, we can still get to Strelsau well ahead of them. I just hope that Michael's thought the whole thing out as well as you have and keeps from murdering the king."

Sapt looked at him with the wild exuberance of a man embarking on a desperate venture. "If he does," he said, "then, by Heaven, you're as good an Elphberg as Black Michael and *you* shall reign in Ruritania!"

5

Forrester knew he had to move fast. Lucas and Andre would have seen the beam flashes, and with no reason to expect anyone except the Timekeepers, they would fire on sight. It would be embarrassing, to say the least, to be burned by his own people. He turned the Observer's body over and quickly started searching it.

Christ, he thought, they're sending children now. He recognized the boy. Bobby Derringer. Mensinger's grandson. He remembered him from RCS, when he had lectured there on temporal adjustments, part of his regular duties in Plus Time. That had only been last year. What the hell was he doing on Observer duty in the field already? He recalled that the kid had an amazing mind. He must have breezed through RCS in record time. Now he was dead. When were those people going to learn that it took more than classroom instruction to prepare people for active duty in Minus Time? As he stared down at the dead boy's face, his feelings were a volatile mixture of sorrow, anger, outrage and self-recrimination. If he had fired just one moment sooner. . . .

His searching hands found what they were looking for. Derringer's chronoplate remote. For a brief moment, he hesitated. The most important thing now was to safeguard the

Observer's chronoplate. He had to get to it at once, but he had no idea what would happen if he activated the remote. The remote would instantly transport him to the location of the chronoplate, but there was no way of knowing what he would be clocking into. On the other hand, if he stayed where he was, he would be in danger from his own people. He knew only too well how they would react. He had trained them himself. That decided him. He hit the button on the small remote, launching hmself into a diving forward roll even as he did so.

He disappeared in midair and an instant later, completed the forward roll upon a wooden floor, coming up with his laser held ready in his hand. Before he could even realize where it was he found himself, before he could recover from the dizzying effects of the transition, his ears picked up a soft, *chuffing* sound and a faint mechanical whirring noise. Instinctively, he fired in the direction of the sound.

The tracking system he had incapacitated had just been zeroing in on him, reacting to his body temperature. It was a small, portable unit that had been set up on a tripod. The chuffing noise had been the sound of its twin turrets firing. In the opposite wall, at the level where his chest would have been had he clocked in standing up, two small needle darts were imbedded in the plaster. He went over to the wall and pulled one out. An M-90 Stinger. Clever. If anyone broke into the safe-house who had no business being there or if someone managed to get hold of his remote and clock in without knowing how to deactivate the tracking system, the M-90s would knock him out for a period of at least 48 hours. You can teach them to be clever, he thought, but you can't teach them the instincts they need in order to survive. They have to pick those up themselves and no one had given Derringer that chance.

He took stock of his surroundings. It was a small room with a well-worn bare wooden floor and white plaster walls grown dingy with age and neglect. The beamed ceiling was low and there was only one tiny window that looked out on a narrow alley with nothing opposite it except the wall of the adjoining building. A ramshackle bed covered with a heavy woolen blanket stood in one corner of the room. A crude table made of old, scarred oak, heavy and blocky, was stood up against the bare wall to his right. Two wooden chairs were pushed in to the table. There was a large porcelain bathtub, a chamberpot, a sofa with faded and torn upholstery, a throw rug before the sofa, a battered reading chair and an old lamp. A wooden chest of drawers with discolored brass handles and a large traveling chest completed the furnishings. With the exception of the damaged tracking system on its tripod, there was nothing to distinguish the shabby room from any other shabby room in the low-rent district of Strelsau's old quarter, except for the ring of border circuits on the floor where he had clocked in. The room was on the top floor of an old four-story building. The window had heavy wooden shutters and the door had a decent bolt. Forrester stood still by the door and listened for a moment, then he unbolted it and opened it a crack. He heard footsteps on the stairs close by and a moment later, two people walked past him down the hall, a man and a young woman. The man was stumbling slightly and mumbling to the woman, leaning on her heavily. She laughed in a sultry way and rubbed his crotch with her right hand. Meanwhile, her left hand reached into his pocket and removed his wallet. Derringer had done well in his selection of a safehouse. No one would notice the coming and goings here.

He closed the door and bolted it again, then turned to face the squalid little room. He spied a bottle on the floor beside the bed. It was three-quarters full, a bottle of Glenlivet unblended Scotch, very nonregulation. Damn kid, he thought, and suddenly tears came to his eyes.

Forrester didn't know why he was crying. He didn't know if it was from anger or sorrow or frustration. His emotions, which he had steadfastly held in check for more years than he could count and which had been under an extremely great strain ever since he had received that letter, suddenly let go, like a cable snapping, and he lost all control of them. They came over him in waves—unutterable grief at the death he might have, should have prevented; frustration at his inability to change what he had done; fury directed at himself and at the woman he once loved. Like some manic depressive run amok, his mood shifted with lightning speed; one moment he wanted to collapse onto the bed and sob his heart out, the next he felt charged up with a trembling fury that made him want to batter down the heavy plaster walls with his bare fists. He had Drakov in his sights and he had hesitated. And Derringer had died. Even when he fired, he could not be sure if it was Drakov's swift reaction or some unconscious impulse that had made him miss the killing shot. He seemed to remember crying out. Had he done that on purpose? In either case, the responsibility was his. He had not been able to kill his own son.

He should have told them. He should have told them at the briefing. He wanted to, but he had not been able to bring himself to do it. He had rationalized. They were the three finest soldiers under his command. They had never failed before. They would not fail now, he told himself. They will neutralize the threat, effect the adjustment, and correct the mistake I made many years ago. Why burden them with the knowledge of who it was I'm sending them to kill? But when they had left, the sour taste of guilt had filled him with immense self-loathing. He had given Drakov life. It was on him to take it away. Elaine—or Falcon—knew that, which was why she had written him that letter. She had known that he would come. It was all there, all the details, she knew it all, even more than he did. And to prove it, she had recounted the whole story for him.

It happened many years ago. The year was 1812 and the place was Russia just prior to the French invasion. He was a young man on his first mission to Minus Time, a newly indoctrinated recruit assigned to the Airborne Pathfinders, as green as a granny apple. The refs had selected that scenario for a campaign, and his unit was floater-clocked into the period for the purpose of scouting out the territory in order to facilitate the temporal conflict. They were to make maps and compile logistics reports. It was supposed to have been a routine mission.

The transition was a complete disaster. Half of his unit was lost in the dead zone coming through. Many came in too low and splattered before they could recover from the effects of the transition and activate their floater-paks. The survivors were widely scattered and, eventually, they managed to get back, but it was one hell of a mess. He came through alone.

He had never made transition before and there he was, on his first hitch, in free fall with a malfunctioning floater-pak. He came in way too low and way too fast. He barely had enough time to realize that he would splatter unless he gained some altitude in one heck of a hurry, so he kicked in his jets and that lousy, misbegotten piece of army ordnance shot him right at the ground instead of boosting him higher. It was all he could do to reduce his speed and try to alter his flightpath so that he didn't corkscrew into the Russian countryside.

He was over a field, traveling at a high rate of speed with a floater-pak that was virtually out of control. He resigned himself to death. He saw the old wooden barn looming up before him and, helpless to alter his direction, he plowed right into it. The barn was old, abandoned. It had seen a great deal of weathering and neglect. Sections of its roof were missing. He went through an exposed latticework of beams and cross-members, managing somehow to turn as he hit so that the pak absorbed most of the impact. It was torn right off him, damaged beyond all hope of repair. He sustained several broken ribs, a fractured collarbone, a broken arm, a broken wrist, a dislocated shoulder, numerous lacerations, and a concussion. Considering the circumstances, it was a miracle he wasn't killed.

He came to in a hayloft. He could still recall the smell. The hay was old and decomposing. It had rained recently and, with the gaping holes in the roof, much of it was wet. A young woman was kneeling over him, a beautiful young woman with green eyes and long, wavy black hair. She was using a kerchief to wipe the blood away from his face. Her hair was brushing his cheeks.

She spoke to him in Russian. He may have mumbled something back, he did not recall. She remained with him, caring for him as best she could, trying to set his bones and ease his pain. Her name was Vanna Drakova and she was a nineteen-year-old gypsy, a runaway serf. They were both very young, both lost, both scared.

It took Search & Retrieve a long time to sort the whole mess out. When no one came after him, he concluded that his implant must have been damaged in the crash through the barn roof. He assumed that he was stranded, marooned in the 19th century.

As the days dragged into weeks and weeks turned into months, he recovered slowly. His bones began to knit, but without proper medical attention, they did not heal properly. Thanks to the drug treatments he had received in the 27th century, he healed with astonishing rapidity, but he would be a cripple—functional, but twisted out of shape. There would be no going back or, in his case, forward to the time from which he came. In his despair, he told Vanna everything.

At first, she did not believe him. Eventually, however, he was able to convince her and more was the pity. He should have kept his mouth shut, but he believed that he would never get back to his own time, much less have his deformity corrected. It seemed important to him that she should know the truth, because by then she was pregnant with their child.

It never should have happened. Strict precautions were observed to prevent just such an occurrence, but Forrester did not react well to the pills they issued in those days. Rather than take the trouble of getting a temporary sterilization, he simply hadn't bothered taking them. It would have taken a mere couple of days of medical leave, but it would have caused him to miss out on his first mission, and he had been too eager to go out to wait until the next one. He had not counted on being intimate with anyone in Minus Time. The possibility had simply not occurred to him. He had not counted on being separated, thinking he was stranded, or falling in love. When S & R finally tracked him down, he didn't tell them that Vanna was pregnant. They would have aborted the fetus. It would have been the best thing all around, but he could not bring himself to go along with it. Leaving her would be hard enough.

He tried to explain things to her before they took him back. They were kind enough to give him the time. It was the hardest thing he ever had to do. He could not take her with him and he had no idea what would become of her and of their child. But there was nothing to be done. There were a lot of tears, both hers and his. She gave him a lock of her hair in remembrance and like a fool, he told her that he would come back for her. He never saw her again.

As if what he had done had not been bad enough, there was yet a further complication, something that never even occurred to him at the time. His family had not been well off and it was always taken for granted that he would go into the service. As a result, they had spared themselves the expense of procuring antiaging treatments for him. As an inducement for recruiting, the Temporal Corps provided antiagathic drug treatments for those unable to afford them during indoctrination processing. The drugs were very volatile. It took a long time for them to stabilize. When Vanna became pregnant, they were still active in his system and were passed on to her in his sperm.

Forrester tipped the unauthorized bottle of Glenlivet back and took a long pull from it. He had a son. Falcon took great pleasure in telling him about him in her letter. His name was Nikolai Drakov and, by now, he'd be 79 years old. She wrote that he appeared to be in his late twenties. She ran into him in London, purely by accident—he thought of Delaney and his fated coincidences. He had made a good life for himself. He was a very rich man, a playboy with a well-known reputation, especially for his astonishingly youthful appearance. She even joked about it. In the circles that he moved in, she wrote, he probably knew Oscar Wilde, which raised the intriguing possibility that he might have been the model for Dorian Grey. The fact that he looked so young had suggested another possibility to her. She thought at first that he was a member of the underground, a deserter from the Temporal Corps. In order to find out the truth, she had seduced him and found out a great deal more than she had bargained for.

He never knew his father, but he knew that his father's name was Moses Forrester and he knew who and what Moses Forrester was. His mother had told him all about his father before she died. She had been raped and killed when Nikolai was just 15. Falcon took him to Plus Time with her. She obtained an implant for him, educated him up to the standards of the 27th century, and indoctrinated him into the Timekeepers. Now things had come full circle.

He was back in his own time again, with her. It was he who had murdered Rudolf Rassendyll, causing the disruption. Drakov was motivated by a hatred which Falcon had fed—a hatred for his father. Forrester could hardly blame him.

Time had bent back in upon itself like some sort of double helix. Coincidence piled on coincidence piled on coincidence, with the Fate Factor tying the whole thing together. Forrester was sure that Finn Delaney would appreciate this little problem in zen physics. He imagined that Finn would be just thrilled to find out who got him into all of this, as would Andre and Lucas be. What could he tell them, that he was sorry?

Nikolai shouldn't be alive, he thought. He's a paradox. At the time he was conceived, I wouldn't have been born for another six hundred years. He should not exist, but he does. And I have to kill him. Or maybe he'll kill me. One way or another, it all ends here.

He tipped the bottle back again, wishing that Derringer had brought more than just the one.

The large grandfather clock in the sitting room outside the royal bedchamber chimed twice. It was a soft sound, coming through the closed doors, one that would not have impinged upon the monarch's sleep, but Finn heard it clearly. He seemed to hear even the slightest sound in his wing of the palace and in the streets outside. He lay on his back, chain-smoking Rudolf's Turkish cigarettes and wondering when he would finally start feeling the effects of the previous day's exertions.

He had been up since five o'clock in the morning, rudely awakened with a hangover to be plunged headlong into his impersonation of Rudolf Rassendyll impersonating Rudolf Elphberg. He was hustled at full gallop to the Hofban station, put aboard a train and drilled mercilessly in the requirements of the part he had to play. He was displayed to all of Strelsau in a grand parade, crowned king in an opulent and lengthy ceremony, driven through the city in a coach while improvising his way through his first meeting with Flavia, toasted in a seemingly interminable banquet, hustled once again on horseback at breakneck speed from Strelsau to Zenda and back again and yet *still* the adrenalin rush would not subside. It felt like being in battle.

He realized that the time had to come when it would hit him all at once, fearing that it would come at the worst possible moment, knowing that when it did come, he would have no choice but to resort to that small but no less potent dose of nitro that he carried. He loathed that horrifying stuff. It made him burn like some apocalyptic roman candle. When it wore off, he had the shakes for hours. The sleep that came thereafter was always filled with hideous nightmares that left him wondering at the sanity of a mind that could manufacture such twisted, tortured visions. He blew a long stream of smoke towards the large canopy above his bed and, for lack of anything better to do on this sleepless night, ran over the events of the last few hours in his mind, trying to get some sort of handle on the role he was assigned, a role in a demented play with only the barest outline of a script.

Poor Fritz von Tarlenheim, his nerves strained to the breaking point by his long vigil, almost had a stroke when he realized that it was not the king who had returned with Colonel Sapt. Finn wondered how he would have taken it if he had known that the man whom he first took to be the king returned from Zenda, but who was actually Rudolf Rassendyll was, in fact, not Rudolf Rassendyll at all, but a soldier from the 27th century named Finn Delaney, who just happened to resemble Rudolf Rassendyll, who just happened to resemble the king. Von Tarlenheim had been badly shaken when Sapt explained to him what had occurred. Finn could only imagine the effect on him if he were to have heard the *real* story.

You see, Fritz, it all has to do with something called the Fate Factor, which controls the flow of time. Most people believe that time is absolute, but in point of fact, it's not. Time is absolute only in a manner of speaking. It depends on where you are in time and what you're doing in time at the time. It's all a question of relativity—temporal relativity, to be exact. It's a bit difficult to comprehend, but don't concern yourself, old sport. The only man who ever came close to really comprehending it wound up committing suicide, so I wouldn't work too hard at trying to understand it all if I were you. Basically, what it comes down to is that my friends and I have come here from the future in order to prevent a group of criminals from the 27th century who call themselves the Timekeepers from altering the historical sequence of events in this tiny fragment of what we refer to as Minus Time. Unfortunately, what's making our job a bit difficult is the fact that not only are we supposed to make certain that events at this particular point in time proceed according to history when we aren't exactly sure of the historical details, but—and this is where it gets a little sticky—these Timekeepers are apparently intent on killing us while we're about it.

I realize it all sounds totally insane, Fritz, but the truth of the matter is that what we have here is a situation in which nothing seems to be happening the way it's supposed to happen and no one is who or what they seem to be. I'm not really Rassendyll. There's a woman here in Strelsau who calls herself the Countess Sophia and it appears that she's involved with Rupert Hentzau and Black Michael, only she's actually involved with the Timekeepers and her name is not Countess Sophia, but Sophia Falco, alias Elaine Cantrell, alias Falcon, a woman whose *true* identity no one seems to know. And while we know that Countess Sophia isn't really Countess Sophia, at this point we have no way of knowing if Rupert Hentzau is really Rupert Hentzau or if Black Michael is really Black Michael. For that matter, Princess Flavia, for all I know, could be a B-girl from San Diego, Sapt could be a hired assassin from Detroit and, come to think of it, Fritz, I'm not too sure about you, either.

Finn crushed his cigarette out with a vengeance, lighting up another one immediately. Best to stop thinking that way, he told himself. That kind of paranoia will make you really crazy. He wondered where in hell Lucas and Andre were. Why hadn't there been any contact? Not that there had been much chance for it, the way he'd been running around. His mind involuntarily returned to the image of Falcon standing on the balcony of the Grand Hotel, watching him with a mocking gaze, smiling. Had she wanted to, she could have taken him out right there and then. Rudolf the Fifth assassinated on the day of his coronation before thousands of witnesses. After that, Michael could have killed the king and there would have been a truly fine mess. So why hadn't she done it?

The only possible answer was that it would not have gone according to her plan, whatever her plan was. She obviously felt that she was in control, so much so that she hadn't even bothered to disguise her presence. She even went so far as to assume an alias as obvious as Countess Sophia. Her arrogance both astonished and unnerved him. The Timekeepers had proved themselves to be formidable adversaries in the past. Falcon was not only a Timekeeper, she was a Timekeeper who had been trained by the TIA. She had killed Mongoose, who had been the TIA's best agent.

He thought of Derringer's safehouse. Derringer had told them where it was, in the old quarter of the city, on a tiny back street. He had explained about the security system and told them how to deactivate it, stressing that if anything went wrong, they were to meet there. However, Finn had no indication that anything had gone wrong. So far. Besides, he would be far more vulnerable on the streets of Strelsau than inside the palace. His orders were to play the part of Rudolf Rassendyll and the last thing Rassendyll would do under the circumstances would be to roam the streets of Strelsau in the middle of the night. He would be alone in this charade, forced to depend upon Sapt and von Tarlenheim for guidance, but ultimately, all alone. Much as Finn wanted to do something, at the moment there seemed to be nothing he could do.

In exasperation, he threw the covers off the bed, got up, belted the king's robe around himself and went over to the windows to unlatch them and let in some air. He pulled the large double windows open and took a deep breath of the cool night air, then jumped about a foot when Lucas said, "Good, I'm glad you're still awake."

He was pressed against the outside wall, supported by a nysteel rappelling line. He was dressed all in black. He had blackened his face as well. Using his legs to push away from the side of the building, Lucas swung out from the wall and in through the open windows, the nysteel line unwinding from the grip handle with a soft, whizzing sound. Once inside, Lucas turned around to face the open window, pressed a small button on the grip, gave the line a couple of sharp jerks. It retracted quickly, whistling back into the handle.

"Where in hell have you been?" Finn said angrily, despite his enormous relief at seeing him.

"Take it easy, Your Majesty," said Lucas, reaching out and taking the cigarette out of Finn's mouth. He took a deep drag off it and sat down on the bed, wearily. He exhaled the smoke in a heavy sigh. "Derringer is dead."

"Oh, hell," Finn said, softly.

"I don't think he even knew what hit him," Lucas said. He held up a hand. "Give me a minute, okay? I haven't slept in 48 hours and I'm exhausted." He rubbed his eyes. Finn gave him another cigarette. Lucas lit it off the butt of the one he had taken from Finn.

"Take your time," said Finn. "You look all done in."

Lucas sighed heavily. "I'll bear up. If I could just catch a couple of hours' sleep, I'd be okay." He inhaled deeply on the cigarette, then lay back on the bed. Finn sat down beside him.

"It happened at around oh-three-thirty last night," said Lucas. "I had taken up a post at the southwest corner of the lodge, where I had a good view of the west side and the rear. Andre was at the northeast corner, where she could see the east side and the front. Derringer took up position a bit farther to the northwest, where he could see part of the front of the lodge and all of the road leading up to it. At about oh-three-thirty, Andre spotted laser flashes. Two quick beams, coming from Derringer's direction, one firing and one returning fire. We couldn't raise Derringer. I had Andre stay put, covering the lodge from her side in case it was some sort of diversion, then I circled round wide to check on Derringer. I found him dead with his neck broken. No signs of a struggle."

"His neck broken?" Finn said.

Lucas nodded. "His laser had not been fired."

"So who—"

"I have no idea. I didn't see a thing. Oh, one other thing. His chronoplate remote was gone."

Finn swore. "We're screwed. By now they will have hit the safehouse and taken the plate. I hope you like the neighborhood. Looks like we might be staying for a while."

"Maybe not," said Lucas. "Derringer did have security setup. Maybe we'll get lucky. If not, we go on with the mission. S & R will come looking for us eventually."

"Yeah, in a few months, maybe, if they're on the ball. Where's Andre?"

"I sent her to check the safehouse. I'll be heading out there as soon as I leave here."

"Take it back from last night," Finn said. "What happened?"

"Nothing," Lucas said, shaking his head. "We expected them to hit us, but they never did. It was pretty nerve-wracking. With only two of us left to cover the lodge, we didn't want to risk trying to get to you and leaving ourselves open. We held tight, expecting them to make their move, thinking maybe they were watching from somewhere and waiting for us to expose ourselves, but it must have been a hit-and-run. When you left in the morning with Sapt and von Tarlenheim, Andre took one of the other horses and trailed you. She was supposed to stick with you until you looked reasonably safe, then head right for the safehouse."

Lucas paused, taking a deep breath. "I had to stay behind and bury Derringer. I picked a spot S & R should be able to find without too much trouble. But that was later. First I watched the guard arrive. Three men went inside the lodge. Detchard was one, I heard his name mentioned. I'm assuming that the other two were also part of Michael's Six. They sent the guard on ahead while they remained behind. Shortly after that, they brought out the king, draped him over one of the horses, and rode off in the direction of the castle. Let me tell you, it was tempting as hell to burn those bastards on the spot. After they left, the old woman came out, carrying a carpet bag, and set off down the road to the village on foot. I waited some more, then went in to check the lodge. I found the king's servant in the cellar with his throat cut. I left him there and went to bury Derringer. I searched the woods in the vicinity, but I didn't find anything. Not that I expected to, but you never know. By that time, it was well after noon. There wasn't anything more I could accomplish there, so I went to Zenda Castle and set up watch on that spot where we were before. I saw one horseman leave, riding hard down the road to Strelsau, then they raised the drawbridge. I didn't think I'd have a chance to contact you before dark, so I stayed put. Just as I was about to leave, two riders came galloping up to the chateau from the direction of Strelsau. One of them was Black Michael, the other one was Hentzau, I think. They lowered the drawbridge, the two riders went in—they rode their horses right through the chateau, which must be a little hard on the housekeeping staff—then the drawbridge went back up again. I figure they're holding the king in that new addition. It was the only part of the castle where lights were burning. It didn't look as if they'd be coming out again, so I headed straight here. It took me a while to time the rounds made by the palace guard, but getting in here wasn't very difficult. So that brings you up to date. I wish I could have brought you some good news."

"Damn," said Finn. They sat in silence for a moment. "He was just a kid."

"Maybe I could have done something to prevent it," Lucas said, his voice strained. "I keep thinking that it was my responsibility."

"As an Observer, he wasn't under your command," said Finn. "It could have been Andre or it could have been you. Blaming yourself isn't going to help. Things are tense enough as they are. They're playing games with us. Falcon had a chance at me during the procession, but she passed on it. It would have been easy. She had me dead to rights."

"You *saw* her?"

"Plain as day and bold as brass."

"You're sure it was her?"

"It was Falcon, all right. No question. She was on the balcony of the Grand Hotel as we rode by. You should have seen her, standing there and grinning at me. She made my stomach do somersaults. She's established an identity here as a visiting aristocrat of some sort. The Countess Sophia, if you please."

"Not very subtle, is she?" Lucas said.

"No, just one look at her would tell you that. That hologram didn't do her justice. She's one of those people who can knock the wind right out of you with just a look. She really puts it out there. Feral."

"Sounds like she impressed you."

"Oh, she did that, all right," said Finn. "That was the whole point. She's really something. Charisma with a capital 'N', for Nasty. Sapt tells me that the lovely Countess Sophia has managed to acquire quite a notorious reputation in the short time that she's been here. If he only knew. He suspects her of being involved in the plot because she's been keeping very close company with Black Michael and Rupert Hentzau. I got a look at Hentzau, but it didn't tell me very much. He seems very young and quite fit, dark and good-looking in a go-to-hell way. According to Sapt, he's the worst of the lot. The other five, Detchard, Bersonin, De Gautet, Lauengram and Krafstein, are all reasonably young, apparently efficient, and generally standoffish. They're not well thought of in court circles. Michael's tarnished his prestige a bit by hiring a bunch of cutthroats. So far, it all fits the scenario, but it's occurred to me that it wouldn't have been very difficult for the Timekeepers to dispose of the real Six and take their places. Anyone could be a ringer in this Chinese fire drill. They've got the mobility and we're the sitting ducks, or at least *I* am. It makes me feel wonderfully secure. Much as I hate to say it, I think our best bet would be for you and Andre to leave me alone to take my chances and concentrate on taking out the Timekeepers. They must have a base of operations around here somewhere."

"I think I've already found it," Lucas said.

Finn glanced at him sharply. "What do you mean, you *think?*"

"Call it an educated guess. A good hunch."

"I've learned to respect your hunches."

"It hit me this morning, when I was crouching in the bushes and watching them take the king away," said Lucas. "Put yourself in their position. You've had some time to set this up. You've considered all your options very carefully. If you wanted to play it safe, if you wanted to have an easily defensable position and still be right on top of things, where would you hole up?"

"Hell," said Finn. "Zenda Castle?"

"Where else?" said Lucas. "It would be perfect. Michael's

got enough to do with keeping up the chateau. It must be costing him a fortune. Why would he waste time and money refurbishing a ruined castle when he doesn't need the room, especially since he has hopes of moving into the palace soon?"

"Derringer told us he'd only seen lights burning in the new addition," Finn said. "The rest of the place has probably been abandoned for years."

"And you've established that Falcon is in close contact with Michael and Rupert Hentzau," Lucas said. "It all fits. She's had the opportunity to visit the chateau. She could have asked to see the castle, dropped a remote in there somewhere when no one was looking, homed in on it later, and clocked right in. There would have been more than enough time to explore the place, program transition coordinates, and establish a practically impregnable base of operations."

"Nice," said Finn. "Now all we have to do is find a way to get into the castle, rescue the king, and flush out the Timekeepers. What could be simpler? Searching that old ruin shouldn't take more than a day or two."

"That's why Falcon didn't kill you before," said Lucas. "Why take unnecessary risks when they can make us come to them? She wants to be certain to get all of us. Their first move was to deprive us of our temporal mobility. Now all they have to do is wait."

"Sure," said Finn, grimly. "The minute we set foot inside Zenda Castle, we'll be on their home ground. Got any ideas?"

Lucas shook his head. "No. Do you?"

"Yeah," said Finn, morosely. "Why don't we just shoot each other and deprive them of their satisfaction?"

"You lied to me," said Drakov.

Falcon did not reply. The moment she clocked in, she began to strip off her elegant gown, shucking her identity as the Countess Sophia as though it were wholly inappropriate for such a dismal setting as the castle turret. Drakov watched her with scorn as she removed every last item of her clothing, laying everything out very carefully upon a clean blanket spread out on the cold stone floor. She was incredibly beautiful, yet she was completely unself-conscious of her nakedness. Aside from the goose pimples that rose upon her flesh, the cold did not seem to bother her. It would be a long time before the warmth of the early morning sun penetrated into the keep, and its light served to give only a little illumination. Falcon strode barefoot across the floor and began to dress in the black fatigues that she had left folded on her cot. She used no wasted motions. Everything about her was methodical, thought Drakov, even the way she made love, though the method there was far more subtle, far more complex, and far more incomprehensible than any that he had encountered in almost 80 years of life. In three months, he would be 79 years old. He looked 30 and, till now, he had felt it. Falcon had aged him, emotionally if not physically, but then she would probably have that same effect on any man, born of a natural union or not.

"What are you complaining about now?" she said.

"Trust," he said. "Or rather the lack of it. You will, perhaps, excuse me if I chafe under my new status as your supernumerary. It is not a role I am accustomed to."

"What in hell are you talking about?" She pulled on the black trousers and sat down on the cot to put on her boots.

"It was never your intention for this to be our secret base of operations," he said. "You mean to lure them here."

"So?" she said, putting on her shirt. "That bothers you?"

"Not by itself," he said. "I can even see a certain logic to it. What bothers me is that I finally see my role in all of this defined. I am to be used as bait and nothing more."

She looked up at him, meeting his gaze, saying nothing.

"In a way," said Drakov, "I am astonished that it took me so long to see it. Yet, in another way, I am surprised that I have even seen it at all. It means, I think, that I am finally beginning to understand you and I find that quite disturbing."

Falcon picked up a pack of cigarettes, took one out, rubbed it against the side of the pack to ignite it, then leaned back against the wall, one leg drawn up underneath her, the other bent at the knee to provide a prop for her right arm. She inhaled a deep lungful of smoke and expelled it through her nostrils. She didn't speak, but her look prompted him to continue.

"He's here," said Drakov. "Or did you already know?"

"I knew," she said. "You saw him?"

"He nearly killed me."

"Only nearly? Then he must be slipping."

"At first, I told myself that you must have arranged it somehow, but I don't see how you could have. Besides, if he *had* killed me, it would have spoiled your plans. For both of us."

"That's true," she said. "What happened?"

"He came up on me as I took the Observer. Even as I struck, I knew he was behind me. I don't know how I knew. I simply knew. He fired as I turned and I felt the beam graze me." He lifted his shirt to show her the burn on his left side, just beneath the large latissimus dorsi muscle. "I activated the remote with one hand and fired with the other. I had no chance to aim. I had one very brief glimpse of him, no more than a dark shape. I never saw his face. In the same instant that I felt the pain of my wound, I was back here again. But it was he. I know it."

"Are you sorry that you missed him?" she said.

Drakov was silent for a moment. "No," he said, finally. "I want to see his face. I want him to see my face when he dies. And I want him to know the reason for it."

"He knows," said Falcon. "It's the only thing that would have brought him here."

"You would have liked it otherwise," said Drakov. "You would rather that you were the reason."

She did not reply. She sat there, smoking, watching him without expression. Nothing in her face gave any indication of what she was really thinking, but then, nothing ever did.

"What is your real name?" said Drakov.

She did not answer.

"Did Forrester know?"

Again, no reply.

"Did anyone? Ever? Or did you just spring full blown, as if from the head of Zeus, with walls and moats and drawbridges, a veritable fortress of isolation and self-containment?"

"Is there a point to any of this?" she said. "Because, if not, I would like to get some sleep. I've had a very long night."

"With Rupert Hentzau."

"Don't tell me that you're jealous. For you, that would be the height of hypocrisy."

"Hypocrisy?" said Drakov, with a slight smile. "That you, of all people, should accuse me of hypocrisy. I called you a fanatic, but I was wrong. Or rather, I was correct in calling you a fanatic, but incorrect in pinpointing your fanaticism. I have no doubt that at one time, your involvement with the Timekeepers was sincere. Insofar as you are capable of sincerity. You were a passionless woman in search of something to be passionate about, but when you found it, not in the struggle to bring the Time Wars to a halt, but in the arms of the man who is my father, it proved to be too much for you. You could not cross your moat and raise your drawbridge and hide behind your walls. You met a man whom you could not control. Worse yet, with whom you could not control yourself. He made you love him and for that, you cannot forgive him."

"You're becoming a real bore, Nicky."

"My apologies. It was my impression that you had grown bored with me a long time ago. But you never tired of Moses Forrester, did you?" He reached into his pocket and took out the ring that she had given him. He tossed it to her. It landed on her lap. "Perhaps you should take this back," he said. "It means much more to you than it does to me."

She made no move to take the ring.

"Does this mean that I cannot count on you?" she said.

"You may count on me," said Drakov. "I will see this thing through to the end with you, come what may. Tell me what it is that you expect of me and I shall do it. But I find it somewhat ironic that the Timekeepers have been reduced to one man whose cause is revenge for the wrong done to his mother and one woman whose cause is revenge for the wrong that she perceives was done to her. Somewhere along the line, the original objective of the great cause became obfuscated. Perhaps it happened with the two of us. However, I am beginning to suspect it happened with the death of Albrecht Mensinger. There is an old proverb that says when one considers embarking upon a course of revenge, one should first build two coffins. I have been giving some thought to designing mine. I'll leave you to make your own plans."

"Where are you going?" she said.

"For a walk through cold, dark corridors. It seems, somehow, the appropriate thing to do."

After he had gone, Falcon glanced down at the ring that he had thrown to her. She crushed out the cigarette, picked up the ring, stood up and walked over to one of the embrasures. She closed her fist around the ring and drew it back, to throw. For a moment, she simply stood there with her arm cocked, then she lowered it. She opened her fist and glanced down at the ring once more. Then she put it back upon her finger.

6

It was almost dawn when Lucas left the palace, and the city was beginning to come awake with a sleep languor. Wagons filled with produce were pulled by toil-weary horses toward the square; here and there a light burned inside a shop as someone made ready to open up for business. No one paid Lucas any mind as he walked through the streets. It was still dark, but if anyone came close enough to see his blackened face, no one remarked upon it.

Though the capital of Ruritania, Strelsau was not a large city, even by the standard of its time. With the exception of a few large estates within the old quarter, houses that held their own with lawns and gardens as defenses against the encroaching buildings, Strelsau was a tightly packed city. Buildings stood close together, sometimes separated by narrow alleyways no more than shoulder width; the streets were cobbled; the architecture a mad jumble of many different styles. The Grand Boulevard of Strelsau would have been just another back street in most other large cities and some of the back streets were no more than hard-packed earth. But for all that Strelsau gave forth the flavor of some medieval city, it was very clean. Despite its lack of character, it had a sort of Prussian orderliness and, in that, perhaps it found what character it had. Bedraggled paupers walked side by side with well-dressed citizens and neither gave the other a wide berth. The sense of community and congruence was obvious; each had a place and each had a function to perform and that was as it should be. Forrester's phrase, "vestpocket kingdom," seemed particularly apropos. Strelsau was warm and cozy. A minicity in a tiny nation with a homey sort of pageantry and spirit all its own. Nowhere was there any sense of urgency. It was hard to believe that here there were two feuding factions, one Elphberg Black, one Elphberg Red, each passionate in support of its chosen champion. It was harder still to believe that here there was a plot afoot to murder the true king and seize the throne. Things like that simply didn't happen in such a cuckoo clock of a town, where doors should open and tiny figures should march out and dance as some folk tune was played to mark the hour. Further, it was beyond any credulity that this romantic little diorama could be the scene of an historical adjustment—surely, nothing could possibly be *wrong* here—and a focal point of temporal continuity. It seemed to make about as much sense as expecting a volcano to burst up through the cobblestones, showering everything with burning rock and ash and burying everyone under molten lava. Yet, in a sense, the earth did churn away beneath the streets, though only Lucas seemed to feel the heat that came up from the stones beneath him.

That secret passageway was a godsend. One of Lucas's biggest worries had been how to keep in touch with Finn while he was in the palace. He had given Finn one of the communicator sets that Derringer had issued them, but it helped knowing that he could actually get in and out of there unobserved, without having to put up with the strain of ducking the palace guard and climbing the walls.

The communicators were designed in such a manner that they could be worn all the time. They were made up of two miniaturized components, a tiny throat mike that could be taped in place over the larynx with a flesh-colored adhesive strip or even secured beneath a small graft of plastiskin, and a small receiver worn inside the ear. Like the pickup, the receiver could be stuck with adhesive within the ear itself, positioned by a pair of tiny tweezers or it, too, could be grafted in by plastiskin. The latter method would involve a minor operation to remove both devices, but it offered maximum adhesion and concealment. With the plastiskin adhesion method, only the closest of inspections by someone knowing what to look for would result in the communicator apparatus's being detected. The equipment was not military ordnance, but the result of trickle-down technology from the law-enforcement field. The average soldier would have no use for such devices, but to a commando team out on an adjustment, they were extremely helpful. Lucas had given Derringer's set to Finn and they had each taken turns putting them in place for the other with strips of plastiskin from a first aid kit. Now, they could simply forget about them. There was, however, one distinct disadvantage to the communicators, and it was for this reason that they seldom used them. Aside from the fact that they were relatively short-range, it was possible for their frequency to be picked up. If the Timekeepers had similar units or compatible equipment, they might be able to home in on their transmissions and monitor their communications. It was a risk Lucas felt prepared to take, since it would reduce Finn's vulnerability somewhat. They would merely have to operate on the assumption that they might be overheard and keep their transmissions short, infrequent, and worded with that possibility taken into consideration.

The sky was becoming gray as Lucas turned into the side street that led to the rooming house where Derringer had set up his base of operations. He had no idea what he would find there. He hoped he would find Andre. He felt reasonably sure he would. If they were very, very lucky, Derringer's security system had protected the chronoplate and they might even have a prisoner from the opposing camp. However, he didn't want to get his hopes up. Luck always had a way of being absent when you needed it quite badly.

He wanted nothing in the world quite so much as a few hours' sleep. Weary as he was, he was on his guard as he entered the rooming house and slowly climbed the stairs to the top floor. He tried to walk softly so as not to make any noise. He could afford to take no chances. The hall was empty. He

moved cautiously. When he came to the door of Derringer's
room, he paused and pressed an ear against it. He could hear
voices. Suddenly sleep was the last thing on his mind. He came
into the room fast and low, his laser held ready before him.
Chairs fell over as the occupants of the room dove in separate
directions and someone yelled his name.

Forrester lowered his weapon. "Too slow," he said.

"For once, I'm grateful," Andre said, shakily. "I didn't
even realize that door wasn't bolted."

"You both need rest," said Forrester. He sounded exhausted himself. "Come have a drink, Priest. There's something I have to tell you."

The morning came with Finn still feeling alert and tense. He
had smoked half a box of cigarettes and his throat was more
than a bit raw. Sapt and von Tarlenheim arrived to find him
dressed, but incorrectly. He had put on his evening uniform
instead of his morning uniform and a change was needed
before he could begin the first of his monarchial duties, which
entailed the greeting of the *corps diplomatique*. There were
papers to be signed, which gave Finn's co-conspirators a nasty
turn for a moment until he claimed that he was unable to write
comfortably due to having injured his hand while hunting in
Zenda. He did so with such a flash of royal petulance that the
chancellor hastened away with many apologies and bows to
search his legal books for precedents. He returned with the
suggestion that "His Majesty could make his mark" with his
left hand. It would be a bit irregular, but it would all be legal
provided that there were so and so many witnesses, all of
whom would have to swear an oath to testify that the signature
was genuine and sign themselves, as well. Sapt did so non-
chalantly, but von Tarlenheim looked pained as he swore
before "Almighty God and My Sovereign Liege" and half his
ancestors, perjuring himself irredeemably both on the secular
and spiritual levels. Finn went through it all with a vague air of
boredom and impatience, grateful for the fact that he did not
have to spend any length of time in conversation with anyone
who knew the king well. Sapt had assumed the role of chief
factotum easily and he ran interference for him admirably, his
stiff military bearing and demeanor proving quite infectious

and lending an atmosphere of formality and dispatch to the proceedings.

It was afternoon by the time that they were finished with the scheduled activities for the morning and took time for a meal, which Finn, as his first royal decree verbally issued, ordered served to them in his chambers. The chancellor, a whipcord thin, middle-aged man with sunken cheeks, immensely mournful eyes, and a habit of pressing his lips together every few seconds, hesitantly reminded His Majesty that there were still a number of people wishing to pay their respects, not the least of them being the Duke of Strelsau, who had ridden in from Zenda and expressed his wish to dine with His Majesty. Finn waved him off without a word and the chancellor departed, clearly not looking forward to informing Michael of the snub.

Sapt chuckled when they were finally alone. "I must say, Your Majesty," he said, giving a slight ironic stress to the title, "you appear to have quite a knack for this sort of thing. I did not sleep at all last night, worrying about today, but my worries have been somewhat alleviated. Still, I cannot help but wonder how long we can keep it up."

"Certainly, we must do *something* and we must do it soon," said Fritz, who also appeared not to have slept at all, though his nerves were far more on edge than Sapt's. "We can't just sit here and do nothing!"

"Better to sit here and do nothing than to do something stupid," Sapt said. "Michael is no fool. It may have been unwise to snub him."

"Why?" said Finn. "You think he might hold it against me?"

Von Tarlenheim giggled. Sapt shot him a venomous look and he instantly put on a sober face. "He may have come with terms," said Sapt. "We should hear him out."

"What kind of terms could he possibly offer?" Finn said. "He's committed himself. There's no way he can let the king go. Somehow, I doubt that under the circumstances, Rudolf would be very forgiving. No, he must kill the king. He has no choice. But fortunately, or unfortunately, depending on whose point of view it is, he'd have to kill me first and he'd have to do it on the sly. It wouldn't do for him to have the act witnessed or to have the 'king's' body found before he could concoct some way to take advantage of it. He'll simply have to play along in the charade until he can find an opportunity to make me disappear."

"He's right," said Fritz. "We must make certain that he has no such opportunity. We must have you watched both day and night."

"I would advise against that," Finn said.

Sapt frowned. "Why?"

"The last thing you want to do is make Michael desperate and force his hand."

Sapt nodded. "You're right again. By God, Rassendyll, there's more to you than meets the eye. You seem to be an old hand at intrigue."

"Let's simply say that I have an extremely strong instinct for self-preservation," Finn said. "This is quite a deadly little game we're playing and the stakes are considerably higher than they were when we began it. Moreover, the odds are hardly to my liking. There are at least seven of them and only the three of us."

"And Michael enjoys the people's favor," added Fritz.

"Well, now maybe there's something we can act upon," said Finn. "If Michael enjoys the people's favor, then Rudolf must be in some disfavor with the people. Why?"

"Why?" said Sapt. "You met him. You saw. He's an irresponsible young fool who cares for little save his own pleasures. He cares nothing for the people or for the duties of the crown. Which is not to say that Michael loves the people any more. He simply knows the art of currying their favor, whereas Rudolf could not be bothered. Rudolf should sit upon the throne by right, there's that, but at least he would leave affairs of state in hands far more capable than his. Michael would take direct control and I daresay that the nation would not prosper for it."

"Then there's the matter of the princess," said Fritz.

"Yes, I was going to mention that," said Finn. "Somehow, it seems the two of you neglected to inform me that I would be alone with her."

"A grievous oversight," said Sapt. "I don't know what I was thinking of. Forgive me, Rudolf. You did not make her suspicious?"

"I don't think so," Finn said. "But I'm going to have to know how things stood between them. From our brief conversation, it was my impression that she is a trifle cool toward Rudolf."

"Cool!" said Fritz. "I like that. Cold as ice, would be more like."

Sapt grimaced wryly. "I never thought that I'd be at all concerned with our friend's romantic dalliances," he said, "but at the moment, I am profoundly grateful that young Fritz here has set his cap at Countess Helga."

"Countess Helga von Strofzin," von Tarlenheim explained, a bit awkwardly, "is lady in waiting to the princess. We are, I suppose one might say, rather close."

Sapt chuckled. This time, it was von Tarlenheim who shot him an irate look.

"From Helga, that is, from the Countess von Strofzin—"

"Let's just call her Helga," Finn said, "to make things simpler."

"Yes, well. From Helga, I have learned that Princess Flavia is resigned to wedding Rudolf, rather than looking forward to it. She bears him little love. Well," he cleared his throat, uneasily, "none at all, to be quite frank."

"Why's that?" said Finn.

"Because, well, dear me, how shall I put it—"

"I'll put it for you," Sapt said, gruffly. "Were Rudolf not betrothed to her from birth, his feelings toward her might well have been different, but as it is, he regards her as a duty, so to speak, and Rudolf has never been the most dutiful of men."

"In other words," said Finn, "you're telling me that he neglects her, takes her for granted?"

"Well, in a word," began Fritz, awkwardly, only to be interrupted by Colonel Sapt.

"In a word, yes," said Sapt. "What the devil's wrong with you, Fritz? This is no time for delicacy." He looked back at Finn. "Rudolf pays about as much attention to her as he does to his saddle. It's there, it belongs to him, he'll use it when he needs it and when not, someone will care for it and relieve him of the bother."

"The man's a damn fool," said Finn.

"See here, now, Rassendyll," said Fritz.

"Be quiet, Fritz," said Sapt. "Rudolf's right. The king's a damn fool. Flavia would make any man a fine and loyal wife. She's intelligent, well-mannered, considerate to a fault and beautiful, as well. What man could ask for more? Rudolf treats her little better than he does his servants. He's a damn fool, all right, but he's *our* damn fool, worse luck, and we must stand by him. But, by God, I'll not condone the way he treats her!"

"The people like her a great deal, I assume," said Finn.

"Like her?" Fritz said. "I should say they like her. She is their darling."

"Then perhaps we should take steps to make her Rudolf Elphberg's darling, as well," said Finn.

"Now just a moment, Rassendyll," said Fritz, anxiously. "Just what are you suggesting?"

"I'm suggesting that if the king were to conspicuously court his future wife, the people might look upon him with more favor. Perhaps having been crowned, the full import of his position has, shall we say, matured him somewhat? Made him take himself, and others, a bit more seriously, as befits a king?"

"*Now just one moment!*" Fritz said, genuinely alarmed now. "You're not seriously proposing to *make love* to Princess Flavia?"

"Why not?" said Finn.

Sapt pursed his lips and nodded. "Indeed," he said. "Why not?"

"*Sapt!*"

"Shut up, Fritz. It's an excellent idea."

"Look," said Finn, "at the risk of seeming crude, I'm not proposing to hop into bed with her—"

"My *God!*" said Fritz.

"Fritz, if you don't shut your mouth, I'll clout you one, so help me!" Sapt said.

"I merely wish to point out," Finn continued, "that it would do no harm to court her. In fact, if the king were suddenly to turn over a new leaf and be more solicitous of her, as well as of his subjects, the people might experience a change of heart toward him. Anything that would strengthen his position would serve as well to weaken that of Black Michael."

"By Heaven, I wish I'd had you in my regiment," said Sapt. "What a second-in-command you would have been! You have a positively brilliant mind for strategy!"

"*Strategy?*" said Fritz, looking from one to the other of them desperately. "Gentlemen! *Please!* For the love of Heaven, we're not discussing some military campaign here! We're talking about a woman! Not just any woman, but the Princess Flavia! I will not stand idly by to see her affections toyed with!"

"What would you rather I do, Fritz," Finn said, "treat her like dirt, as Rudolf did? She seemed like a very nice woman to me. Far too nice to be treated like a saddle, as Sapt here put it."

"No, certainly, I would not wish that—"

"What, then?"

"Well. Well, I. . . . Well, that is, I. . . ."

Sapt grinned. "He has you there, Fritz."

Von Tarlenheim bit his lower lip.

"Fear not, Fritz," Finn said. "I give you my solemn word of honor as an Englishman and a gentleman, as well as a former officer in the service of Her Royal Majesty, the Queen Victoria, that my conduct toward the Princess Flavia will be nothing less than honorable with the observation of all the usual proprieties. So there. You have my word of honor. If it will not serve, then sir, I must perforce offer you my glove."

Von Tarlenheim instantly stiffened to a position of attention, every inch the gentleman and cavalier. "With my utmost respect, Mr. Rassendyll, that will not be necessary. The word of an English officer and gentleman is certainly good enough for Fritz von Tarlenheim and I will not have it said otherwise. If anything that I have said led you to believe that I have in any way impugned your honor, sir, I humbly tender my apologies and hasten to assure you that nothing can be further from the truth."

"No apologies are necessary, my friend, as no offense was taken," Finn said. He stood up and offered von Tarlenheim his hand. "I appreciate your concern and regard you well because of it. Let us say no more. We understand each other."

They shook hands.

"Now," said Finn, "let's get down to business, shall we? When I agreed to undertake this masquerade for you, I had no idea that it would ever go this far. Needless to say, neither had you, but that is not the point. The point is that we now find ourselves in a devil of a mess. If we are to get through it alive, much less with any hope of rescuing your king, I am going to require a great deal of help from you."

"That goes without saying," said von Tarlenheim. "We owe you everything. Without you, the king would surely have been dead by now."

"And he may well be, for all we know," said Sapt, gloomily.

"No, the king still lives," said Fritz.

Sapt looked at him sharply. "How do you know?"

"Because when Michael arrived in Strelsau this morning, he brought only three of the Six with him," Fritz said. "Which can only mean that the remaining three have been left behind in Zenda to guard the king. There would be no need of their having been left behind to guard a dead man."

"Then there is still hope," said Sapt. "Michael hasn't lost his head. I was afraid he might. He's realized his position. The question is, has he found a way to extricate himself from it?"

"There is only one way he can extricate himself from his position that I can think of," Finn said, "and that would be to kill me."

Sapt nodded wordlessly.

Von Tarlenheim licked his lips nervously. "I can think of one choice open to us." He swallowed hard. "We could kill Black Michael."

"If you could get past his bodyguards," said Finn. "Besides, killing him would not guarantee the king's safety. If you did that, the Six would have no one left to give them orders or to pay them, true, but why should they allow you to get off the hook? If we are to assume that they are professionals, gentlemen, we must also assume they would realize that with Michael dead, they would have no protection. The moment that they learned of Michael's death, they would kill the king and flee or, better yet, if they were smart, they would flee with the king as hostage. Then, the moment they were safely beyond your reach, they would kill the king and disperse, each to his own fate." Finn shook his head. "No, your best chance to keep the king alive is to keep Michael alive. His removal would throw them into disarray, but not for very long."

Sapt stared at Finn with growing interest. For a moment, Finn had a crazy feeling that the old soldier had actually figured it all out, though of course, that was impossible.

"What are we to do, then?" said von Tarlenheim, helplessly.

"It appears to me that there is only one thing that we *can* do," Finn said. "We cannot hope to attack the castle in force. Even if there were some way we could get the entire army to support us—and how would we do that without tipping our hand?—Michael could easily kill the king. Where would be your proof? By the time you could take the castle, Michael would have had an opportunity to destroy Rudolf's remains a dozen times over."

"*Lord*, Rassendyll," said Fritz.

"Listen to him, Fritz," said Sapt, watching him intently. "This is a grim business we're about and we can spare no time to phrase matters delicately."

"We cannot hope to prevail upon Michael to release the king," said Finn. "He has everything to lose by doing so and nothing at all to gain. There is no pressure we could bring to bear upon him that would be great enough to bend him to our will. Agreed?"

"Agreed," said Sapt.

"What does that leave us, then?" said Fritz. "What if we tried to bribe the Six? We could pay them more than Michael pays them and induce them to change sides."

"That would be unwise," said Sapt. "One can never trust a mercenary. They have only their own gain to care for. They could burn the candle at both ends."

"What's to be done, then?" said von Tarlenheim.

"We have only one choice left open to us," Finn said. "We must take Zenda Castle by ourselves."

"You're mad," said Fritz von Tarlenheim. "It would be impossible. Besides, you only just finished telling us that Michael could kill the king if any such attack took place."

"If it were an open attack, yes," said Finn, "but not if it were accomplished by stealth."

"But *how?*" said Fritz.

"There has to be a way," said Finn. "Sapt, you strike me as the sort of man who would inspire great loyalty amongst his troops. Are there any such who once served under you that you could count on?"

"I can think of a few," said Sapt, "senior officers now in Strakencz's regiment and some who have retired from the service. They are not taken in by His Lordship, the Duke of Strelsau. They remember him all too well as a young officer. Still, they are only a handful, and how can we enlist their aid without telling them the truth?"

"Perhaps we will not have to tell them the truth," said Finn. "Or we can tell them the truth and bend it slightly."

"What do you mean?" said Fritz.

"Well, there *is* a prisoner in Zenda Castle," Finn said. "Do we have to tell them it's the king?"

"Go on," said Sapt, intrigued.

"Suppose we had a potential international incident upon our hands," said Finn. "Suppose some very influential foreign gentleman, a friend of the king's, had run afoul of Michael somehow—we needn't say how—and Michael had imprisoned him in Zenda Castle in order to teach him a lesson? He is, after all, the Duke of Strelsau and holder of the estates and lands of Zenda. He could easily charge someone with a crime and execute the punishment."

"True," said Sapt. "He has that authority."

"Well then, let us assume that the king has been made aware of this, say that the ambassador of the nation that this imaginary gentleman is from has secretly approached the king and asked him to intervene on this gentleman's behalf. All very behind the scenes, to avoid an unpleasant incident involving governments, and so forth. Our imaginary gentleman is a very important man. The king, also secretly, remonstrates with Michael to release the man in order to avoid political repercussions. Michael is intransigent. You can see how this would pose a serious problem. Moving against Michael openly as his first official act would be a bad decision for the king. It would reopen wounds that are still all too fresh in Ruritania. Michael, of course, would realize this. That would be his advantage in the situation. So, in order to avoid political unpleasantness, the king intends to continue bargaining with Michael. However, should all his appeals fall upon deaf ears, he is prepared to move, in secret, against Zenda Castle in order to rescue this imprisoned gentleman. Afterwards, of course, he can claim total ignorance of the affair and insist that it all must have been done by foreign nationals, lodge a strenuous protest with the ambassador concerned, which imaginary ambassador will of course take it no further and the entire affair will be brought to a close. That is how you will present it to your men, Sapt. They are to stand by, prepared to move at a moment's notice in this most secret mission, to rescue this imaginary gentleman from Zenda Castle in case all negotiations fail."

"By God, Rassendyll," said Sapt, "you astonish me! The plan is positively brilliant! Still, it has serious flaws. I cannot muster enough men to take the castle. And even if they could, how would we protect the king?"

"That is where I come in," said Finn. "I will have to swim the moat and find a way to get inside by stealth. I will have to find out where the king is being held, then lower the drawbridge for you so that your attack can be made by surprise. If you can gain access to the castle, you will not need a lot of men. You will storm through the chateau on horseback and in the ensuing confusion, I will make my way next to the king and guard him with my life."

"But how can you hope to accomplish that alone?" said Fritz.

"One man, alone, might penetrate the castle and escape detection," Finn said. "If we attack at night, we may have a chance. But you will need to move with all possible speed once the drawbridge has been lowered. Our only advantage is in surprise."

"It just might work," said Fritz, "though the plan is insanity itself. You would be taking a tremendous risk. The odds are almost certain that you would be killed."

"The odds are certain that I will be killed if we do not make the attempt," said Finn. "In fact, if we do not, we are all dead men. You cannot watch over me indefinitely. If a man is a target for assassins, then he will surely die eventually. Sooner or later, Michael's mercenaries will have me and once I am out of the way, Michael can contrive to stage Rudolf's death in some manner that would not implicate him and that would serve him at the same time, just as you told me earlier, Sapt. With Michael in power, you can be sure that your lives would not mean a thing. In the event that I should disappear before the king is freed, my friends, I can only urge you to do likewise. Michael would waste no time in having you two murdered once I was disposed of."

"In the event that Michael has you killed," Sapt said grimly, "then he signs his own death warrant, come what may. Rest assured that you shall be avenged. On that, you have *my* word of honor and I care not what the cost."

Finn felt a strange tightness in his chest. He and Sapt had known each other for scarcely three days, yet he knew—as did Sapt—that there had formed a strong bond between them. Physically, Sapt was older by a good many years, having never had the benefit of antiaging drugs that could extend his lifespan. Biologically, Finn had lived longer than Sapt had. The worlds that each existed in were separated by over seven hundred years. Yet, they were the same. Both cut from the same cloth. Both subscribers to a code of ethics that neither of them could have stated, yet each understood on some subliminal level that came not from the intellect, but from somewhere in the gut. Buddhists believed that that was the center of one's being and perhaps, Finn thought, they knew something that no else did. Or, that all men knew, but few remembered.

"There is one thing more," said Fritz, oblivious of the electric interplay that had just taken place in some fraction of a second between the two other men, a spark that had made them lock gazes quickly and then, just as quickly, look away, like guilty lovers. "The marriage between the king and Princess Flavia was to have taken place after the coronation. Each day it is postponed brings more disfavor on the king. It will be interpreted as an insult to the princess that the king would make her wait upon his bidding until such time as he is pleased to wed her. There, Michael has us. That we have dared allow an imposter to be crowned is bad enough. For that, Lord help us, our souls will have to answer on the Day of Judgement. But to allow the princess to enter into holy wedlock with that same imposter would be unthinkable.

Whatever it is we are to do, we must do it soon, else all is lost."

"All the more reason for me to court 'my' future wife," said Finn. "It will buy us time. I would imagine that the court at Strelsau is not all that much different from the English court in one respect at least. Both surely have their gossip-mongers. With a word in the right ear or two, it can quickly go about that the king, having experienced some profound awakening—perhaps in the midst of all the holy solemnity of the coronation ceremony—has also realized or, let's say, has had forcibly driven home to him the sudden knowledge that he is about to wed a woman whom he has never taken the trouble to know. At least, on the level of a husband-to-be. If he postpones the marriage in order that he might romance the princess, court her favor rather than simply take her as his due, wouldn't that be regarded as romantic gallantry or some such thing? Would it not make Rudolf seem—well—somehow more human?"

Sapt smiled and shook his head. "You English!" he said. "You and your romantic poets and drawingroom novelists! Flavia has known Rudolf all her life and he has never regarded her as anything more than part of the palace furniture. Why should she believe in such a sudden change in him?"

Finn raised his eyebrows. "Why? Well, perhaps she won't. But I'll tell you a secret about women, Sapt. It has to do with what women know about men, but what men themselves do not know about each other. Women know that men are creatures of emotion. Whereas we ascribe that attribute to them, the fact is that a woman understands her emotions far better than a man does. We men are the ones who are entirely creatures of the heart. We accuse women of it like guilty little boys pointing fingers at their playmates in order to spare themselves responsibility. The truth is that women understand us better than we understand ourselves. If we are foolish or inconsistent, they are not surprised. They expect it of us."

Sapt made an incredulous face. "I never heard such addle-brained nonsense in my life!"

"Then you, Sapt, will never understand a woman."

"I think it's worth a try," said Fritz. "What have we got to lose?"

Sapt looked at him with astonishment. "*You* think it's worth a try? A moment ago, you were outraged at the very idea!"

Finn chuckled. "You see?" he said.

Von Tarlenheim flushed deeply and began to stammer a reply when there came a knock at the doors and the chancellor entered with a letter for the king. Finn thanked him and dismissed him, then opened the letter.

"What is it?" Sapt said.

Finn read aloud:

"If the king desires to know what it deeply concerns the king to know, let him do as this letter bids him. At the end of the New Avenue there stands a house in large grounds. The house has a portico with a statue of a nymph in it. A wall encloses the garden; there is a gate in the wall at the back. At twelve o'clock tonight, if the king enters alone by that gate, turns to the right and walks twenty yards, he will find a summerhouse, approached by a flight of six steps. If he mounts and enters, he will find someone who will tell him what touches most dearly his life and his throne."

Finn tossed the letter down onto the table, so that Sapt could take it. "Somehow, I didn't think it would be signed. Do you recognize the hand, Sapt?"

The old soldier frowned, gazing at the letter. "Not I."

"Would you know Black Michael's?"

"It is not his. Yet, that means nothing. He could have dictated it. It's a trap, for certain."

"Well, we shall have to see, won't we?" Finn said.

"Surely, you're not thinking of going?" said von Tarlenheim.

"Why not?"

"Why not? Don't be a fool, man, you'll be killed!"

Sapt rose. "I shall go and find out who delivered that letter to the chancellor."

"Don't bother," Finn said. "Our letter-writer prefers to remain anonymous. I doubt he would have delivered this in person. Besides, I don't think this is a trap. Would Michael be so obvious?''

"No, but he might be so devious," said Sapt. "He might think that we would not credit him with being so obvious and so fall into the trap.''

"There is that," said Finn. "Nevertheless, there's only one way we will know for sure."

"No," said Sapt, shaking his head. "I cannot allow it. The risk would be foolhardy.''

"Sapt, would you countermand your king?" said Finn.

"This is no time to jest," said Fritz.

"Who's jesting? Something in this game has got to give. We won't get anywhere if we sit around here hoping for the best. If someone wants to kill me tonight, I'll do my best to stay alive, but I think that someone wants to talk. I'd like to listen to what he has to say. It might guide us in our plans.''

"I shall go with you, then," said Sapt.

"As far as the garden wall," said Finn. "From there, I go alone.''

Sapt glowered at him. "Don't take your role too seriously, *Your Majesty*," he said. "You're *not* the king, you know."

"Maybe I'm not the real king, but I'm the only one you have at the moment. If I decided to take a walk tonight, how would you stop me? Call out the guard?''

"I'd stop you by myself if need be," Sapt said. "Don't think I couldn't.''

"Perhaps you could," said Finn, "but then I could call out the guard, you see. Fit of royal temper, don't you know? A night in jail would do you a world of good.''

"Damn you, Rassendyll—''

"Come on now, Sapt. Where's your spirit of adventure?''

"Very well. You win.''

"You're both insane!" said Fritz.

"You want to come?" said Finn.

Von Tarlenheim looked from him to Sapt and back again, then rolled his eyes and shrugged helplessly. "All right, we are all three insane, then. Why not? I am already a blasphemer, a perjured liar, and an accomplice to a fraud. I may as well be a fool, too.''

"By the way," said Finn, "whose house is it we're going to, does anybody know?"

"Everyone but you," said Sapt. "The house is Michael's residence in Strelsau. Just a coincidence, I suppose."

"Do me a favor, Sapt," said Finn, "please don't ask me to explain, but don't *ever* use that word to me again."

7

Drakov wandered alone through the dank, deserted corridors of Zenda Castle. In his right hand, he carried a small flashlight, one capable of throwing out a wide beam or of being used as a highly concentrated light source, emitting a beam of light almost as thin as that of a laser. At the moment, he had it set in the middle of its range, so that it illuminated only the corridor before him.

It was damp, it was cold, and it was quiet. The silence was broken only by the sound of his boots upon the stone and by the chittering of rats. There were thousands of them inside the castle, some approaching the size of housecats. Most swarmed in the dungeons below. From the lower floors of the abandoned main sections of the castle, their noise was like the distant sound of monstrous birds. It was a fitting atmosphere for black and brooding thoughts. As he walked, he brushed aside spider webs the size of bedsheets and crushed the bodies of long-dead insects beneath his boots. Just like Count Dracula, he thought, striding through his dark domain. Drakov, Dracula, even the names were similar. But the year was 1891 and the book would not be published for another six years yet. Perhaps Stoker was working on the manuscript somewhere in England at this very moment.

It never ceased to amaze him how he knew such things

through the subknowledge of his implant programming, that a veritable library of information could be stored upon a tiny sliver in his brain, available to him with the speed of thought. Subknowledge. Knowing things he didn't know he knew until he thought about them. That was one of the true miracles of Falcon's 27th century. He had become a part of it, but there was no place for him there. There was really no place for him anywhere. He should never have been born.

Moses Forrester would not even have been born for hundreds of years at the time he was conceived. For years, he had not really understood how a man could father a son before his own birth. The whole thing had seemed supernatural to him, despite his mother's attempts at explanation, and he had felt himself to be a demon issue, accursed from birth. Born of an impossible union, victim of a hate that could never be appeased. How to take revenge upon a man who had not even been born yet? How to reach across almost a thousand years to find him?

It had always been important to his mother for him to know his history, to know who and what his real father was. She had impressed upon him early on that he was different, that he was very, very special. She had been so proud, never suspecting how the story terrified him. He had always listened silently, never asking any questions, never saying anything, afraid to say the wrong thing, afraid of learning more.

He had been born while Moscow burned. He was one month premature. His mother's midwife was an old, drunken Cossack who looked after the wounds of the irregulars who harrassed Napoleon in his retreat, supporting in their disorganized way the attacks made upon the French by Kutusov's army. A severe winter was setting in and no one believed that the baby would survive. He not only survived, he grew strong and never sickened, not even when grown men succumbed to the fierce cold. They were taken in by a young army officer who led the irregulars, Captain Nikolai Sorokin. It was his name that had been given to the child. With the invaders driven out, they returned with Sorokin to St. Petersburg, where Sorokin—who knew the truth about Vanna Drakova, that she was a runaway serf—invented a fictional background for her. She became the sister of an army officer who never existed, who had died in the campaign and whose last wish was that Sorokin should care for her. They married and there was hope of a good life at last, but it was not to be.

Sorokin was a leading member of the secret Northern Society, which was one of several radical groups whose goal was to bring an end to the autocracy. Drakov was thirteen when Sorokin's hopes were dashed in the tragic Decembrist Uprising. Sorokin had escaped the slaughter in the Senate Square, only to be arrested and brought before the Tsar, who personally ordered his exile to Siberia. They followed so that Vanna could be close to him. Drakov knew that she had never loved him, at least not as Sorokin loved her, but she thought him a kind and good man and she owed him gratitude and loyalty. They were released from that obligation by Sorokin's death. He succumbed to influenza within the year, dying in his prison cell.

Vanna died soon afterward, murdered by a rapist, an ugly, smelly Georgian who took advantage of the fact that her only protector was a child of 15. When Drakov attempted to go to her defense, the rapist slashed him across the face with his knife, then kicked him repeatedly until he could no longer move. He left him bleeding, had his way with Vanna, and left her dead. Falcon had told him that the scar could be easily removed when she brought him to the 27th century, but he would not consent to it. The scar served as a daily reminder to him of what Moses Forrester had brought his mother to. It always kept the memory alive.

He survived being orphaned at 15. He survived Siberia to make his way with an old fur trader to the Russian settlements in Alaska, where he took up the fur trade, learning to hunt, learning to live in the wilderness. At the age of 20, he was on his own again. He still looked like a child. Many tried to take advantage of him. He learned how to protect himself. He learned to fight and he learned to kill. He already knew how to hate.

At the age of 24, he became a seaman, working on a trader's schooner. They hunted seals in the Pribilofs with great success. By the age of 38, he had his own ship. He was known as the youngest captain in the Pribilofs, for few suspected his true age. It was something he had learned to conceal, though he could not explain why he looked so much younger than he was. Still, seamen were always superstitious and after a time, stories began to circulate about Captain Drakov, who miraculously did not seem to age. By then, he had made his fortune. The time had come to travel once again to some place where he was not known. He sold his ship the year that the Americans acquired Alaska and traveled to Boston. He was 55 years old and he looked like the son of a man that age.

He purchased a large mansion on Beacon Hill and set about making a new life for himself. He learned about investing in the stock market and within a few years, he had multiplied his fortune many times. He was thought to be some European nobleman and he soon became much sought after in Boston society. He, the illegitimate child of a runaway serf, rubbed shoulders with the scions of the finest families on the Eastern seaboard. But notoriety led to curiosity and it wasn't very long before people began to inquire into his affairs, into his history. It did not seem very long before it was time to move once more.

He arrived in England in his seventieth year. He had no need of looking for an occupation. He had millions. He had everything a man could want—wealth, youth (to all appearances, he was quite young), position; the scar so ignobly received was believed to have been inflicted in a duel and so added an adventurous mystique; he could easily indulge the lavish tastes he had acquired. He entertained the finest minds in all of Europe, became a patron of the arts, sought all manner of diversions. Still, no matter what he tried, he could not find a sense of self. He was a shadow with substance, a creature who could not possibly exist, yet did exist, blessed—or cursed—with eternal youth. Why did he not age? Why did he never become ill? After a time, he was not the only one who wondered about such things, as people who had known him in America arrived in London and the gossip began anew. Only this time, he decided that he would not run away. He had had enough of running from himself. Let the speculators speculate, let the gossips gossip; let the curious wonder. He no longer gave a damn.

He became a figure of mystery and infamy. He was rich enough and he had become powerful enough to do as he pleased. He no longer cared what others thought. Doctors clamored to examine him, to conduct tests to see if they could determine the secret of his youth. He gave them all the back of his hand. Officials who became curious about his background were quickly silenced by the expedient of bribing their superiors. He quickly learned that each man had his price, some higher than others, but none so high that he could not afford to pay and never miss the loss. Women were irresistibly drawn to him, fascinated by the virile power of a man who seemed to be forever in his prime. He entertained them all, but he had none of them. He was still a virgin, unwilling to risk bringing a child into the world, a child whose father would have been a man born of some sort of supernatural union. He had no wish to pass on the curse. He remained chaste, until he met Sophia Falco.

She appeared one day in London, a woman of intrigue and mystery, apparently a rich countess from the Mediterranean. No one seemed to know much about her background. She was like quicksilver; elusive, charming, breathtakingly beautiful and compelling in a strange and savage way, like some predatory feline. She was full of animal grace and power. She fascinated him. They seemed to be two of a kind, each determined to live life solely on his own terms, with no thought for the opinions or concerns of others. Drakov was unable to resist her. He had never before met a woman who possessed such strength and independence, who affected him so profoundly.

All the while, she was penetrating his defenses, suspecting the truth about him, a truth not even he himself knew. She thought him to be a member of the temporal underground, a soldier who had deserted from the armies of the future. She thought she could make use of him and of his resources. When she finally learned the truth, for by then he could no longer keep it from her, she laughed. He could never forget that laugh. In it was contained a wild joy, grim realization of some grotesque joke that he was unaware of, bitterness, and even grief.

Each time he fantasized confronting Moses Forrester at last, having his father helpless before him, much as Rudolf Rassendyll had been, he always heard her laugh again. It had been a laugh that he had heard only that one time, for she laughed rarely and never quite like *that*, and each time he experienced anew the gripping fear that he had felt when he first heard it. There was an understanding in that laugh. He felt himself reflected in it, a pathetic caprice of fate, a sad and ultimately meaningless joke that served only to unite events, having no significance in and of itself.

He longed to make that fantasy reality, to confront his father, to see his face in the flesh, to hear his voice, to make him real and to demand some sort of an accounting. *Look* at me, he wanted to tell him. I exist! I think, I breathe, I feel! Did you even once consider *me* when you released your poisoned seed in a paroxysm of lust? Did you ever give any thought to what would become of the young girl who gave herself to you, to whom you whispered words of love, to whom you promised to return, all the while knowing you would leave her, never to come back? It was not enough for you to use her. It was not enough to shame her. You had to leave her with a hope that could never be fulfilled. Where were you when she gave birth to me in a ramshackle wooden cabin in the dead of Russian winter? Where were you when she was being violated? Damn you, where were you when she died?

Ultimately, at the bottom of it all, was one central question that was posed by all the other questions, a question that he knew he could never bring himself to ask directly. *Where were you when I needed you?*

"Is that, then, the final measure of a man?" he asked himself, speaking aloud to the damp walls, to the spiders, to the dust. "That his life is not complete unless he needs someone? Is *that* why she laughed, because she understood that both of us, who had lived as though we never needed anyone, really needed you?"

Falcon did not have to say it. He saw that she had once again put on the ring. Which of us has the greater need, he wondered. Which of us hates you more? It began in the ruin of a peasant's barn and it was somehow fitting that it would now end in the ruin of some long-departed noble's castle.

He had come to a large central chamber, feeling the hazy disorientation of one who is caught in the delicate awareness of that moment between wakefulness and dreaming. He stood in the arched entryway to a cavernous room, a hall cloaked in dust and darkness. He widened the beam of his flashlight.

The ceiling was high over his head and vaulted. The stone sconces for the torches that had not blazed in years were carved into the shapes of gargoyles. A wide stone stairway curved gently to an upper floor and spiders made lace curtains between the columns that supported it.

Once ornate tapestries hung upon these walls. Once long oaken tables stood here, groaning beneath the weight of medieval feasts. Once wolfhounds sprawled beneath those tables, catching morsels thrown to them by raucous celebrants. Once logs piled high inside the spacious fireplace burned brightly, making dancing shadows on the walls. Now the place was permeated with an aura of decay. The hearth had long been cold; the floor was veined with cracks and the current celebrants were spiders, rats, and lizards, creatures that regarded his intrusion with indifference. They seemed to accept his presence as if he belonged here, a lifeform that remained long after others had departed, a shade of some bygone age, a dream with substance, indeed, one of the undead, like the vampire count who lived only to hunger ceaselessly and never have his appetite appeased.

Drakov leaned back against the wall and slowly slid down to a sitting position on the floor. He had lived in squalid huts, in cramped cabins aboard ship, in staterooms, in well-appointed homes, in luxurious mansions, yet never had he felt more in his place than he had come to feel inside this mausoleum of a castle. He had started off hating it, but it had grown upon him. It felt like home now.

He switched off the flashlight and sat there in the darkness, feeling the weight of time upon him. It was almost like being asleep, only he did not have to close his eyes.

And he did not have to dream.

Rupert Hentzau's face shone with an expression of pure joy behind his fencing mask as he lunged at his opponent. His lunge was neatly parried, followed by a lightning beat and riposte, then a disengage. Both backed off, then sprang forward once again, their sabres clanged against each other four times quickly, then another disengage. Again, steel on steel singing, three staccato notes followed by a grinding as each attempted to bear the other's sabre down, then a quick scraping of blade against blade, three more strikes, cut, parry, riposte and Rupert scored a touch, whipping off his mask with a triumphant cry. His opponent's mask also came off, revealing a cascade of long ash blond hair.

"Hah!" cried Rupert, his light blue eyes glittering with excitement. His black hair was tousled, hanging down over his boyish face. White, even, perfect teeth flashed in a wide grin. "By Heaven, you fence well! Would that I could cross swords with your father. He must have been the very devil of a swordsman. He taught you well, Sophia."

Falcon smiled. Her father had been a small, studious man, slight of frame and weak of wrist. He would not have known a sabre from a foil. His field had been genetic engineering. Her fencing instructor had been a woman, a weapons training specialist in the Temporal Army Corps. What would Hentzau have made of that, she wondered.

He stood there, breathing heavily after their long exertions, staring at her with undisguised lust. Then he flung his sabre away from him and took her in a strong embrace, crushing his lips to hers. She raked her fingers through his hair, returning the kiss and grinding her body up against his; then she pulled away.

"Not now, Rupert," she said huskily. "Michael could walk in at any moment."

"Hang Michael!" He sought to kiss her again, but she put her hands upon his chest and pushed him away firmly.

"Control yourself," she said.

He scowled petulantly. "I've been doing little else. I don't see why we waste time. All we have is here and now."

"There is somewhat more to life than here and now," said Falcon, glancing at him archly. "Perhaps one of these days, you will realize that." The arch look became coy. "Maybe when you're older."

"Older! Like Michael, you mean?"

"Michael is not so very much older than you are. He is, however, more mature in some respects."

"The devil with Michael! I don't see what we need him for.

I don't see why we dawdle. We should finish the whole thing and have done with it!''

"How many times must I explain it to you?" she said, wearily. "We need Michael to fall back upon if our plan fails. The man Rassendyll has nerve and we need Michael to play against him.''

"I can see that, I suppose," said Hentzau, "but it all seems needlessly elaborate to me. My patience is wearing thin.''

"Your impatience may yet be the death of you, my love," she said. "You must learn to wait.''

"Well, I shall wait until tonight, at least," he said.

"What about tonight?" said Michael.

He stood in the doorway, holding the door open. Falcon glanced at him sharply, wondering if he had heard. He gave no sign of it. Hentzau could not appear to care less.

"We were discussing the dinner tonight," she said, moving toward him. She came up to him and gave him a soft kiss on the lips. "Rupert is impatient to get back to Zenda to check upon the prisoner. I told him that he should wait until tonight. I would feel better knowing he was here to guard me while you were at the dinner. They might try anything to work against you. They could try to kidnap me and use me to make you release the king.''

"But what makes you think that you will be remaining here?" said Michael.

"You're sending me away?"

"I will do no such thing. You shall attend the dinner with me." He glanced down at her fencing apparel. "In fact, you had best be getting yourself ready." He frowned. "I don't know why you bother practicing your fencing. It is one thing for a girl whose father had desired a son to play at it, but it is useless for a woman. It is unseemly.''

"She plays at it rather well," said Hentzau, with a smirk. "You should try her, Michael.''

"Don't be ridiculous. Now run along, dear, and prepare yourself.''

"Is it wise to take her to the dinner?" Hentzau said. "I mean, it would hardly ingratiate you to Flavia. You might do well to cultivate the favor of your future queen." His eyes mocked them both. "A man in your position may find two women burdensome."

"Take care of your insolence, Rupert," Michael said. "When the time comes, I shall take Flavia as is my due. As to what she thinks or doesn't think, I could not be less concerned."

"What about yourself, Countess?" Hentzau said, addressing her, but baiting Michael. "Have you no thoughts upon the matter?"

"Flavia can warm his throne," she said, smiling. "I shall be the one to warm his bed."

"You see, Rupert?" Michael said. "Sophia and I understand one another."

Hentzau gave an insouciant chuckle. "I would caution the man who believes he understands his woman."

Michael narrowed his eyes. "That will be enough! I shall tolerate no veiled insults to Sophia in my presence."

"Why," said Hentzau, innocently, "was I insulting the countess? May Heaven forbid! I meant no such thing."

"Stop it, both of you," she said. "Dissension in our ranks serves only Sapt and von Tarlenheim. We must be patient. Time is on our side. We can afford to wait, while each day makes the imposter's position more precarious. They are doubtless growing desperate by now and desperate men are vulnerable men."

"You see, Rupert, how she always thinks of my interests above all else?" said Michael.

"*Our* interests," she said. "It is in all our interests for you to become king. Isn't that right, Rupert?"

Hentzau smirked and inclined his head slightly.

"I shall go get ready, then," she said. "Rupert, thank you for indulging me. I know I could never give you a good match, but it was kind of you to humor me. It helped alleviate some of my worries."

"Anytime, Countess," Hentzau said.

They left him in the training room. "I have a few matters to attend to," Michael said. "I will see you when you have dressed. I wish you to look particularly ravishing tonight, my dear."

"Your wish is my command. *Sire*," she added, significantly.

When she was alone in the bedroom, she shut the door and bolted it, then sprawled down on the bed with a bottle of whiskey. She took a long drink. It helped to wash the bad taste out of her mouth. Hentzau was a pleasant diversion as a lover, but he was growing more tiresome by the day. It was wearying to play constantly to his juvenile sensibilities, to his swaggering braggadocio, to his arrogance and conceit. He was an excellent swordsman, but he had condescended to her during their match. She had to use all her concentration to fence even more poorly. It would have been interesting to see how it would have gone had he given his all. It might have been an excellent match, indeed. She was reasonably certain that she could take him if he were in earnest. She had originally thought to use him further, but she had long since dismissed any such notion. He was too self-centered, too unpredictable, too much of a boy with a cocksure sense of his own uniqueness. If Michael had walked in on them one moment earlier, she had no doubt that Hentzau would have welcomed it as an opportunity to kill him. He simply didn't care. He did, indeed, live only in the here and now, with no thought to any consequences.

Michael, on the other hand, was the complete opposite: a planner and a brooder, a born intriguer. However, his moodiness and his possessive attitude were stultifying. Keeping the two of them in line and away from each other was a full-time job. Fortunately, the same tactics worked well on both of them. They were men and being men, were easy to manipulate. All it took was an appeal to their hormones. It was easy, but it was both annoying and time-consuming. Now this demand that she attend the dinner at the palace as Michael's showpiece. She grimaced as she realized the *double entendre* nature of the thought. Her first instinct had been to beg off. Michael might not have liked that, but she could easily have managed it. Then, it occurred to her, *why not*?

Why not attend the dinner? It would make Delaney squirm. There she would be, face to face with him, and he would be unable to do anything. It would serve to demoralize the bastard. Perhaps he would give himself away somehow. It was certain that they were planning to make their move soon, perhaps even tonight. Maybe something in his manner or in his face would give it all away.

To Rupert and to Michael and to Nikolai, she counseled patience, yet she herself was beginning to chafe at the bit. She was concerned about the others, Priest and Cross. She had no idea where they were or what they were doing. Surely, they would not be idle. And Moses would be with them now. That would only serve to spur them on, give them more confidence. The leader had come to join his troops in battle. She wondered what was going through his mind.

He would be thinking of his son. His son, the Timekeeper. His son, who hated him with an all-consuming passion. His son, whom he would have to kill. Would he be thinking at all of her, of how she had used Nikolai to lure him here? Would he be recalling the nights that they had spent together, both in Plus Time and in the field, of the love that they had shared, of her proposal to him?

She drank more whiskey. It had been another life. A part of her, a very essential part, had been suppressed so that she might avoid detection. During that life, she had been unaware of her true self, but afterwards she had remembered. She remembered both her real self and everything that had happened while she had been Elaine Cantrell. The whiskey always helped to dull the memories, but it could not obliterate them.

There had been a desperation in Elaine Cantrell, some sense of imminence perhaps motivated by subconscious knowledge of the hidden part of her. She had sought escape. There had been strong impulses driving her, impulses she had not understood then but knew now as programmed imperatives she had vainly attempted to resist. In order for Elaine Cantrell to be able to function in her role, it had been necessary for her to be the sort of person who would abhor what her real self did. She had found solace in the arms of Moses Forrester and for a time she believed that she might find escape as well. Escape from an imminent *something* that would not resolve into a clear picture. She had proposed marriage to him one night—a new life, a new beginning. They could leave the service and find stability. As civilians, they could enjoy a peaceful existence. No more uncertainty. No more traveling through time. No more pressure, no feelings of impending disaster. They could have a permanent home that would be their own. They could have children. *A son, Moses. We could have a son.*

He turned her down.

She offered him what other men would have accepted upon any terms and he turned her down. To add insult to injury, what she offered him he had accepted from some ignorant peasant girl. The child that Vanna Drakova had borne should have been hers. She flung the bottle away, cursing Lachman Singh. He had done his job too well. Elaine Cantrell should have been dead, but a large part of her still lived. Well, soon it would be put to rest. Relief would come at last with the death of Nikolai Drakov.

She lured Forrester here to destroy him, but not in the manner that he thought. She would not try killing him herself. She would leave that job to Nikolai. If Drakov killed his father, she would, in turn, kill him, and then the slate would be wiped clean. And if Forrester prevailed, it would be a much more exquisite revenge. She would let him live with the knowledge that he had killed his own son. Either way, he would die. The Timekeepers would also be avenged and a massive timestream split would occur. As with the ancient Japanese, who would not surrender until they had experienced firsthand the awesome power of atomic energy unleashed, so would the war machine be forced to face the final consequences of their folly. She would go down in history as the woman who had single-handedly brought the Time Wars to a halt. And this time, history would not be changed.

8 ⸻⸻⸻⸻⸻⸻

They were admitted to Flavia's chambers by Countess Helga von Strofzin, a pretty girl scarcely out of her teens. She was delighted to see Fritz von Tarlenheim. Finn left them alone in the sitting room as he went in to see the princess. Flavia had dressed for the occasion, already prepared to attend the dinner so that her king would not be kept waiting while she changed. She curtsied deeply with a rustling of organdy.

"Come, come, no need of that," said Finn, taking her hand and bringing her up straight. "Surely we can dispense with formalities in private."

"As you wish, Rudolf," she said. "May I offer you some wine?"

"No, I don't think so, thank you."

She raised her eyebrows. "Not even your favorite port?"

"I have favored port too much of late, I think," said Finn. "It is one thing for a prince to be somewhat overfond of wine, but a king should be more abstemious."

She looked surprised. "What brought this on?"

Protocol demanded that he sit first before she could be seated. Despite the fact that he was not standing on formalities, Finn knew that she would not sit down until he did. He settled on the large divan.

"To be honest, I'm not really certain," he said, putting a

118

note of puzzlement into his voice. "Things suddenly began to feel somehow strange."

"How strange?" she said, sitting down beside him and turning so that she could face him. They sat close together, yet there was still a distance separating them. He knew he would not close it in a single day, but he could make a start, for Elphberg's sake.

"I wish I could explain," he said. "I am not quite sure when it all began. Perhaps it began when we rode together from the cathedral to the palace. Perhaps it started afterward, when I was alone in my bedchambers. Nothing had changed outwardly, but everything seemed somehow different suddenly. I experienced a vague unease. I stood before the mirror, still dressed in the uniform in which I was crowned, and I said to myself, 'Well, there you are, Your Majesty. King Rudolf the Fifth.' Only somehow, I did not feel like a king. I felt like a little boy who had dressed up in his father's clothing. The clothing looked impressive, but it did not quite make me feel grown-up. It didn't seem to fit. It was too large for me, somehow, despite its having been excellently tailored to my form."

Even as he spoke, he was starting to feel cheap.

"I began to feel foolish," he continued, noting that Flavia was listening with growing interest. "It felt like, well, you know— Oh, well, I suppose *you* would not know, but it felt like the morning after one becomes paralyzed with drink. You wake up and absolutely everything is wrong. You can't see straight, your head is splitting, your stomach feels as though someone had lit a fire in it. You feel terrible and the first thought that enters your head is 'Why on earth did I *do* that last night? What possessed me? I must have been insane. I'll never, *never* drink again, not so much as one sip.' Only of course, it doesn't last long. The feeling goes away and one does drink, even to excess and the entire process repeats itself. It's a never-ending circle, like a puppy chasing its own tail. The only difference is that eventually, the puppy grows tired of the game and has enough sense to lie down."

He glanced at her and saw that the beginning of a smile was tugging at the corner of her mouth.

"Does any of that make any sense at all?"

She licked her lips and nodded. "I think so. But I'm not certain that I completely understand your meaning."

"Well, for that matter, neither am I," said Finn, grinning ruefully. Delaney, you miserable bastard, he told himself, you're working a fast-talking con on a naive young girl who has already resigned herself to a loveless marriage. Now you're trying to turn her head in another man's name to suit the purpose of the moment.

"It was a most peculiar feeling and I thought that it would go away. I said to myself, 'You're tired, Rudolf, worn out from all the nonsense of that ridiculous parade through town and kneeling for what seemed like forever while that mitered idiot—" she frowned, but Finn continued in character— "sprinkled holy water over you and chanted nasally in Latin. You drank too much at the banquet and did not eat enough. You simply do not feel yourself.' And that was the answer, you see. I did not feel myself. And the feeling did not go away. It only grew and grew and it began to give me headaches. I was not ill; there was no fever, but I felt like an old woman with the vapors. I knew that I needed to talk to someone, to attempt to describe how I was feeling, only who was there to talk to? Sapt? He had no patience for such nonsense. I was not up to hearing yet another lecture from that old bear. Von Tarlenheim? What would Fritz know? He's just a boy. I'd only confuse him. The chancellor? He'd merely sit there pressing his lips together and then run off to search his documents for some precedent."

Flavia chuckled. "And so you came to *me*?"

Finn shrugged. "I have no idea why, I must confess. Why should I burden you with this nonsense? Yet, the moment it occurred to me to speak to you, it seemed like the most sensible thing to do." He frowned. "Perhaps I *am* ill."

"You do not look ill to me," she said. "Perhaps you *were* ill and are just now beginning to recover."

"Recover? From what?"

"Perhaps from growing pains?"

"Don't be ridiculous," said Finn. Not too much at once, he thought. Let's have a little of the "old" Rudolf. "What would you know about growing up? You're still a child yourself."

"Am I?" she said. "When was the last time you took a good look?"

Finn gave her an appraising glance, half-humorously, then made his face grow a bit more serious. "Come to think of it, I may have judged a bit hastily." He grinned. "A dowager you're not, but neither are you a child. Kings marry little girls upon occasion, but it appears that *this* king will marry one that's grown."

Her gaze held his for a moment, then slid away. "I had wondered if you had come to speak of that," she said.

"So does half the kingdom wonder, by all accounts," said Finn, gloomily. "To tell the truth, I am loathe to set the date just yet."

"I see," she said, softly, looking down.

"No, Flavia, I don't think you do. We have known each other all our lives, yet if we were to wed now, each of us would be marrying a stranger."

She glanced back at him abruptly.

"I mean, what do you know of *me*, really? You know something of my actions, but what do you know of my thoughts? For that matter, what do I know of you? Royal marriages are seldom made of love, I know, but why should a king or a queen be denied what even the lowliest peasant can enjoy, the security of being able to wed someone that they know and care for?"

"Care for?" Flavia said, uncertainly.

"Well," Finn said, looking away, "in your case, that may not apply. Oh, I know that you care for me as your king, but I do not delude myself that you care for me as a man. I have given you no reason to. Nor can I care for you as a woman. How can I care for someone I have never taken the trouble to know?"

Flavia looked at him intently. "Rudolf . . . am I to take it that you are—" she became a little flustered. "Are you proposing to *court* me?"

Finn pretended to look embarrassed. He did not have to pretend too hard. "It does seem rather ridiculous, does it not?"

She shook her head, which he saw out of the corner of his

eye, but he acted as though he had not noticed.

"Here we are, already betrothed, with the entire kingdom knowing we shall wed, and I come to you like some stammering suitor. I should have thought to bring flowers, I suppose."

"Flowers? From you?"

"Why not? I can give flowers if I choose to! Is that so very foolish? You find it amusing?"

"No. No, I find it . . ." she shrugged, at a loss for words. "I don't know. Remarkable, I suppose. Somehow, I cannot picture you bringing flowers. Rudolf, what *is* this? What's gotten into you?"

Finn stood up, irately. "Damned if *I* know," he said. "I feel like a complete fool."

"You are not sounding like a fool," she said. "But, Lord knows, you do not sound like yourself."

For a moment, Finn took that literally and wondered if his mimicry was slipping, then he realized that it wasn't what she meant. She stood up and came to stand by his side, putting a hand on his arm and turning him slightly so that she could look into his eyes.

"What is it?" she said. "Is this some sort of joke? Have you come to play a prank on me, the way you did when we were children? Are you having second thoughts about the wedding now that you are king? Is that what this is? You propose to court me so that at some time during. . . ." Her voice trailed off and she frowned.

"What?" said Finn.

She stood back from him a moment, then came up close to him again. "Have you *grown*?"

Oh-oh, thought Finn. Get her off this tack, but fast!

"Grown? What are you talking about? How could I have grown? I was speaking seriously and you decide to address yourself to the question of my *height*? If you don't want to discuss this, why then, say so! Don't attempt to change the subject!"

She squeezed his upper arm where her hand had rested. "And your arm is larger, too," she said. "It was not so firm or large when we danced together at the last ball. You've been training?"

"Of course I have been training," Finn said, suddenly feeling that he was losing control. "I am king now. I should be more fit, I must take better care of myself. I have responsibilities."

She backed off from him slowly, shaking her head and staring at him with bewilderment. "I find it hard to believe that you are Rudolf," she said. "I do begin to believe that you really *have* changed!"

"I am the same man I have always been," said Finn. "I've just been thinking about things; that's all."

"That, in itself, is quite a change," she said. Then she flushed. "Forgive me. I did not mean to be insulting."

"It seems that I shall have a sharp-tongued queen," said Finn. "Well, a man could do far worse. So, do you agree or don't you?"

She looked baffled. "Agree? To what?"

"To our spending more time together. To my bringing you flowers if I choose to. To carriage rides through the city streets. To walks in the country or some such thing; I don't know, what do people *do* when they are courting?"

She stared at him, wide-eyed. "Those sort of things, I suppose. How would I know? No one has ever courted me before."

"A fine pair we make," Finn said. "I know. Let's call in Fritz and Helen. We shall ask them what they do."

"Don't you dare!" she said.

"Such a reaction! Now I *really* want to know what it is they do."

"She blushed. "You would only embarrass both of them. Leave them be, please. We shall spend more time together. You shall bring me flowers. We will go for carriage rides and walks. That all sounds quite sufficient. I shall do whatever you command."

"Well, now you've ruined it," said Finn.

"I'm sorry. I did not mean it that way. You may court me if you wish. I would be delighted." Her brow furrowed. "Is that what one should say?"

"It'll do, I suppose," said Finn. "Well. Shall we make a beginning, then? Would you do me the honor of allowing me to escort you to dinner?"

"But I thought that was all arranged already," she said.

"I've already dressed, you see, and—"

"*Damn* it, Flavia, will you or won't you?"

"Oh, I see. Forgive me. Yes, of course, I would be very pleased to have you escort me to dinner, Rudolf."

Finn offered her his arm. She took it. As they came out into the sitting room, Fritz and Helen were sitting very close together. They instantly sprang apart the moment that they saw them.

"Well, come on, Fritz, plenty of time for that sort of thing later," Finn said. "We have a dinner to attend."

Sapt carefully eased himself over the stone wall, keeping low so that he would not make a silhouette. He dropped down soundlessly onto the grass below, wincing slightly as the impact jarred his back. I'm too old for this sort of thing, he thought. I should be in the old soldier's home, sitting in a cane chair with a pipe in my mouth, a glass of warm milk at my elbow, and a wool blanket over my lap. Instead, I'm scaling garden walls like some septuagenarian Don Juan. Damn that Rassendyll, anyway.

Still, the man was a surprise. Who would have guessed that a real soldier lurked beneath that dandy's exterior? How quickly he had assumed his role! How effortlessly he seemed to have taken control of the situation, almost as though he were a real king! He had the makings of one, that much was certain. He would have to be sure to ask him what rank he had held in the English army and in which regiment he'd served, what sort of action he had seen. The man was no dilettante playing at strategy. He knew what he was about. If only Rudolf could be more like him! Rassendyll would make a damn sight better king than he would.

He quickly pushed that thought aside. Even thinking it was treasonous. Staying low, he moved across the tree-sheltered lawn in the darkness, taking careful stock of the surroundings. Rassendyll would expect a detailed report. He was surprised that he hadn't asked him to draw a map. Perhaps he would. Strange, he thought, how he makes me feel. He can't be but half my age. Yet it is as though *he* is the experienced veteran. It's the mark of a born leader. A true officer. One who leads by both example and charisma. It was something one could learn, but not at so young an age, certainly. Rassendyll appeared to come by it naturally. How had the English army allowed him to get away? He still had years of good service left in him. Perhaps there was some disciplinary problem. That was the trouble with men like that. They made outstanding officers if they could survive their superiors early on in their careers. Men with such natural abilities did not do well under inferior officers. It was a question that he would not ask. Such things were better left unspoken.

He crossed the wide expanse of lawn quickly, heading toward the little summerhouse situated at the end of the garden near the statue of a nymph. It was a small, latticed gazebo, open at both ends, set up on a platform of cobblestones arranged in a pattern of concentric circles. Situated on a slight rise, it gave a commanding view of the landscaped garden and the sloping lawn on the opposite side. Sapt immediately noted that it was fairly isolated, with no bushes or trees anywhere close to it that would afford good concealment for an ambush. However, it would be dark enough at midnight to enable one or more people to approach the little summerhouse completely undetected, especially if they came up on it from one of its latticed sides. He didn't like that. He didn't like anything about the whole affair, but Rassendyll was firm on going, damn him. In a way, Sapt could even understand it. If it was managed carefully, this meeting could mislead the enemy, giving them the impression that they were desperate enough to try anything. It all rested with Rassendyll. If he was right, then perhaps it would not be a trap, though the opportunity for it would be excellent. Something about it simply didn't smell right, though. Was Michael being so obvious merely to be devious? Did he hope to buy the imposter off? Or was it even Michael who had sent the note? Rassendyll was correct in saying that there was only one way in which they would learn the truth. Still, it would be a risky business.

Sapt began to look for probable avenues of retreat in the event that something should go wrong. It did not look promising. Open ground upon all sides for a distance of at least some thirty or forty yards. A running man would make an easy target, but there the darkness that would serve any possible assassins would serve Rassendyll, as well. He could still be brought down, though. The question was, how to minimize those odds?

If he thinks that I will remain meekly behind the garden wall, Sapt thought, he's in for a surprise. There had to be a spot somewhere from which he could keep watch and provide covering fire if the need arose. He began to look around, trying to keep to concealment as much as possible. It was past eight, but there was still a chance he might be seen. It was not that dark yet. He checked the place where Rassendyll would be entering the garden according to instructions. Then he began to walk along the inside of the wall, circling the garden, glancing continuously back at the summerhouse, estimating lines of fire. He found several places where he could wait and watch, but the distance was a bit too great to ensure good visibility in total darkness, even with his excellent vision. He would have to get considerably closer. However, there was no way that he could get closer to the summerhouse from where he was without being in the open. He glanced back towards Michael's house.

If there would be trickery afoot, they might be expecting someone to be protecting Rassendyll from a position somewhere between the garden wall and the summerhouse. But between the summerhouse and Michael's house? Cautiously, Sapt made his way towards the west wing of the mansion, where French doors opened out onto a flagstoned patio that overlooked the garden. From the end of the patio, a flight of stone steps led down into the garden and to a path leading up to the summerhouse. At the bottom of this flight of steps were two very large stone planters in the shape of urns, one on each side. If he were to conceal himself behind one of them, up against the stone wall of the steps, he would be invisible unless someone coming down the steps were to look down over the side and see him. He took up position there to see what sort of view it could afford him. Not bad, he thought. Far from ideal, but closer to the summerhouse than if he stayed by the garden wall on the opposite side. He crouched down, took out his pistol, and sighted. If Rassendyll made his escape towards the garden wall, anyone inside the summerhouse would have to take up position on that side in order to shoot at him. He could barely make out the dark shape of the gazebo now; it would be worse still later. He lined up his sight on the entrance to the summerhouse, locked his arm, and slowly brought it down to rest upon the top of the stone urn. He sighted once again from rest. Yes. It would do. Without moving his arm, he reached with his other hand into his pocket and brought out two of the wooden matches he always carried to light his pipe. He stuck the matches into the earth inside the planter on either side of his wrist, then moved his arm. The matches would remain there as sighting posts. He carefully lowered his arm again, so that his wrist rested exactly between the two matches, and sighted once more. It would serve. Even if he could not see well, using the matches to line up his aim would enable him to shoot anyone who stood in the arched entryway of the gazebo.

Above him on the patio, he heard footsteps. He froze, cocking his pistol. He looked up, but could not see who it was because the wall blocked his view. It was just as well, because it meant that he could not be seen, either.

"I told you not to come here!" Sapt frowned. It was Sophia's voice, kept low, scarcely above a whisper.

"I am growing tired of taking orders from you," another voice said. It was a man's voice, resonant and very deep. "I am growing tired of waiting."

"You're a fool!" she said. "You want to ruin everything?"

"You know what I want. I want it over and done with. I want him dead. As for the rest of your intrigues, I could not care less. It no longer matters."

Sapt did not recognize the voice. Moving slowly, he began to edge around the urn so that he might see who it was.

"I thought you said that I could count on you," she said. "Is that how much your word means?"

The man snorted derisively. "*My* word? What about yours?"

"What are you talking about?"

Sapt had edged around enough so that he could see Countess Sophia from the waist up, the rest of her blocked from his view by the stone steps. He could not see the man to whom she was speaking. Slowly, he began to crawl up the steps.

"What have you done with the other plate?"

Sapt frowned. *Plate?* Why would they be discussing plates while they spoke of murder?

"I've moved it."

"Where?" he said. "Why didn't you tell me?"

"Because—"

"Sophia? Sophia!"

"Michael!" she said. "Go. Quickly. I'll explain later."

"You will explain now."

"Sophia, we'll be late!" Michael called.

"Go, I said!"

Sapt crawled up two more steps. The French doors opened and Michael came out on the patio. This should prove interesting, thought Sapt.

"Sophia! What the devil are you doing out here?"

"I thought I'd come out for a breath of air while I waited for you, Michael. Are you ready to leave now?"

"I have been ready for the past hour! I was waiting for you!"

Is Michael blind? Sapt risked crawling up one more step, staying low, now only yards away from them. He could see the patio clearly. He could see both Michael and Sophia. But no one else.

"Well, let us go, then," said Sophia. "We can arrive fashionably late."

"Why cannot women ever be on time?" said Michael. "Come, the coach is waiting."

They went back into the house. Sapt had his pistol out as he crawled up the few remaining steps. He was alone upon the patio. How could that be? There were only two ways for the man she was speaking with to go. One would have taken him into the house through the French doors, where Michael was. The other would have taken him down the steps into the garden, directly at him. He had not gone past Michael and it was impossible for him to have gone down the steps without stepping on me, thought Sapt. Unless he vaulted the patio wall. . . .

He could only have vaulted on one side, the side closest to where he had been standing. Going the other way would have brought him across Michael's field of vision and his own. Sapt went over to the wall upon that side. He looked down over it into a fish pond with water lillies floating in it. It was wide enough that a man could not possibly have leaped over the wall and cleared it. There would have been a splash. Only there had been no splash. And there was no place on the patio itself where the man could have hidden.

"What the *devil*?" Sapt whispered aloud. "How could the man simply disappear?"

9

They entered the main dining room of the palace after the chamberlain had announced them to see everyone standing at his place. It made Finn think of a scene out of an historical romance, all those medals and epaulets and sashes, moustaches and muttonchops and beards, bodices and ribbons and chokers and cameos, necklaces and rings and bracelets, pomp and circumstance and splendor. He wondered what would happen if he ordered a hamburger. And a beer. Some french fries on the side, with steak sauce. Being a king, he decided, was very overrated. The job had certain perks, but it had to be tiresome to constantly be the focus of so much formality and pointless ceremony. The occasion, Sapt had explained to him, was a "state dinner" and its purpose seemed to be nothing other than to give the lords and ladies of Ruritania, the ministers and high-ranking officers, the ambassadors and their factotums, assorted minor functionaries and hangers-on a feeling of importance at being privileged to share a table with His Majesty. It made Finn think of the 20th-century British monarchy. A showpiece royal family. They didn't actually *do* anything except be a royal family. A nominal royalty, they lived a life that could be described as a photo opportunity in exchange for drawing exorbitant salaries just so their "subjects" could bask in the trivial and pointless glamor of their existence. While the economy of the nation that had once been a major world power continued in a constant downward spiral, they lived in palatial residences (plural, of course, we must have summerhomes and country estates and stables and riding to hounds), spent enough on clothing to feed an average middle-class family for several years, had their little romances extensively documented and their family squabbles agonized over in the press, all the while being treasured like prize canaries in a cage by people dazzled by and starved for their celebrity. Meanwhile, the matters of government were left to politicians, far less glamorous and cultured but much more workmanlike. It would have been the same, undoubtedly, with Rudolf. He would have enjoyed all this, thought Finn. What was it about people, he wondered, that even in so-called egalitarian societies, they seemed to eschew the very concept of class, all the while creating it on all levels of their culture?

As they moved up to the table to take their places, Fritz and Helga began to walk toward the far end, but Finn caught Helga by the sleeve and indicated the place next to his, where there were two empty seats on his right.

"Oh, no, Sire," Helga said, blushing. "Surely, it must have slipped your mind, but that is the Duke of Strelsau's place."

"Well?" said Finn. "Where is he?"

Fritz cleared his throat. "It seems that he has not arrived, yet, Sire. Doubtless, he has been unavoidably detained."

"Well, then, he shall unavoidably sit elsewhere," Finn said, to the shocked stares of the assemblage. "I have no desire to separate the princess from her close friend and companion. Suppose I should run out of conversation halfway through the meal? Everyone knows what a boring fellow I can be. Flavia would have no one to talk to. Strakencz there, Lord love him, is half deaf and she would have to shout into his ear. Most discommodious for both of them. No, it would never do. Sit down here and you, Fritz, take the place next to hers. I insist."

"As you wish, Your Majesty," said Helen, her face very red at being the focus of all the attention. Von Tarlenheim suppressed a smile as he sat down next to her. Several of the diners looked outraged, but none dared speak.

"Well, then, that's all settled," Finn said.

Platoons of servants began to bring out silver serving trays with platters of food upon them. Finn was naturally served first. He waited until literally everyone else at the table had their food before him. Everyone was watching him expectantly. Finn glanced at Flavia.

"What are they all staring at?" he said, in a low voice.

"I believe that they are all waiting for you, Sire," she said.

"Oh." He glanced up and down the table. "We seem to be bereft of churchmen this evening."

The diners exchanged puzzled glances.

"Well, in that case, Marshal Strakencz, perhaps you would be so kind as to say grace?" said Finn.

Eyebrows were raised up and down the table.

"Beg pardon, Sire?" Strakencz said, leaning forward towards him.

"Grace, Strakencz."

"Race? What race?"

"*Grace.*"

"Eh?"

"GRACE! GRACE! Oh, the hell with it. Bow your heads, everyone."

Hesitantly, as if a little shell-shocked, they all bowed their heads, staring up at him out of the corners of their eyes.

"For what we are about to receive, may the good Lord make us all truly thankful," Finn said. He crossed himself and, after a brief hesitation, they all did likewise. Von Tarlenheim was biting his lower lip and attempting to keep his shoulders from shaking.

"Well?" said Finn. "What the devil are you all waiting for? Eat!"

There was a muted noise of plates and silverware.

"Talk!" said Finn.

A strangled sound escaped von Tarlenheim's throat. They began to converse among themselves, stealing furtive glances at Finn to see if he approved. At that moment, Michael arrived with Falcon on his arm. All conversation instantly ceased. Flavia looked up at "Countess Sophia" and pressed her lips together tightly.

"Your Majesty," said Michael, with exaggerated formality, giving Finn a piercing look. "Please accept my apologies for having been detained. It was inexcusable. Allow me to present the Countess Sophia, who is visiting with us from Florence."

Finn stood up. There followed a hasty scraping of chairs as everyone else stood, also. Their eyes met.

"Your Majesty," said Falcon, with just the barest trace of irony in her voice. She curtsied deeply, inclining her head, but staring up at him as she did so, her gaze boring into him.

She had electrified the room merely by her presence, and from the expressions on Flavia and Helen's faces, it was clear that what Sapt had said about her notoriety was not an understatement. Flavia looked uncomfortable, but Helen looked scandalized. It was with an effort that Finn kept himself under control. Not this time, he thought. You won't get to me this time. I can play this game as well as you, bitch.

"Countess," Finn said, making a very small bow. "I'm very pleased to see you face to face at last. I've heard so much about you."

The silence in the room was thick. Michael noticed that his place at the king's right was occupied. He stood behind von Tarlenheim's chair stiffly and cleared his throat.

"Sit, everyone, sit," said Finn. "Oh, Michael, I've made some small alterations in the seating arrangements, since I did not know if you would be coming. There's bound to be a place for you down there, somewhere." He indicated the far end of the table with an airy wave. Michael stared at him, astonished.

"Come, Michael," Falcon said, taking him by the arm. Michael did not move. He stood there, glaring at Finn, slowly turning a deep crimson while Finn ignored him totally, concentrating on his food. Finally, he allowed himself to be led to the far end of the table.

"That was unwise, Rudolf," Flavia said softly. "You have humiliated him in front of everyone. He'll never forgive the insult."

"It serves him right, for bringing *her* here," Helen whispered fiercely.

"Your Majesty," Falcon said loudly, overriding all the other conversations, "Michael tells me that there is to be a royal wedding soon."

Instant silence.

"Indeed?" said Finn, meeting her gaze steadily and refusing

to be intimidated. "I was under the impression that it was general knowledge. I'm surprised you hadn't known, Countess. It was my understanding that in the short time you've been with us, you've become fairly intimately involved in Ruritanian affairs."

Several people gasped. Michael stiffened, the color draining from his face.

"I was wondering if the date for the royal wedding has been set yet," Falcon said, giving him a faint smile. "My visit here will end before too long and I would be loathe to miss it."

"What, leaving us so soon?" said Finn. "What a pity. The young men of Strelsau will be crushed."

Michael slammed his knife down onto the table.

"No more so than I would be if I were to miss your wedding, Sire," she said. "Will it be soon?"

"I hope so," Finn said, "but it appears to me that it would be a bit presumptuous of me to set the date when Flavia and I have had so little time to spend together of late. Affairs of state are pressing, but affairs of the heart are no less important, don't you think? I am determined to set aside some time for us to be together. I haven't had much time to be a proper suitor. Time is so precious, wouldn't you say?"

"Indeed, Sire. Why waste it?"

Heads turned like those of spectators following a tennis match.

"I have a very high regard for time," Finn said. "I intend to make wise use of it. A man and a woman, even a king and queen, need time to spend together. Time for romance. What is marriage without courtship, after all?"

"What is courtship without marriage?" she countered.

Flavia's hands were white-knuckled on the table at the veiled implication.

"Courtship without marriage?" Finn said. "An affair, I should think. Isn't that right, Countess? Is that what you call it, an affair?"

"Eh?" said Marshal Strakencz, a bit more loudly than he had realized. He was having trouble following the conversation and he had been leaning close to the Minister of the Treasury, who had been keeping him abreast of it by speaking directly into his ear.

"Affairs, Strakencz," Finn said.

"Your pardon, Sire?"

"COUNTESS SOPHIA AND I ARE DISCUSSING AFFAIRS!"

"What about her affairs?" said Strakencz.

Michael shoved his chair back so hard it fell. He was on his feet, his face white, his lips quivering with rage.

"Are you all right, Michael?" Finn said, solicitously. "You look pale. Are you ill?"

In a choking voice, Michael said, "If Your Majesty would please excuse me, I find that I suddenly feel unwell."

"Of course we'll excuse you, Brother," Finn said, rising to his feet. Everyone else followed suit. "I will send the royal physician to attend you."

"That will not be necessary, *Sire*," Michael said, spitting out the words. "I am quite certain that I will be feeling a great deal better before too long."

"I *do* hope so," Finn said. "Countess, you will watch over him, won't you? My brother has always had the most delicate of dispositions. The least little thing upsets him."

"Come, Sophia," Michael said. She stared at him furiously, but there was nothing she could do. As Michael stalked out with her, she glanced at Finn and gave him an almost imperceptible little nod. Once they were outside, she turned on Michael angrily.

"You fool," she said. "You acted like a child in there! That was the most pathetic display of—"

Michael struck her hard across the face.

"I had turned a deaf ear to the gossip," he said, "and it has brought me humiliation! I've been made a fool of by that bastard in front of the entire court! He will pay dearly for that. But as for you, you trollop, I have reached the limits of my tolerance. I do not know what sort of morals they have where you came from, but from now on, you will act as befits a proper lady. You will speak only when spoken to, you will dress more demurely, you will take care of your manners, and you will go nowhere without a proper chaperone. And if I ever catch you alone with any other man, I will have you whipped like a common slut!"

He turned and got into the coach. She climbed in after him,

assisted by a liveried footman who had witnessed it all. She waited until the coach got rolling.

The servant who opened the door of the coach when they arrived at home staggered back with a cry at the sight of her blood-spattered gown. He ran when she told him to get Hentzau. Rupert came quickly. His eyes grew wide when he saw her.

"Sophia! Sophia, what—"

"Shut up and help me with him," she said.

Hentzau looked into the coach. He sucked in a sharp breath. "Good God!" he said.

Michael was sprawled senseless on the seat with a handkerchief stuffed into his mouth. His face was covered with blood. One eye was swollen shut. His lip was badly cut, his nose was broken, and several teeth were missing. Hentzau turned to her.

"*What happened?* Are you all right? How did—" he had taken both her hands in his and now he stared down at her cut knuckles. He looked up at her with an expression of disbelief.

She jerked her hands away. "Bring him inside," she said, then turned and went into the house.

Forrester handed the night scope to Lucas and pointed. "The keep," he said. "Use maximum magnification. Zero in on that small turret sticking out from the tower at about eleven o'clock."

Lucas held the scope to his eyes. "I don't see anything," he said. "What am I looking for?"

"The embrasures," Forrester said.

"I still don't see . . . wait."

"What is it?" Andre said.

Lucas handed her the scope. "It's hard to spot. You can barely make it out. They've got a laser tracking system set up in that turret. It sweeps across the entire compound."

"I can't see anything."

"Keep watching. Look for a slight hint of movement."

"Got it." She grunted. "Looks like floater-paks are out, then." She put down the scope. "What's next?"

"An evening swim," said Forrester.

"Shit," said Lucas.

"Come on, it's not that cold," said Andre, turning the scope toward the moat.

"That isn't what bothers me," Lucas said. "I must have been hanging around Finn too long. I think his paranoia is starting to rub off."

"What do you mean?" said Forrester.

"If they were careful enough to guard against a floater-pak assault, they might have taken precautions about the moat, as well. How do we know they haven't doped it with nasty little microorganisms?"

Andre shivered. "God. What makes you think of these things?"

"Your standard, basic-issue cowardice," said Lucas.

"Okay, so we don't swim the moat," said Forrester. "We bridge it."

"Nysteel line?" said Andre. Forrester nodded.

"Moon's full," Lucas pointed out. "Nice night for silhouettes."

Forrester glanced at him irately. "Did you just come along for moral support, or what?"

"I'm just doing my job, Colonel. You want to give the orders, go ahead."

"Not me, son. I'm not going to pass up a chance to see my executive officer perform his duties in the field. This is your command. You make the decision. Hand-over-hand and get shot, or the Australian crawl and have your balls fall off or something."

"Some choice."

"Come up with another alternative."

"I'm working on it."

"What time is it?" said Andre.

Forrester glanced at his watch. "2130 hours," he said.

"I feel nervous about Finn," she said.

"He can take care of himself," said Lucas.

"He doesn't even know the colonel's joined us," Andre said. "He's not going to like not being informed."

"If there was a chance to tell him, I would have," Lucas said. "But Finn's right. Our best chance is to leave him to play it out while we concentrate on the Timekeepers. He'll have enough trouble with Black Michael and his mercenaries without having to worry about Falcon.''

"We're wasting time," said Forrester. "Priest, have you come up with a workable approach yet or are you worrying about microbes being released into the air now?"

"The hell with it," said Lucas. "I'll swim the moat and take my chances."

"Suit yourself," said Andre. "If it was up to me, I'd use the boat."

"*What* boat?" both men said, simultaneously.

"The little one pulled up by the bank there and tied to the shore," said Andre.

"Give me that," said Lucas, taking the scope and training it on the spot she indicated. "A boat," he said, grimacing. "Who the hell goes rowing in a moat?"

"Children?" she said. "Rat catchers? Microorganism fishermen?"

"All right, all right," said Lucas, irately. He glanced at Forrester. "Did you see that boat?"

Forrester shrugged.

"You didn't see it, either, did you?" Lucas said.

"Cheer up, Priest," said Forrester. "Maybe it'll sink half way across."

They picked up their packs and made their way down to the bank of the moat on the west side of the chateau. The boat Andre had spotted was tied up to a small bush and two oars were stowed beneath the seats. It was an old wooden double-ender, far too small for more than one adult. The size of the oars also confirmed Andre's guess that it was intended for use by children, probably those of the chateau's serving staff. There was a tiny fishing net in it, along with some line wound around a stick, a rusty old hook embedded in the wound-up line.

"A toy," said Lucas, miserably. There was some water pooled in the bottom of the boat. "It's only big enough for one of us, if it doesn't sink."

"I'll go," said Andre. "I'm the lightest. Give me the remote."

Forrester handed it to her. "We'll cover you from the bank," he said. "Don't take any chances. We can't afford to lose the remote unit."

She grinned. "Thanks for your concern, sir."

Forrester glanced up at the sky. A large bank of clouds scudded across the moon. "Now," he said. "Move it."

She climbed down into the boat, unshipped the oars, and pushed off. Taking care not to make any splashing sounds, she rowed carefully and slowly, putting her back into it in an effort to get as much momentum as possible from the short oars. She kept rowing in a straight line across the moat, making the most of the cloud cover. It didn't take long before the prow of the small boat touched softly against the moss-covered stone of the castle.

She stowed one of the oars inside the boat, using the other one to slowly propel herself alongside the castle wall, taking care to keep the boat from making too much noise as it scraped softly against the lichen-covered stone. Little by little, she circled round toward the front of the castle. She rounded a corner and the back of the chateau became visible, its whiteness looking ghostly in the moonlight. The drawbridge was raised. Between her and the drawbridge, jutting out over the moat, was the most recent addition to the castle, the only part of it that appeared to be inhabited. She could see lights burning in several of the windows above her. She touched her larynx, activating the throat mike, then thought better of it and turned it off again. No point in alerting them if they were scanning for communications. They probably weren't, but this was no time for taking chances.

As she propelled herself forward in the boat, she kept a close watch on the lighted windows above her and almost missed seeing the dark shape in the water that suddenly loomed before her.

She nearly hit it. At first, she could not tell what it was, but then she saw that it was a large length of pipe, about four feet in diameter. Moving with extreme caution, she brought the boat up alongside it.

There was some rust upon the pipe, but it could not have been in place for very long. One end of it went into the water and, feeling with her oar, she could tell that it ended perhaps two or three feet below the surface of the moat. The other end of it was butted up against a small window in the wall just above her, level with the top of her head. It covered the window entirely, but it was not quite flush and as she examined it, a faint line of light appeared around it.

She drew back, instinctively, then balancing carefully, she stood up in the boat, steadying herself with one hand on the iron pipe. She heard voices, but she could not make out what was being said. Shielding her laser with her body, she carefully burned a small hole into the iron pipe, dipped her hand into the water, sprinkled it, then put her ear up against it.

"—should eat more, Sire. You haven't touched your food."

"I am not hungry, Detchard. Tell my brother to have done with it and kill me. I am dying by inches here."

"The duke does not desire your death, Your Majesty," Detchard said. "At least, not yet. When he does, behold your path to heaven."

A moment later, Andre heard the scraping sound of metal hinges, quite close by, followed by two taps upon the inside of the pipe. The sounds rang in her ear and she pulled her head away, briefly. When she put her ear back up against the pipe, she heard part of what Detchard was saying.

"—restful at the bottom of the moat, Your Majesty. Your grave and our escape route, should they be so foolhardy as to attempt a rescue. However, rest assured. We shall not leave you to drown. Drowning is an unpleasant death, I'm told. We shall be sure to kill you first before we place your weighted body in the pipe. We would not wish for you to suffer greatly."

"How very kind of you," the king said, flatly.

"I'm sorry," said Detchard. "I, for one, have nothing against you. You're not a bad sort of fellow. I've tried not to treat you ill, insofar as Michael would allow. I give you my word that when the time comes, your end shall be swift and as painless as possible."

"Most considerate of you," the king said. "When do you think that will be? I grow weary of waiting."

"Not too much longer, I should think," Detchard said. "I would not dwell on it, if I were you. You need your rest."

"For what?" said Rudolf.

"Yes, well, I see your point. Good night, Your Majesty."

She heard the sound of a heavy door opening and closing

and the faint crack of light around the pipe disappeared. A moment later, she heard the sounds of the king sobbing softly.

Bastards, she thought. Prisoner or not, it was no way to treat a man. Why torture him with explanations of how they would dispose of him? She sat down in the boat. From Michael's point of view, she had to admit that it was a simple and effective plan. If anyone tried to take the castle, they would kill the king, weight his corpse, then lift it up and slide it into the pipe. It would sink to the bottom of the moat in some twenty feet of water and be buried in the mud. If necessary, they could then slide down the pipe themselves and swim the moat to safety. Otherwise, they could release the pipe, it would sink into the moat, then they could close the iron grate over the window and who would ever know that the king had been held prisoner there?

She examined the pipe to see how it was fastened over the window. She could not tell. She tried a gentle shove at it, then she tried again, more firmly. It would not move. It had to be attached somehow from inside. It would be a simple matter to cut through it with her laser. The grate across the window could be taken care of in the same way. She licked her lips anxiously. The thought of that poor man sobbing in the darkness made her want to do it at once, but she steeled herself against the temptation. Now was not the time and she was not the one to do it. Besides, getting the king out of the castle would be the very least of their problems. At any rate, now Finn would know where Rudolf was being held.

She looked all around her carefully, noting every detail of her surroundings. Immediately on the other side of the pipe, there was a section of protruding stone wall. Beyond it, an expanse of moat and the drawbridge. There was a lighted window some fifteen to twenty feet above her. She looked still higher. The wall was straight and smooth all the way up to the tower until, near the top, a small turret stuck out from it. No, not a turret, but a balcony of sorts, shaped like a turret, but open on the front and sides. She breathed in sharply as she saw that someone was standing on the balcony, looking down at her.

She heard a soft, coughing sound and in the next instant, felt a tremendous blow to her left shoulder. It knocked her to her knees and almost over the side of the small boat. She dropped the oar. She clapped a hand to her shoulder and felt the flow of blood. She also felt the blunt end of a nysteel dart, the tip of which had penetrated through her skin and deep into the bone. There was a line attached to it.

She cried out as she was yanked out of the boat to rise quickly through the air as the nysteel line retracted with a soft *whirring* sound. She was being reeled in like a fish. The moat seemed to drop away beneath her and in the next moment, she felt a strong arm encircling her neck, dragging her over the side of the balcony. She lost consciousness.

Forrester shook Lucas hard. "Take it easy! Lucas, damn it, relax!"

"I can't believe it! I just can't fucking believe it! They got her and I just stood here and *watched!*"

"I was here, too, remember? There was nothing we could do. We didn't even have a shot. She went up so fast that if we tried to burn the line, we might've burned her, instead."

Lucas gritted his teeth. "*Christ!* They just harpooned her! What if she's dead? What if that rappelling dart severed an artery?"

"Then she's dead," said Forrester. "Stop blaming yourself. There was nothing you could do."

Lucas clenched his fists. "She must have broken a beam or something. I was a fool not to consider that. Dammit! *Now* what do we do?"

"We wait. If she isn't dead, it'll be in their interest to keep her alive. They'll want to question her. And they'll want to keep her alive to make sure we try to get her back. If we're lucky, she'll have a chance to drop the remote somewhere before they discover it on her."

"And if we're not lucky, then they'll be smart enough to search her first and then we'll be clocking right into a trap."

"So we take the chance," said Forrester. "That's what we're paid for."

Lucas shook his head, calming himself down with an effort. "No."

"What do you mean, no?" said Forrester. "Damn it, Lucas—"

"Are you taking over command of the adjustment?" Lucas said, in a level tone.

Forrester stared at him fixedly. "No, Major. It's your play. You're in command."

"Right. Then we split up. That way, if it's a trap, they won't get both of us. One of us homes in on the remote and clocks in blind. The other goes in from outside, the hard way."

"You sure that's the hard way?"

"You have any preference?" Lucas said.

Forrester's lips were tight. "It's my son we're up against," he said grimly. "If there are any chances to be taken, I'm the one to take them. I'll clock in blind. What the hell, I'm technically A.W.O.L. anyway. If I survive, I'll probably be facing a court martial when I get back. No point to risking my second-in-command, as well."

"Moses—"

"What?"

Lucas took Forrester by the upper arms in a strong grip. "Friend to friend," he said. "Don't allow yourself to feel guilty. That's what she wants."

"I know," said Forrester.

"You hesitated once and a man died," said Lucas.

"*Damn* you."

"Drakov made his own choices," Lucas said. "Would Vanna have approved of them?"

"Back off, Major," Forrester said, tensely. "I know what I have to do."

"I wouldn't have thought you to be the sentimental type," said Lucas harshly, "but you've shown me a side of you I hadn't seen before. You knew what you had to do when S & R found you and you didn't do it. If your little playmate had been given an abortion, none of us might be in this mess."

Forrester grabbed Lucas by the shirt front with one hand and drew back his fist. He hesitated.

"See what I mean?" said Lucas. "Go on, Moses. Hit me. Think it'll help?"

Forrester let him go and turned away, fighting to get himself under control. Finally, with a note of forced calm in his voice, he said, "I know what you're trying to do, Priest. I can even appreciate it. Just the same, when we get back from this, I'm going to take you apart."

"Just hold onto that thought," said Lucas.

Forrester turned to face him, his face expressionless. "Count on it, Major."

10 ⎯⎯⎯⎯⎯⎯⎯⎯⎯⎯⎯⎯

"I have never seen anything like it," Hentzau told Bersonin. "I tell you, Karl, he was beaten senseless!"

The lanky mercenary gave Hentzau a highly dubious look. "And you think the *countess* did it?"

"She did it, for a fact," said Hentzau. "Go and see for yourself if you do not believe me. Look at her hands. Her knuckles are cut from knocking out his teeth. Evidently, Michael had the temerity to strike her. She took her pound of flesh, I can tell you. The coach is spattered with his blood."

"Really, Rupert," said Bersonin, smiling as if his leg was being pulled, "you expect me to believe that a mere woman—"

"A mere woman who can handle a sabre better than many men I've met," said Hentzau. "I tell you, she's an animal! God, she's absolutely magnificent!"

"You must be mad."

"Mad, am I? Well, we shall see who's mad. We shall see who calls the tune from now on, Michael or Sophia. You wouldn't care to place a little wager?"

"I think—"

He was interrupted by Falcon entering the hall. She had changed from her evening gown to a riding costume that lacked only the jacket. She wore a white lace shirt and waistcoat of black leather, tight black breeches and high black boots. She was pulling on her gloves as she came in. Her ash-blonde hair was pulled back, and she had removed all of her makeup.

"Where is Albert Lauengram?" she asked Bersonin, crisply.

"Just one moment, Countess," said Bersonin, somewhat patronizingly. "First, there are a few questions which—"

"I shall ask the questions, Karl, and you shall provide the answers. Now, where is Lauengram?"

"I think you presume a bit too much, Madame," Bersonin said, in a tone of rebuke. Hentzau watched this interplay with a faint smile upon his face. "I take no orders from you."

"And I will take no insolence from you, Karl. Now, I shall ask you only one more time. *Where* is Lauengram?"

Bersonin glanced at Hentzau and smirked. "I follow Michael Elphberg," he said, "not his concubine."

Her eyes seemed to flare. "Really? In that case, you are no more use to me than Michael is. Your sword, Rupert."

With an arch look at Bersonin, Hentzau drew his sabre and casually tossed it to her. She caught it easily by the hilt.

"Never say I didn't warn you," Hentzau said.

"You must be joking," said Bersonin.

"Draw your sword, Karl," Falcon said.

"Against a woman? I'll not. This is ridiculous."

"Fine, then." Before Bersonin could react, her sabre swished through the air between them, opening up his cheek from the left ear to the jaw.

Bersonin cried out, staggering several steps back, his hands going to his face. They came away bloody. He stared at her with livid fury. Wiping his bloody hands upon his breeches, he drew his sabre. "Have it your way, then. Michael or no Michael, you'll die for that."

Hentzau swung a chair around, sitting in it backward with his arms crossed upon its back, watching as Bersonin sprang at her. She parried his thrust effortlessly, disengaged with astonishing speed, beat his blade out of the way and opened up his other cheek.

With a howl of fury, Bersonin attacked, fully intending to cut her to shreds. Instead, to his amazement, he found himself at once on the defensive. The clang of steel on steel filled the hall as she drove him back, refusing to give quarter. He backed up against a table, faked a thrust and rolled backward across it, putting it between them so that his longer reach would give him an advantage. Falcon vaulted the table, coming down lightly on the other side. Bersonin lunged at her while she was in mid-air, but even before she landed, she parried his thrust, turned his blade, and went on the attack.

Lauengram chose that moment to walk in. He had been eating in the kitchen and pressing his suit against one of Michael's pretty young serving girls. Having heard the sounds of fencing, he had come to see what was transpiring. At the sight of Bersonin dueling the countess, he froze, mouth agape.

"*What in God's name . . ?*"

"Here," Hentzau said, reaching back and pulling out another chair. "Sit down and watch this, Albert. It should prove interesting."

Eyes wide, Lauengram ignored the chair and simply stood there, mesmerized by the spectacle. Bersonin, an accomplished swordsman, was dueling with a *woman* and he seemed sorely beset.

Bersonin himself was in a panic. He could do absolutely nothing with her. Her blade was everywhere, slashing his shoulder, pricking his upper arm, deflecting each of his thrusts and lunges. She had cut him half a dozen times and he had yet to score a touch. He realized with a sudden horror that she was actually toying with him, that he, who had killed more than a dozen men in duels, was no match for her. He recoiled from that lightning blade, from those lambent, ferocious eyes that fixed him with a devilish fury, turning and running from her. He ran about ten steps, turned quickly to face her once again and threw down his sword.

"Enough! I yield! I wish no more of this!"

"Well, I do," said Falcon. She swiftly changed her grip upon the sabre and threw it, like a javelin. It pierced Bersonin's chest, the tip of the edged blade ripping through flesh and sinew to protrude from his back. Bersonin glanced down at it with a look of utter disbelief. Slowly, his hands came up to grasp the blade, as if to reassure him of its reality; then he toppled forward and collapsed upon the floor.

"*Dear God in heaven!*" Lauengram whispered, awestruck.

Hentzau stood and clapped his hands. "Bravo! Bravo! An inspired exhibition! You have been holding back on me, Sophia! Never did you fence so well in practice!"

She turned to face them both. "Does anyone else wish to question my authority?" she said.

Lauengram slowly shook his head from side to side, unable to tear his eyes away from her. He had never in his life seen a woman fight like that. He, himself, had been no match for Bersonin and she had disposed of him as casually and with as little apparent effort as a fencing master in a match with a new pupil.

"Not I!" he said.

"And I am yours unswervingly!" cried Hentzau, flashing a handsome grin. "By God, Sophia, what a pair we two shall make! You were wasted on that fool, Michael. Together, we shall—"

"Be quiet, Rupert," she said. "Have someone clean up that mess. We are leaving tonight for Zenda Castle. I want the two of you to take Michael in the coach and depart at once. Inform the other three that I shall be taking charge. Should they have any reservations, you can inform them also of what happened to Bersonin. Tell them as well that their pay is to be doubled henceforth."

"Is there to be a change of plan then?" Lauengram said, hesitantly.

"I will give you my instructions when I meet you there," said Falcon. "Go now."

She turned and walked calmly up the staircase toward her bedroom on the upper floor.

"I must be dreaming," Lauengram said. "That is no woman. It is Satan with breasts."

"Ah, but what breasts!" said Hentzau.

"What do we do now?" said Lauengram.

"Do? Why, we do what Satan tells us," Hentzau said, grinning. "Didn't you hear? Our pay is being doubled. Go on with you. Get Michael and drive His Would-Be Majesty to Zenda. I'll join you later.''

"She said for both of us to go," said Lauengram.

Hentzau winked at him. "I have some unfinished business to attend to."

He went over to Bersonin's corpse and retrieved his sabre, examining it to see that it was not damaged.

"I believe that if she were really Satan, you would still not be deterred," said Lauengram. "I shall have to have a long talk with the others. We did not bargain for this."

"Do what you will," said Hentzau. "As for me, I go my own way."

"You always have. But you may have gone out of your depth this time," Lauengram told him. "A woman like that is no fit mate for any man."

"Yes, well, I am not just any man," said Hentzau. He tossed off a casual salute to Lauengram and followed Falcon up the stairs.

He had one very immediate purpose in mind, but his thoughts were racing. Suddenly, everything had changed. The balance of power had shifted and new opportunities were beginning to present themselves. He had to consider them all quite carefully. He took the stairs two at a time, then moved briskly down the hall towards Sophia's rooms. He paused outside and tried the door. It was unlocked. He smiled to himself and pushed it open.

She was not there. He called her name several times, but there was no answer. He frowned as he walked through the suite, determining that it was in fact empty. Where the devil had the woman gone? Systematically, he searched every room on the floor. There was no sign of her. Outside, he heard the coach driving away and he went to a window in time to see it turn into the street with Albert driving. Had she gone in the coach? But no, she had ordered both of them to go and she would have wanted to know why he was absent. She had to be still in the house somewhere. He searched every room in the mansion, ignoring the frightened servants until it finally occurred to him to question them, but no one had seen her. It was as if she had simply disappeared.

Hentzau sat down and ordered one of the servants to bring him some wine. He smoked a cigarette. Clearly, there had to be a way out of the house he did not know about. But what was the woman up to? The thing to do now was to consider all the aspects of the situation and find the one that would most benefit Rupert Hentzau. He would have to alter his own plans for tonight now.

On the other hand, he thought, perhaps not. One had to explore all options.

It was late and the streets were mostly empty as the royal coach drove from the palace.

"It was very kind of you to see me home," said Flavia. "It was not necessary, you know."

"A fine suitor I would be," said Finn, "if I simply had the coach deliver you to your door as if you were a package."

Flavia suppressed a smile. "It would not have been the first time," she said.

"I've treated you dreadfully, haven't I?" said Finn. "I don't know what could have been wrong with me. From now on, I shall make it up to you, I promise."

She looked at him and smiled. Finn felt wretched. The worst part of it all was that he really liked her. He had never been very good at concealing such things and she obviously was responding, which had been the whole idea. However, now he was beginning to have regrets, for her sake.

"Poor Michael," he said to change the subject. "He did not even stay for dessert."

Flavia shook her head. "You pushed him too far, Rudolf. There was murder in his eyes when he looked at you tonight."

"Is that what it was? And I believed it to be indigestion!"

"You may joke," she said, "but where before he may have envied you, you have now given him more than enough reason to truly despise you. You made him out to be a fool in front of everyone. I beg you to be wary of him, Rudolf. I fear that he may stop at nothing."

"You worry too much," Finn said. "It is merely the rivalry of brothers and nothing more."

"Surely you do not believe that."

"Well, perhaps not," said Finn, "but he brought it on himself. He should not have had the woman bait me in that manner. Especially in your presence."

"I do not think that I have ever met a woman quite so brazen in my life," said Flavia. "I had heard about the countess. One cannot avoid such gossip; but seeing her tonight, I believe it all. That woman would be capable of anything."

"Undoubtedly," said Finn, thinking that it was the understatement of the year, if not the century.

"She is very beautiful, though, is she not?" said Flavia, not looking at him.

"I suppose," said Finn, "if one cares for the type."

"Do men . . ." she hesitated. "Do men find such women to be desirable?"

"I am sure that many do."

"Do you?"

"That is an impertinent question."

"Forgive me. I did not mean to be—"

"Oh, for goodness sake, I was only joking," Finn said.

"Oh. I see."

"In answer to your question, I will be frank. In a word, yes."

"You are forthright, at least."

"I had not finished. It is one thing to respond to a woman physically, and don't blush. Remember that you asked."

"I did, indeed."

"And it is quite another thing to look beyond the senses and consider a woman—or a man, for that matter—for what goes on inside the head. In some cases, as was the case with me for far too long, I fear, nothing goes on at all. In others, what goes on within is a far cry from what appears without. In Countess Sophia's case, I have the strong impression that what goes on within is very like snakes writhing."

Flavia shuddered. "Lord, Rudolf, what a thought! I had not suspected that your imagination was so lurid."

"Drink can do that to a man," said Finn, wryly.

"And how do you perceive what goes on inside my own head?" she said, with a slight smile.

"To answer that would be impertinent of me," said Finn.

"How diplomatically you avoid the question," she said, chuckling.

"Diplomacy, in many situations, is merely a tool to prevent one's looking foolish," Finn said.

"How statesmanlike you are becoming!"

"It comes of spending hours on end with Sapt," Finn said. "Once I began to actually listen to him, I discovered him to be the very font of wisdom."

"I simply cannot stop marveling at the change in you," she said. "You are like a different man." She pursed her lips and cocked her head to one side, saying in a joking manner, "I am beginning to suspect that you are not Rudolf at all, but some imposter who is his double. Tell me the truth, what have you done with the *real* king?"

"The truth? He's being kept in the dungeons of Zenda Castle. It's all a plot of Michael's."

The coach came to a halt before her house.

"That was a poor jest," she said. "The way Michael looked at you tonight, I can almost believe that he would be capable of such a thing. Remember, Rudolf, that you have no heir as yet. If anything should happen to you, the throne would surely go to Michael."

"Are you so frightened for me?" Finn said.

The sincerity in her face stabbed him to the heart. "You have changed so, Rudolf, almost overnight, it is as if . . . as if you *really* were another man. I feel as if we have met for the first time. You spoke of what appears without and what goes on within. Without, you are the same Rudolf I have always known and yet, within, I seem to sense a stranger, one who has shown me but little of himself, yet who compels me in a manner that I find both frightening and delightful. I feel as though I am only now starting to know you. I care about what happens to you, not only as my king, but as a man. Forgive me, but I did not think that such a thing would ever come to pass. I beg you to be watchful. Michael and those ruffians he has retained fill me with foreboding. Guard yourself well."

She leaned forward quickly, kissed him on the lips, and then hurried from the coach. Finn stared after her for a long time before he directed the coachman to drive back to the palace.

Sapt and von Tarlenheim were waiting for him. Both men had dressed in dark-hued clothing, the better to provide concealment in the night. Von Tarlenheim tried once more, unsuccessfully, to dissuade him from keeping the mysterious appointment, then resigned himself to the inevitable. Finn quickly changed into clothing similar to theirs and they left by the secret passageway. Sapt pressed a revolver into Finn's hand.

"Do not hesitate to use this if you find you must," said Sapt. "Remember, if we lose you, then we lose everything."

Finn took the revolver with a smile. "Thank you for your concern," he said, laconically.

"Don't be a fool," said Sapt. "You know damn well what I mean. Our first concern is for the throne, as it must be, but I would not wish to lose a friend, as well."

They rode on horseback to Michael's house, reining in a short distance away from the wall that circled the estate.

"This is as far as you two go with me," said Finn. "If all goes well, I shall return shortly and we will ride to Zenda."

"And if not?" said von Tarlenheim, nervously.

"I promise to be careful. But just in case, you have your watch?"

"Right here."

"If I do not return in half an hour, then you can assume the worst," said Finn. "It will then be up to you to free the king."

"Come what may," said Sapt, "we make our move tonight. Good fortune to you."

Finn dismounted and crossed the street, heading for the entrance that the letter specified. He felt very much alone. Taking a chance, he tried raising Lucas and Andre on his comset. From where he was, the safehouse was within range, but there was no response. He nodded to himself. All right, then, they were proceeding on their own, as he had thought they would. The Timekeepers had to be their first concern. He did not like not being able to contact them, but it was just as well. His had now become the secondary role in the mission. Theirs was far more difficult. They would be at Zenda Castle, trying to find a way to get inside. Perhaps they were making their move at this very moment. If he was lucky, they might complete their part of the mission by the time that he arrived with von Tarlenheim and Sapt. Then they could provide him with a backup if the need arose. If not . . . he decided not to think about if not.

It was dark and quiet in the garden, the only sounds coming from the crickets in the flower beds. Keeping to the side of the wall, he avoided the pathway, circling round to where he could see the little summerhouse. Sapt had briefed him on the layout. If Michael wanted to trap him here, he could not have picked a better spot. On the other hand, though he was sure it was a trap, it might not be Michael who had set it. On the chance that it was Falcon, he had to walk into it. He had seen her twice now and been helpless to act both times. The third time, he swore, would be the last.

He sank down to his knees, then sprawled flat on the ground, lying on his belly. It was thoughtful of Sapt to have provided him with a revolver, but he preferred the silence of the laser. He held it in his hand, ready to fire. Slowly, he crawled forward across the open space that separated the garden wall from the gazebo, approaching the small structure from the side, where its latticed wall would at least impede the visibility of anyone who might be inside. Assuming, of course, that anyone was in there waiting for him. If not, then he would not go in. Either way, the gazebo would be an easy target, especially to someone equipped with a night scope.

As he crawled forward, coming closer, he saw the glow of a cigarette inside the summerhouse. He frowned. Surely they would not be that sloppy, unless it was meant for him to see, to decoy him into a false sense of security. He was tempted to take a shot, but that would pinpoint his location to anyone who might be watching. He crept closer. He was beginning to sweat. A match flared briefly and he saw that it was Hentzau, leaning casually against the arched entrance of the summerhouse and smoking. He was close enough now that if he whispered, Hentzau would hear him. He spoke his name, once, softly.

Hentzau started slightly, peering out into the darkness. "Hello? Is that you, play-actor? Show yourself."

"And be shot for my trouble?" Finn said, moving immediately as he spoke.

Hentzau chuckled. "You're safe enough, Your Majesty," he said, sarcastically. "I merely wish to speak with you. There is no one else about. They have all departed for the castle. Save for the servants in the house, you and I are quite alone."

Finn hesitated.

"Look, I assume that you have not come unarmed," said Hentzau. "You could shoot me easily. Come, man, where are you?"

Finn bit his lower lip. What the hell, he thought, if you're going to step into a trap, step into it. He stood, tensely, prepared to leap at once to either side.

"Ah, there you are," said Hentzau. "Not very kingly, creeping about like that."

"Was it you who sent the letter?" Finn said, putting the laser away and holding the revolver Sapt had given him so that Hentzau could see it. He looked at it without concern.

"You would not shoot me," he said. He spread his arms out away from his sides. "You see, I am unarmed. Not even a sword. I left it in the house. Surely, an English gentleman would not slay an unarmed man?"

"Don't bet on it," said Finn. "I find the temptation very difficult to resist."

"Do you? Well then, if you can manage to resist it for the next few moments, I have a proposition I would make to you. The duke offers you a million crowns and safe conduct across the frontier. What do you say to that?"

"That isn't even a temptation," Finn said.

"You refuse?"

"Of course."

Hentzau grinned. "I told Michael that you would. I said that you would never trust him. Cigarette?"

"No, thank you."

"As you will. Only trying to be friendly."

"No need to try."

"Has His Majesty done me the honor to fasten a particular quarrel on me?" said Hentzau, mockingly.

"You hardly seem worth the bother," Finn said. "How is the king?"

"Alive," said Hentzau. "For the time being, at least. Look

here, I've made you a proposal from the duke, now hear one from me. Attack the castle boldly. Let Sapt and von Tarlenheim lead. Arrange the time with me.''

"I have such confidence in you,'' Finn said, wryly.

"Tut, I'm talking business now. Sapt and von Tarlenheim will fall. Michael shall fall, as well. You can leave that to me. The king will take a short swim to the bottom of the moat and two men will be left—I, Rupert Hentzau, and you, the King of Ruritania. Think it over, play-actor. You could extend your tour indefinitely. Wouldn't that be a hand to play? A throne and a pretty princess for yourself and for me, say, some small compensation out of His Majesty's gratitude? This house, for example, and the chateau would do quite nicely.''

"I admire your loyalty to Michael,'' Finn said.

"Loyalty is an admirable attribute,'' said Hentzau. "In a hound. So long as my own interest can be served, what care I which side I throw in with? Consider the opportunity, Rassendyll. When will you ever get another such as this?''

"Where does the countess stand in all of this?'' said Finn.

"Ah, you have deduced, of course, that she is with us,'' Hentzau said. "A most fascinating woman, Countess Sophia is. The stories I could tell you. . . .''

"Tell me a few,'' said Finn.

"Really? Does that mean you are considering my offer?''

"Let us say that I have not dismissed it out of hand,'' said Finn, convinced now that Hentzau was acting on his own. He was clearly an opportunist, seeking to advance himself. "Where does she fit in if I accept your offer?''

"Yes, well, she doesn't, I'm afraid,'' said Hentzau. "More is the pity. In a way, it would be a tragic waste, and yet, I am not so great a fool to think that I could manage her. There's a woman that no man could manage. She sits securely in the saddle, that one. Poor Michael was unwise enough to strike her for something that she said to him tonight and, hard to believe though it may be, she beat him bloody.''

Finn raised his eyebrows. "I believe it.''

"Do you really? Bersonin didn't, poor chap. She killed him earlier this evening. Now she means to take charge of the whole affair and I believe she will, too. She's a bit too unpredictable for my taste. She's all woman, but she speaks and fights like a man. No, the moat would be the best thing for her, I'm afraid. And we shall see to it that the others fall, as well. A clean slate, just you and I to divvy up the booty. What do you think?''

"I think that if you play your cards right, you could go very far," said Finn. "This house and the chateau, you say? Is that all you would want?"

Hentzau smiled. "And the means to support same, say, a dukedom? For services rendered, don't you know?"

"How would we explain the death of Michael? What reason would we give for attacking Zenda Castle? It seems to me that there are some flaws in your plan which you have not considered," Finn said.

"In any great venture, there's bound to be a certain element of risk," said Hentzau. "We can concoct some sort of story. With all the principals disposed of, who will gainsay us?"

"I must admit that you intrigue me," Finn said. "How many in the castle?"

"As of tonight, there will be Michael, though he's feeling somewhat out of sorts I would imagine, Sophia, Lauengram, Krafstein, De Gautet, Detchard, and myself. I leave to join them presently. The chateau is staffed with servants, but they do not know what Michael is about and cannot be counted on to fight, in any case."

"I do not care for the odds," said Finn.

"The odds do not worry me," said Hentzau. "They will not expect anything from me and in that lies my advantage."

"Just the same," said Finn, "I would prefer to take greater care of myself in this. Circumstances could arise in which your own best interests would become realigned with Michael's, suddenly."

"You would have to take that chance," said Hentzau. "I will not insult you by asking you to trust me, but consider where my greatest benefit would lie."

"Nevertheless, I would like it better if I could be there to encourage you," said Finn. "Suppose that you could arrange to get me inside the castle. Then, at a given signal, I could have Sapt and von Tarlenheim start the attack. We could arrange to have the drawbridge lowered at the precise instant. Then, in all the confusion, you and I could strike and they would be beset upon both sides.''

Hentzau threw back his head and laughed. "By God, I like the way you think! We are cut from the same cloth, you and I. We understand each other."

"And neither of us is a very trusting sort," said Finn, smiling at him.

"I can see that," Hentzau said. "You have not put down your pistol the whole time. Still, we can share a common ground. I stand to gain a great deal by throwing in with you and you will surely reap much more reward than whatever they have promised you for taking Rudolf's place. You will have to trust me to get you into Zenda Castle without turning you over to the others and I, in turn, will have to trust to your good faith to keep our bargain once you are king in earnest. I think that once I have helped you gain entry to the castle, mine will be the greater risk. Still, I will chance it. With a kingdom to gain, I do not think that you would begrudge me my small fee."

Finn put down his pistol. "I have decided to accept your offer."

Hentzau held out his hand. "Somehow, I thought you might. I suggest that we act soon."

"Tonight."

"*Tonight?*"

"Why not?"

"Why not, indeed? What will you tell Sapt and von Tarlenheim?"

"I'll think of something," Finn said. "I could say that there has been dissension in the ranks, that you and Michael have clashed over Sophia and in revenge, and also for a fee, you have agreed to turn on him."

"It's near enough to the truth," said Hentzau. "I like that. They will believe it. You have a devious turn of mind, my friend. It should stand you in good stead as king."

"Let's not waste anymore time, then," Finn said. "How will you get me inside the castle?"

"Let me think a moment. Ah, I have it! Listen carefully, here is what you must do. . . ."

• • •

Sapt crouched behind the urn, his revolver ready, cocked and positioned between the two tiny firing stakes that he had earlier improvised. Whoever Rassendyll was meeting, he was taking a long time in there. He wished that he could hear what was being said. Just as he was starting to think that he could not bear it one moment longer, he saw a dark shape exit the summerhouse, heading towards the garden wall. It had to be Rassendyll. He prepared to fire. Half expecting a shot to ring out and shatter the stillness of the night, he heard instead a jaunty whistling coming towards him and moments later, Rupert Hentzau came striding past him, up the stairs and into the house.

He had almost put a bullet into him and now that the opportunity was past, he cursed himself for wasting it. He wanted nothing quite so much as to kill the cocky young blackguard, but an assassin's shot was not his way. Hentzau had given him no reason to shoot. That, in itself, puzzled Sapt. He was convinced there would be treachery. What had they discussed? What *rapprochement* could the two men possibly achieve?

The moment Hentzau went inside, Sapt hurried after Rassendyll, taking care not to close the distance between them for fear that Rassendyll would think that he was being pursued and fire at him. Rassendyll had already rejoined von Tarlenheim by the time Sapt came out of the garden and ran across the street.

"Sapt, damn you!" Finn said, furiously. "You were supposed to remain behind!"

"Forgive me for disobeying your orders, *Sire*," Sapt said. "It seems to me that sometimes you believe you really are the king. I was concerned for your safety, but apparently my worries were ill-founded. Did you have a pleasant chat with young Hentzau?"

"Hentzau!" said Fritz.

"You didn't kill him, did you?" Finn said.

"No, though I regret it. I could not bring myself to shoot from ambush like a common highwayman. Curse me, though, I should have done it!"

"It's well that you did not," said Finn. "You would have

killed our best chance to save the king. Hentzau has changed sides, agreeing to betray Michael for a price.''

"Surely you do not trust him?" said Fritz.

"No, but I think I can trust his greed and his ambition," Finn said and he quickly recounted the details of the meeting. Sapt swore savagely when he had heard the story.

"The man is thoroughly corrupt!" he said. "I would not have thought that even he could sink so low!"

"And he believes you will betray us?" said Fritz.

"Of course," said Finn. "I've met his sort before. His ethics are defined by expediency. It's simple enough, if a little dangerous, to deal with such a man, once you understand his motives. The fact that I did not react with outraged shock at his suggestion predisposed him to believe that I would give it serious consideration. After that, it was a *fait accompli*. Were he in my place, he would leap at such an opportunity. He believes that I am doing this because the two of you have promised me a reward.''

"So he judges you by his own standards," Sapt said, nodding. "How fitting that it shall be his downfall. Well, we have no time to lose. I will assemble my men at once and tell them that we strike tonight to free the prisoner of Zenda.''

"I'll ride to the castle directly from here," said Finn.

"I'll go with you," said von Tarlenheim. "Two will be safer on the road than one.''

"All right, then," Finn said. "Make speed, Sapt. It all depends on you now.''

"Your part is no less significant," said Sapt. "Remember, above all else, the king must be protected.''

"If any harm comes to Rudolf," Finn said, "it will be over my dead body.''

Sapt held out his hand. "You are the most gallant gentleman I've ever known, Rassendyll. God go with you.''

He mounted his horse and galloped off at top speed through the streets.

"Heaven help us," said von Tarlenheim. "It all rests with a mercenary, an imposter, a group of aging soldiers, and a young nobleman who's quaking in his boots. Shamed as I am to admit it, I'm afraid.''

"There's no shame in that," said Finn.

"You're not afraid, though, are you?"

"Me? Fritz, my boy, I'm scared spitless. More than you will ever know."

"Have . . . have you any loved ones?" Fritz said.

"No," said Finn. "No one who would miss me very much."

"That's where you're wrong," said Fritz.

Finn clapped him on the shoulder. "Come on, let's ride."

They mounted their horses and galloped off into the night.

11

Andre came to in a small, cold, drafty room. She was tied down to a cot, her hands at her sides, her feet stretched out straight. Instinctively, she tested her bonds and found that she could barely move, only enough to keep the circulation going. The knots that she was tied with were seaman's knots and they were quite secure. She could move her head to look around and when she did so, she saw him. He was seated some fifteen feet away from her, on the cot on the opposite side of the room, against the wall. He was tall and muscular, dressed in surplus black base fatigues that were standard base uniform issue to the Temporal Army Corps. He had thick, curly black hair and a handsome face that would have been almost Byronic except for the fact that it was striking rather than pretty, the effect heightened by the long scar upon his cheek. His brilliant green eyes watched her steadily, their gaze uncomfortably direct.

"Corporal Cross," he said in a deep, mellifluous voice, "your position may not be very comfortable, but it was the best that I could do under the circumstances. I have also done what I could for your shoulder and I've given you something for the pain."

"Why bother?" she said.

"Because whatever else I may be," he said, "I am not a barbarian."

She grimaced. "I'd say that was open to debate. Where am I? Where are the rest of your people?"

He smiled. "You can stop trying to activate your comset with your chin. I have removed it. As to where you are, you are in a turret atop the keep of Zenda Castle and besides myself, there is only Falcon. At the moment, I would imagine that she is at Michael Elphberg's home in Strelsau, but she should be here before too long."

"There are only two of you?"

"We are all that's left," he said, with a trace of bitterness. "However, our number should be quite sufficient to the task."

"So you must be Drakov," Andre said.

"He told you?"

"You mean your father?" She made a wry face. "Yes, he told me."

Drakov sat silent for a moment. Finally, he said, "How does he speak of me?"

"How do you think? How should a father feel about a son who's become a terrorist?"

"He hates me, then. Good."

"Believe that, if you like. I imagine you need some sort of justification for what you do."

Drakov smiled faintly. "I might well say the same for you, Corporal Cross. I've seen your dossier. You were a 12th-century mercenary, were you not? What was the term used then, a 'free companion?' Rather an ironic choice of words, wouldn't you say? Have things changed so very much now that you live in the 27th century? Or do you merely serve different paymasters?"

"I'm a soldier," she said. "When I kill, it's in the line of duty. I don't murder innocent people."

"I see. Is it duty, then, which determines who is innocent and who is not?"

"Spare me. If you're going to kill me, get it over with. Don't talk me to death. I'm not exactly in the mood to discuss the philosophical implications of war, thank you. Least of all with you."

"Have I struck a nerve, perhaps?" said Drakov. "I am merely seeking to understand your motivations. You are the first soldier of the Time Wars I have ever spoken with. Being the son of such a soldier, I am naturally curious. Besides, I do not intend to kill you. Falcon claims that honor. I desire only the death of Moses Forrester."

"Why?"

"If he did not tell you that, I should think you would be able to infer it."

"Humor me."

He smiled again. "If you think to stall for time, save yourself the trouble. I am well aware that your friends are gaining entry to the castle even as we speak. It does not concern me." He held up a small rectangular box. "We have had time to prepare for them, you see." He turned the box so that she could see the tiny screen. "Your Major Priest is in the act of rappelling up the castle wall at the moment. He should be able to gain access to the parapet with little difficulty. It will be interesting to see how far he manages to go from there. Shall we observe his progress together?"

"You bastard," Andre whispered.

He stiffened. "Yes, I am that. Only I know who my father is. And tonight, he shall know his son at last."

Treading water, Lucas aimed and fired the nysteel rappelling dart at the projecting edge of the bottom of the tower high above him. He heard the faint *chink* as it became embedded in the stone and he put his full weight upon the line to test it. It held.

Holding firmly onto the grip handle, he thumbed the button and was yanked free of the moat to rise rapidly into the air. In seconds, he was at the level of the parapet. He thumbed the switch, stopping his ascent, and braced himself against the tower wall with his legs. Then he swung out and to the side, giving himself some slack at the same time. His momentum carried him over the edge of the parapet and on top of the castle wall.

Immediately, he dropped down, crouching very low. Cautiously, he moved to the far end of the parapet, towards the open, arched entryway that gave access to the tower. The stone stairs within spiraled up to the top of the tower and down to the lower levels. Down was the way he had to go, and the narrow passageway afforded no concealment whatsoever. He swallowed hard, took a deep breath, and slowly began his descent, holding his laser before him.

Forrester watched from the bank of the moat as Lucas swung out over the edge of the parapet and dropped down out of sight. He glanced at his watch. They had agreed on giving Lucas a head start of twenty minutes. By that time, if all went well, he should at least have reached the keep. Assuming all went well. However, Forrester was not going to give him that head start. He bent down and opened the case containing the chronoplate. He removed the border circuits and started to assemble them.

He was virtually certain that he would be clocking right into a trap. It did not concern him very much. In fact, he was counting on it. He did not think that he would be killed at once. Death was not the only goal of their vendetta, he felt sure of that. It would be the end result, but before death, there would be punishment. Punishment for wrongs real and perceived. Real on Nikolai's part, he thought. No, after all these years, his son would certainly have something to say to him. And that would give him time. Time in which to set things right, once and for all. Time in which to set off the small device he wore strapped to his chest, beneath his shirt. It was not very bulky and he hardly knew he had it on. The small casing fastened directly over his breastbone contained TD-131, a substance outlawed in the 27th century and consequently no longer manufactured. It was last used, with devastating results, in the Final Conflict of the Middle East in the early 21st century. It was a total diffusion nerve gas. Its effects were lethal and instantaneous. It would quickly and effectively resolve all of his problems. He smiled at the thought of Priest's baiting him, psyching him up and trying to redirect his anger. It was a touching, if sophomoric gesture.

"You have no need to worry, Lucas," he said softly. "This time, I won't hesitate."

The sound of galloping hooves made him look up. A coach was rapidly approaching the courtyard in front of the chateau. It was all starting to come together. The pivotal moment in time. The fulcrum of the Fate Factor. He stepped into the circle of the border circuits as it began to glow. Reaching into his pocket, he pulled out a small, enameled box.

"Forgive me, Vanna," he said.

The circle flared and vanished.

She knew that more than anything, Nikolai hated rats. Since his childhood in Siberia, he had loathed the creatures and more than once while they were within the castle, she had seen him draw back in disgust at the sight of them. There were many about in the lower floors, but here, in the long-abandoned dungeons of the oldest sections of the castle, there were thousands of them. Their chittering filled the air with a deafening noise as she descended the slimy stone stairs to the lowest level of the subterranean dungeons. The air was rank with their smell and with the stink of stagnant water. The moody Russian had taken to stalking like a ghost through the dank castle passageways, immersing himself in gloom and black despair, but he would never venture here.

Her boots sloshed in fetid water up to her calves as she proceeded down the musky passageway, using her laser to clear the rodents out of her path. It was like walking through a sewer. The smell was overpowering. Once, her foot touched something that slithered away beneath the surface of the water, making ripples with its passage. She suppressed a shudder, steeling herself against the mounting nausea. Something dropped down off the ceiling and scuttled through her hair. She made frantic brushing motions and finally dislodged whatever it was. She didn't want to know.

At the end of the passageway, which was only slightly wider than her shoulders, there was a short flight of steps. She climbed them slowly, for they were very slick with slime. Her feet had left the water by the time she reached the third step and, after six steps more, she came to a small landing and a sharp turn to her right. The rats receded before her like a furry brown wave, screaming in protest. She killed the more aggressive ones. There were so many, she could not avoid stepping on their bodies as she moved forward. Some of them still squirmed.

There was another passageway at the top of this second flight of steps. She used her sword to clear away the spider webs that had been painstakingly reconstructed since her last passage here. She passed heavy wooden doors fastened upon rust-encrusted hinges, the barred windows in them covered with a patina of corrosion. Behind those small yet heavily constructed doors, ancient bones of prisoners who had been long forgotten even while they lived gave mute testimony to unremembered crimes and sentences. In one cell, a brown skeleton hung suspended from manacles set deep into the wall, its head bent down in shame, its jaws agape in a never-ending silent scream. At the end of this passageway, there was one door that had fallen into the cell, deprived of the support of its aged hinges, which had been burned through.

The cell was tiny, no more than a cubicle. Falcon had to bend down low to enter it, stepping upon the fallen door. Rats so large their tails looked like snakes glared at her ferociously. She killed several and the rest retreated from her, all save one, which crouched upon the small case on the floor and snarled at her. She put away her laser, took out her sword and slashed at the creature viciously. The rat avoided the swift stroke, leaping off the case and darting into a small fissure in the wall.

She crouched down and set her light upon the floor, opening the case. She assembled the border circuits on the floor of the cell and set the plate for time and destination, programming the transition coordinates from the chronoplate's data file. Then she checked the plate's remote unit and slipped it into her pocket. Now, in the event that anything went wrong, their second chronoplate was preset with the coordinates for her escape. Drakov did not know its location. It was just as well that his usefulness to her was almost at an end. He was becoming quite difficult to control. If not tonight, she thought, then soon. Very, very soon. She could sense it. She did not know what it was, whether it was merely a strong intuition or the perception of the confluence of forces gathering together. She had a strong sense of imminence and every nerve fiber in her body fairly tingled with anticipation. She removed the other remote from her other pocket, the one slaved to the chronoplate up in the turret. Drakov had not been there when she had clocked in. Out wandering through the castle corridors again, she thought wryly. The man was becoming an emotional basket-case. At least he had had the sense to take the security monitor along with him.

She heard a scuttling behind her and turned quickly to see several large rats converging upon her from the corners of the cell. She stood quickly, almost hitting her head on the low ceiling, slashing at them with her sword. One of them darted close inside and fastened onto the toe of her boot. She kicked it off, then hit the switch on the remote. The first thing that she saw upon materializing in the turret was the form of Andre Cross, tied down onto the cot. Drakov sat casually upon the other cot, his eyes on the screen of the security monitor.

She smiled broadly. "So," she said, "it's happening at last."

Drakov glanced up at her expressionlessly. "She was nosing about in a small boat just outside the king's cell."

"Well done, Nicky," she said. "Any sign of the others?"

"Priest just climbed the wall and entered the south tower. No sign of Forrester or Delaney."

"Then they'll be attacking on two fronts," she said. "Delaney will make a try for the king while the others concentrate on us. It's just as I anticipated. Excellent. Excellent."

She glanced at Andre.

"Andre Cross," she said. "I've been waiting a long time to meet you."

Andre stared at her, saying nothing.

"Your friends and I have an old score to settle," Falcon said, "but it will have to wait. There's one other little matter to be taken care of before I can get around to you. I'll be back soon, Nicky."

"Where are you going?" he asked, surprised that she was leaving now that the commandos were making their move at last.

"There's plenty of time," she said. "Relax. I'll be back after I kill the king."

"Remember," Finn told von Tarlenheim, "the moment

that the drawbridge comes down, give Sapt the signal and then ride to join the assault."

"You can count on me," said Fritz.

"Remember one thing more," said Finn. "Hentzau's foremost concern will be that you and Sapt must die. Neither of you must lead the attack, for if you do, Hentzau will shoot you down."

"I'll have a hard time convincing Sapt," said von Tarlenheim. "You know how he is."

"Tell him that with the king's life at stake, this can be no time for heroics," Finn said. "He's no fool; he'll see that."

"Rassendyll," said Fritz, reaching out and taking Finn by his upper arm. "May the Lord protect you."

Finn smiled. "And you, Fritz."

He lowered himself into the moat. The water was chilly, but not uncomfortably cold. Finn breaststroked slowly and strongly across the water, taking care to make no splashing sounds. He swam straight towards the lighted section of the castle, just to the side of the massive portcullis. On the first floor of the castle, some fifteen to twenty feet above the surface of the moat, the lights were on in several of the windows of the new addition to the castle. Recent changes had been made to it, most notably in the installation of actual glasspaned windows, capable of being opened outward. It was towards one of these windows that Finn swam, the third one from the corner. As he came closer, he saw that it was opened and, as agreed upon with Rupert Hentzau, a rope hung from it, trailing down into the moat. He grasped it firmly and began to climb up the side of the wall, hand over hand, bracing himself with his legs. He paused just below the window and listened. Then, hearing nothing, he climbed a bit higher and peered in.

It was a large and ornate chamber that had been turned into a bedroom. A thick, opulent carpet covered the stone floor, leaving an open border for about a foot around it near the walls. Several paintings of moustachioed and bearded military men hung upon the walls. The illumination was provided by several oil lamps, with a number of large hanging lamps for mineral oil and candles being suspended from the ceiling by chains. The room contained a large stone fireplace, with tongs, pokers, and a coal scuttle beside it. There were two old broadswords crossed high over the mantel, below a medieval shield emblazoned with the Elphberg coat of arms. There were two armchairs upholstered in plush purple velvet to either side of the fireplace and a settee somewhat to one side, similarly upholstered. Directly across from him was a handsome sideboard that held a number of ceramic pieces and several bottles of what appeared to be port. Beside the bottles there were several glasses and a gasogene. There was also a marble-topped washstand with jugs and basins on it and, on the opposite side of the room, against the wall, a large canopied bed upon which Rupert Hentzau reclined, fully dressed, smoking a cigarette and staring at the ceiling. He was alone inside the room.

"*Hentzau!*" Finn whispered.

Hentzau sat up in bed and glanced towards the window. "Ah, it's you, play-actor! Have a pleasant swim?"

"Never mind the witticisms, just help me in," said Finn.

Hentzau came over to the window and stood there, looking at Finn clinging to the rope. He grinned, made a small "gun" with his thumb and forefinger and made a popping sound with his mouth.

"You see?" he said. "How easily I could have dissolved our partnership. Perhaps now you will trust me a little more."

"I'll trust you to help me inside," said Finn.

Hentzau reached out and took Finn's hand, pulling him into the room. He then untied the rope and let it drop into the moat.

"You're dripping on the carpet," he said. "You'd best change, unless you wish to leave a trail of water behind you. My clothes will be tight on you, but I think that we can manage to squeeze you into a pair of Michael's boots and breeches and perhaps one of my larger shirts. This was Michael's room, you know. I've decided that he would be more comfortable in my old quarters. They're a trifle smaller, but then I don't think he will protest. I've locked him in."

While Finn changed into the white breeches, high black boots, and loose, flowing white shirt that Hentzau gave him, Rupert quickly explained the situation to him.

"The king is in the dungeon directly below us," he said, "the first room off the stairs. There is a guardroom outside it, where Detchard and Krafstein will be stationed now. The way to reach it is by going out the door here, turning to your left, going down the corridor and across the main hall of this part of the castle. You will see several passageways leading off this hall. The largest one, with the great vaulted arch above it, leads to the main section of the castle. The one you want is immediately to its left. It leads to a stairway going down to the lower level, the upper level of the dungeons. It isn't even properly a dungeon. They were once servants' quarters and have now been converted to hold a considerably more illustrious tenant. The actual dungeons are below the main section of the castle, but they need not concern you. You would not wish to go down there in any case; they are teeming with rats. You will have to watch yourself when you cross the hall. I will try and make the way clear for you, but you shall be completely in the open and you will have to move quickly. Should anyone see you, I will do my best to prevent an outcry, but it would be better all around if you avoided being seen. Now, once you have reached the stair, you go down one flight and you will reach a landing. From there, the stairs turn sharply to the left. At the bottom, you will be near the entrance to the guardroom. I suggest that you pause upon that first landing and listen carefully. If the way seems clear, proceed down to the bottom. Take care to look before you step off the bottom stair. If either Detchard or Krafstein are anywhere near the middle of the room, they will be bound to see you. You will need to find a place of concealment. There is a short passage of sorts, a hall between the bottom of the stairs and the guardroom itself. It is no more than seven or eight feet long and there are no doors there. However, if you press yourself against the wall on either side, just before the archway, you will be in a shadowed corner and more or less hidden from sight. Once you have gotten that far, your greatest problem will be if either Krafstein or Detchard should decide to go upstairs for any reason. If they do, they cannot avoid seeing you. In that case, you will lose the advantage of surprise with one of them, at least.

"Here is a pistol for you. I advise you to shoot Detchard

first. I do not know if he carries his pistol on him, but he always carries a knife and his reactions are devilishly quick. He'll have that knife in you before you blink. So I advise you not to miss. As for Krafstein, he always goes armed, but he is nowhere near as quick as Detchard. He does, however, shoot well. Think you can handle it, play-actor?"

"Just make sure you do your part," said Finn. "If that drawbridge does not come down, I'll make certain to save a bullet for you."

"If the drawbridge does not come down," said Hentzau, with a grin, "then save that bullet for yourself. It will mean that I have died in the attempt and I would advise you to kill yourself rather than be taken by the countess. There's a bitch with a thirst for blood that is unmatched. She once showed a bit too keen an interest in the implements of torture down there. I believe she chafes to try them out on someone."

"I'll keep that in mind," said Finn.

"Are your people in position?"

"By now, they should be," Finn said. "The lowering of the drawbridge will be their signal to attack."

"Good. Once you have achieved the stair, I shall count to twenty, then lower the bridge. It shall be rather noisy, I'm afraid, so you had best be ready."

"What about the others?"

"You leave them to me. Just dispose of Krafstein and Detchard as quickly as you can, then enter the king's cell and do away with him. There is a grate across the window of his cell that swings away. Beyond it is a pipe. Place the king's body in the pipe and weight it, you will find all you need there ready to hand. Once the king has gone into the moat, release the pipe and it shall drop in after him. Then, Your Majesty, hasten to me, for I will require protection from your friends."

"Very well," Finn said, nodding. "When do we go?"

Hentzau walked over to the door, opened it, peered out then nodded at Finn. "Now," he said.

Albert Lauengram reached the top of the stairs, glanced quickly down the hall, and then moved swiftly to the door of Hentzau's old room. He paused, listened, then turned the key in the lock and swung open the door.

Michael Elphberg was sitting on the edge of the bed, bent over, his head in his hands. When Lauengram came in, he looked up quickly. His face was puffed and bruised. His nose was splayed across his features at an odd angle and several of his teeth were missing. Both his lips were cut.

"So," he said, "they've sent you to do me in, have they?"

Lauengram held a finger to his lips. "Hush, Your Lordship," he said softly. "Not all have turned on you."

"What do you mean?" said Michael, sitting up straight and staring at Lauengram with the beginnings of hope.

"Though she has promised to double our wages," Lauengram said, "we are not keen to throw in with her. There is more honor—and more profit, to be sure—in following a king . . . Your Majesty."

Michael stood. "Who is 'we?' "

"Detchard, Krafstein, De Gautet and myself," said Lauengram.

"And Hentzau?"

"We did not ask him," Lauengram said. "He seems too enamored of the countess and too anxious to receive his doubled wages. Besides, it was he who locked you in here, remember."

"Yes, I remember all too well," said Michael. "You can tell the others that their pay is to be tripled henceforth and that they may look forward to more once I have attained the throne. As for Hentzau, he does not live out the night."

"We had already agreed on that," said Lauengram. "And the countess—"

"That she-devil is *mine*," said Michael, vehemently. "Give me your pistol."

"I would prefer to keep it," Lauengram said. "Should we run into Hentzau—"

"Then I will shoot him down like the dog he is!"

"No offense, Milord, but my hand is steadier."

"What, then, are you afraid? You have your sword."

"Aye, and I'll not draw it against Hentzau. With a gun, I do not fear him, but I am no match for Rupert with a blade."

"Would you question your king?" said Michael, holding his hand out.

Reluctantly, Lauengram handed him his pistol.

"Where is Hentzau now?" said Michael.

"In your chamber right below us," Lauengram said.

"And the others?"

"Krafstein and Detchard are with the king. De Gautet keeps watch for Hentzau in the main hall. As for the countess, she has not arrived as yet."

"Then she shall have a nice surprise when she comes to join us," Michael said. He squared his shoulders, drawing himself up, and walked past Lauengram into the corridor.

Lucas moved slowly down the stairs, wishing that he could risk using a light. He moved in almost total darkness and the hairs prickled on the back of his neck. He kept close to the wall, feeling his way along, moving one careful step at a time. He had almost reached the upper floor when the stone stairs beneath him simply stopped. He flailed for balance and almost fell into the yawning darkness beneath him. He caught his breath, backed up a step and took a small flashlight out of a pouch upon his belt. A whole section of the stairway was missing. He let his breath out slowly. So much for not risking a light. He shone the beam across from him to see where he could go from there. Nowhere. If the stairs began again, they began around the curve of the tower further down. There seemed to be only one way that he could go.

Clipping the light onto his belt, he fired a dart into the stone step on which he stood. Then he clipped the nysteel line onto it. Crouching on the edge of the step, he carefully lowered himself over the side and slowly played out the line from the handle, descending into the darkness. He had gone no more than thirty feet when he heard a very faint whirring sound. Instantly, he let go of the handle and fell. He fell perhaps another ten or fifteen feet, landing hard on the stone floor below him. He looked up.

The space above him was bisected by two bright laser beams. He rolled quickly and two more beams stabbed down at the spot on which he had landed. He moved quickly back once more, but he was in the clear, out of the line of fire. He was in a long corridor that stretched out into the darkness.

Now I know why it was so easy, he thought. Portable defense systems. He was like a rat in a maze. Knowing what he could expect now was of damned little help. There would undoubtedly be more such surprises in store for him ahead. The question was, how would he avoid them?

Not using a light now would be a far greater risk than using one. He shone the beam ahead of him. It was a long, straight corridor, following the line of the parapet above. It ran for some twenty yards or so, ending in a wall at the far end. At that point, it turned to the right, though whether it ran straight or led to another stairway, he could not tell. Going back the way he came was out of the question. It would expose him to the laser beams again. He shone the light upon the walls and on the ceiling, but it revealed nothing. He then turned the light off and held the night scope up to his eyes. No infrared beams, either. That still did not mean that the corridor was safe. Some of those systems, like the one Derringer had used to protect the safehouse, operated on biosensors.

"Well, come on, Lucas," he said to himself aloud, "you can't just stand here. Be a good little rat and go for the cheese."

Keeping close to the wall, he started forward, straining to hear the slightest sound. The only thing he heard was the sound of his own breathing. It seemed incredibly loud. He was about a fourth of the way down the corridor now. So far, so good. All he had to do was reach the opposite end of the castle and at the rate he was moving, it would take him until mid-afternoon of the following day. It would never do.

He glanced at his watch. Forrester would be making his move in a few moments. Lucas took a deep breath, bit his lower lip, and set off at a dead run towards the far end of the corridor. It seemed like the longest sprint that he had ever made. He reached the far wall, practically slamming into it. Pressed up against it, his face to the cold stone, he gulped in deep lungfuls of air. His knees felt like rubber.

Something whistled through his hair at the back of his head. Something else plucked at his shirt in several places. As he dropped to the floor, sliding down the wall, he heard a soft pattering sound, as if a handful of gravel had been thrown against the wall to his left. He snapped his light on and saw the silver gleam of numerous needle darts lying on the floor beside him, where they had bounced off the wall. He heard a very soft *chuffing* noise and flattened himself upon the floor, try- ing to become a part of it. Dozens of deadly little metal insects droned over his head, pattering against the wall like silver rain. He fired his laser, sweeping the corridor to his right; then he lay still, scarcely breathing. After a moment, he slowly raised himself to all fours, then moved down the corridor, ready to flatten out again instantly.

The machine was mounted on a tripod at about the level of his knees. He had knocked it out, but it still gave him the shivers as he imagined that little cannister spinning slowly, bringing up the next barrage.

"Christ," he whispered. "These people are really serious."

Then he noticed the tiny security monitor attached to one of the legs of the tripod. In disgust, he kicked it over. So much for the element of surprise, he thought. It seemed like a no- win situation. They knew exactly where he was and they could follow his progress as he tried to make his way to them. They wouldn't even need many more such units. All they needed was a few neat little booby traps placed at strategic points be- tween the turret where they made their headquarters and all routes of access to it. The odds of his avoiding all of them were infinitesimal. They could move about the castle at will, simply deactivating their defense systems as the need arose. He had no such luxury. He had to do it the hard way.

He was on the upper floor of the castle now. He had planned on getting through this section, going down to the ground level, and then crossing the open courtyard in the center of the castle to get to the old keep. Now, he saw that they had anticipated him. It was doubtful that they would have rigged up anything covering the courtyard, but then, they didn't need to. Even if he managed to get that far, he would be in the open. If Michael and his men did not spot him, the Timekeepers surely would.

He had to think like them. He had to try to anticipate where they might have placed their weapons systems. It stood to reason that there would be more of them the closer he came to the keep. Obviously, it was a good idea not to go that way, except he had to go that way.

There *has* to be a way, he thought. He couldn't get to them from above. The parapets provided hardly any cover and their tracking system would pick him off as soon as he came near the keep. It also seemed now that he could not get to them from the inside. Sooner or later, one of the devices would get him. What was left?

He could try working his way back to the new section of the castle. If he could manage to avoid Michael and his mercenaries, maybe he could make his way to the open courtyard in the central portion of the castle, but then he would be wide open trying to cross it and he would still have to get inside the keep and climb up to that turret. It was a certainty that they would have their highest concentration of defensive systems placed there.

There was only one chance he had that he could think of. It stood to reason that the Timekeepers would need to be able to deactivate the systems for their own safety when they moved about inside the castle. That and the monitor he had found on the last device suggested that they all had to be tied in to a master control unit. It would not need to be very large. If Forrester could somehow manage to knock it out, then he had a chance. Otherwise, it was only a matter of time before his luck ran out.

There was no point to maintaining communication silence now. They knew that he was here. He activated his comset.

"Colonel," he said. He waited a moment. "Moses, damn it, I'm in a lot of trouble! *Moses!*"

There was no response.

12

"Make no sudden moves, Father," Drakov said. "Keep your arms well away from your sides and stand perfectly still."

Forrester saw Andre lying before him, tied down onto a cot. She was securely bound and her shirt was torn open at the shoulder where she had been treated for the wound made by the rappelling dart. She looked pale and weak. When she saw him, she pressed her lips together grimly and slowly shook her head from side to side.

"Now, very slowly," Drakov said, "turn around."

With a gut-wrenching sensation, Forrester complied. It was a blow to him to see how strongly Drakov resembled his mother. He had the same lustrous, curly black hair and the same wide mouth. He had the same high cheekbones and patrician nose, the same dusky complexion, even his bearing was similar to hers, proud and languid, self-possessed. Yet the eyes, with their unwavering gaze, were his father's eyes. Forrester saw that they were a brilliant emerald green, just like his own, deeply set and smouldering. He saw the long knife scar on his son's cheek and thought of Falcon's letter, of the taunting manner in which she had written of how he had received it. His knees felt weak suddenly and there was a pressing sensation in his chest. He looked at Drakov, standing by the wall and gazing at him coldly, aiming a laser directly at his midsection. My son, thought Forrester. God help me. And God help him.

"Using only the fingertips of your left hand," said Drakov, "remove your weapon and drop it to the floor; then remove your belt in the same manner."

Forrester did as he was told. He had tried to prepare himself for this, but it hadn't helped. He felt physically ill. It was difficult to breathe.

"You will keep your arms spread out from your sides," said Drakov. "I do not intend to risk searching you. If you have other weapons secreted on your person, be advised that if you make even the slightest motion, you will find yourself an amputee. You will move only when I tell you and exactly as I tell you. Is that clear?"

Forrester nodded, hoping fervently that his emotions did not show.

"Now, move backward, slowly, until you are against that wall there," Drakov said, indicating the direction with a nod of his head.

When Forrester had done so, Drakov cautiously moved forward and picked up the items Forrester had dropped, placing them well out of reach without taking his eyes off Forrester for an instant. Forrester stood perfectly still with his back against the cold stone wall, his arms spread out as if for an embrace. The irony of this posture was not lost on him.

"What now, Son?" he said.

"Son," said Drakov, bitterly. "How easily you say that."

"You called me 'Father' easily enough."

"No, not easily at all," said Drakov, with a quiet intensity. "I've thought of you a great deal over all these many years, but that hasn't made it any easier to call you 'Father.' Still, I have long dreamed of this moment. Falcon will be returning shortly. It should be quite an interesting reunion. Tell me, how does it feel to finally meet your son face to face?"

"It feels very sad," said Forrester. "I pity you."

"You can pity yourself," said Drakov. "I am what you made me."

"I didn't make your choices for you," Forrester said. "I am responsible for you, but not for what you have become. I won't take all the credit. Or the blame. You think your mother would have approved of the way that you turned out?"

Drakov tensed. "Why should you care? She meant little enough to you."

"That's where you're wrong. She meant a great deal to me. More than you will ever know."

"Did she?" Drakov said, softly. "Is that why you abandoned her?"

"I had no other choice," said Forrester, trying to keep his voice level. "I couldn't take her with me and I couldn't have remained with her, much as I wanted to. I tried to explain all that to her. I thought she understood. If you think that it didn't hurt to have to leave her, not knowing what would become of her, or of you—"

"Spare me your rationalizations," Drakov said, scornfully. "You shamed her, then left her when she needed you the most. Even then, she loved you. She died loving you. Yet, as I look at you now, I see no trace of the man she spoke of. I see only a pathetic old man trying to excuse his actions. You did not deserve her love."

"I'm not trying to excuse anything, Nikolai," said Forrester, feeling the sting of his son's words. "I'm only telling you the truth. Not that I expect it to change anything. I can understand why you hate me. I don't blame you for it. What I can't understand is what that hate led you to become."

"I seek neither your understanding nor your acceptance," Drakov said with a hard edge to his voice. "I seek only justice."

"This isn't justice, Drakov," Andre said. "I don't think you realize just what's at stake here. Falcon's using you. This is more than a temporal disruption. You've endangered the timestream itself. It doesn't have to be this way. If you'd only listen, if you'd only let us help you—"

"Help me?" Drakov said, speaking to her without taking his eyes off Forrester even for an instant. "How would you propose to 'help' me? A reeducation procedure, is that what you had in mind? Is that what you mean? Help me to 'adjust'? No, I don't think so, Corporal Cross. I have been to your 27th century and I have seen its perversity firsthand. I will not have my mind conditioned so that I would respond like some happy, brainwashed citizen of your great technocracy."

"No one's talking about brainwashing," Andre said. "I've gone through it. It's more like therapy than anything else. True, there are cases where personalities are altered, but that's for psychotics. I don't think you're psychotic, Drakov. I think you're just hurt. Reeducation can help you deal with that. It can make you understand why things happened the way they did."

"I find the very idea obscene," he said.

"And terrorism is not obscene?" said Forrester.

"Labeling me a terrorist makes it convenient for you to moralize, but otherwise, it's meaningless. One man's terrorist is another's freedom fighter. History, I have learned, is written by the winners, not the losers. If the losers ever have anything to say, they merely make excuses for having lost, in order to cast themselves in the most favorable light. Unfortunately, what history does not say is that if there is obscenity in violence—and I am not denying that there is—there is far greater obscenity in the fact that it is the only thing most people understand. Particularly *your* people. Mensinger tried using reason, did he not? Where did it get him? All I do is employ the only means left available to me in making war on war. If what I do becomes historically significant, then history will judge me. You, however, are in very poor position to pronounce judgment on my morality. Violence is your stock in trade."

"*Moses!*" Lucas's voice came over Forrester's comset. "*Damn it, Moses, I'm in a lot of trouble! Moses!*"

Forrester could not respond. Drakov was watching him alertly and he could not risk moving to activate his throat mike.

"*Moses, I don't know if you're receiving me, but if you're not, I guess it doesn't matter. They've got the whole interior of the old part of the castle rigged with defense systems. They have to be centrally controlled somehow, probably through some kind of remote unit. If you can't get them turned off, I'll never make it to the keep. Can you hear me, Moses? Colonel?*"

"*Stay put, Lucas.*"

"Finn? Where are you?"
"In the castle, with Hentzau."
"With Hentzau? *What the hell—"*

"What are you doing, play-actor?" Hentzau called out softly, seeing Finn hesitate in the corridor behind him. "Come on!"

"I'm coming," Finn said. "Just catching my breath." He lowered his voice to a whisper. *"I can't talk now, Lucas. The castle is about to be attacked. Stay put. I'll try to get to those defense systems."*

"Come on, Rassendyll, damn you!" Hentzau said. "Stop dawdling!"

This is it, thought Forrester. All the elements had come together and the key moment in temporal continuity had finally arrived. Only where was Falcon?

"In order to deactivate those systems," Drakov said, "Sergeant Delaney will first have to deactivate me."

He held up the control unit and Forrester abruptly realized that he had relieved Andre of her comset and was wearing it himself. He had heard every word.

As Hentzau stepped out into the main hall, De Gautet left his position of concealment behind an arras and raised his pistol, aiming it at Hentzau's back.

"Stand where you are, Rupert!"

Hentzau stopped, then casually turned around. "Well, well," he said, with unconcern. "What have we here? Dissension in the ranks?"

"Some men do not change sides as easily as you," said De Gautet. "We feel that our interests would be better served allied with the duke, rather than with your ambitious countess."

"I see," said Hentzau. "Well then, if you're going to shoot me, best be quick about it. There's a man creeping up behind you."

De Gautet laughed. "Really, Rupert, if you think—"

Finn seized him. He tried to grab the gun, but it went off,

the shot echoing through the hall. As they struggled, Hentzau drew his sabre.

"Run, play-actor! Take care of the king! Leave this cowardly dog to me!"

Finn shoved De Gautet away from him and the man fell sprawling. Fully expecting Hentzau to run him through, he began to spring across the hall, knowing that the shot would have alerted all the others. When he glanced over his shoulder, he saw to his amazement that Hentzau had put his foot down upon the pistol and was waiting for De Gautet to get up and draw his sabre.

"What are you doing?" he shouted. "Kill him, for God's sake!"

"It won't take but a moment," Hentzau called over his shoulder as the two men engaged.

Finn pulled out his own pistol, aiming at De Gautet, but Hentzau kept moving into his line of fire. "Get out of the damn way!" he yelled.

"You're wasting time, play-actor!" Hentzau shouted.

Cursing the arrogant young fool, Finn turned and ran headlong down the stairs, crashing into Krafstein, who was running up the stairs with his pistol drawn. They both went down and Finn lost his revolver as they rolled to the bottom of the stairs, onto the first landing. Krafstein flailed at him, but Finn brought his knee up sharply into the man's groin, then rammed the heel of his palm up into his nose, breaking it and driving the bone splinters deep into the brain. Krafstein went limp and Finn shoved him away, reaching for his laser. He felt a sharp blow just below his left shoulder, beneath the collarbone. He raised his weapon and fired, hitting Detchard squarely in the face. Detchard screamed once, briefly, then fell dead.

Finn glanced down to see the hilt of a dagger protruding from his chest. He felt no pain. Not yet. He wondered if he would even have the time.

"Stay put, my ass," said Lucas. "I'm getting the hell out of here."

He ran down the stairway to the next level, abandoning all

caution. It had all come apart. He couldn't raise Forrester and the attempt to rescue Rudolf was under way. For all he knew, both Forrester and Andre were already dead. They had all run out of time. If he could only get to a window in the outside wall, he could dive out into the moat. Then, as the castle was assaulted, he could try to take advantage of the confusion to get in the only way that was left open to him: the drawbridge to the portcullis. It would be better to face a hail of bullets from Michael's mercenaries than to take his chances with laser beams and needle dart barrages and God only knew what else. He turned a corner and an auto-pulser opened up on him.

He felt a searing pain in his thigh as the blast of plasma grazed him and a wave of incredible heat passed close to his head. He just barely managed to duck back around the corner in time. The stone walls were covered with blue flame. His clothing was smoldering and he smelled cooked meat. His own. The skin on the entire right side of his face felt as though it had been ripped away. It was roasted, cracked and blistered from the temple all the way down to his jaw. He could not see out of his right eye. He reached up gingerly and felt liquid seeping down his cheek.

The pain was unbearable. He leaned back against the stone wall for support, gasping, slamming his left hand hard into the wall in a desperate effort to focus on some other part of his body, to keep the pain from blotting out everything else. He reached into his pouch and pulled out a warp grenade. They were issued only to the adjustment teams, only one per team, and they were to be used only as a last, desperate resort in case of an emergency. This qualified. Perhaps the review board wouldn't think so, assuming that he made it back, but at the moment, he could not care less. All bets were off.

Finn stepped over the body of Detchard and aimed his laser at the lock on the cell door. The knife still protruded from his chest. He did not dare to pull it out. It could be the only thing holding an artery together. He half-expected to drop dead at any moment. He reeled and almost fell. He couldn't seem to make his fingers respond.

Damn, he thought, *now* it finally gets to me! With a knife

stuck in his chest, the reserves of energy he had been functioning on finally gave out and he was on the verge of collapse. His
limbs simply were not responding. He felt like a marionette
with its strings cut. He was beginning to disassociate. He had
to buy himself more time.

Using all his concentration, he removed the small ring from
his left hand. It felt as though he were drunk, unable to coor-
dinate his movements. He managed to work the tiny catch and
the needle snapped out. With everything swimming all around
him, he pressed the needle up against his neck and injected the
tiny dose of nitro directly into his carotid artery. The effect
was instantaneous. It felt as though he had injected himself
with white phosphorous as the nitro slammed into his brain.

"*Aaargh!*" He jerked bolt upright, ready to tear the door
down with his bare hands, ready to attack the stone walls with
his teeth. He steadied his right hand with his left, trying to
keep it from shaking.

"*Finn! Finn, where are you?*"

"*Outside the king's cell with the top of my fucking head
coming off!*"

"*What? Oh, Christ, are you on nitro?*"

"*Hell, yes!*"

He fired his laser at the lock.

"*You'd better move it, then. I'm about to make a lot of
noise up here.*"

"*What's going on? You sound terrible. Are you all right?*"

"*No, but I might live. Hold your ears. I'm setting off a
warp grenade.*"

"*Are you crazy?*"

"*Probably. Good luck. I'm out.*"

Finn burned through the lock and kicked the door open.

Rudolf slowly raised himself from his cot. "Cousin Rudolf!
I heard shots! Are. . . ." his voice trailed off when he saw the
knife. His eyes grew wider still. "Good Lord, man, you've
been stabbed!"

"Never mind me," said Finn, practically lifting him off the
cot. "Can you walk?"

"You say that to me with a knife stuck in your chest? It is *I*
who should be helping *you!*"

"Well, let's see if we can help each other stay alive long enough for Sapt and von Tarlenheim to reach us. We're not out of danger yet."

De Gautet's sabre scraped against Hentzau's blade as he bore down on it and De Gautet's eyes were wide with panic. He knew he was no match for Hentzau. He also knew that the shot would bring the others and he was hoping desperately that they would come before Hentzau finished him off. He gave way to Hentzau's pressure and leapt backward, forcing Hentzau off balance momentarily, but Hentzau's recovery was swift. However, it bought De Gautet enough time to unsheath his dagger and hurl it at him. Hentzau dodged it and it missed him by inches, striking the wall behind him and falling to the floor.

"Ah hah!" cried Hentzau. "Close, but not close enough! I'm afraid I have no more time for you, my friend. It's too bad you didn't throw in with me."

"No, Rupert, please—"

Hentzau took his own dagger and threw it with a quick and easy motion. It plunged into De Gautet's chest. De Gautet's hands came up to clutch at it. He staggered one step forward and collapsed onto the floor. As Hentzau turned to run to the drawbridge and release it, a pistol shot cracked sharply and he felt the bullet pass close by his ear.

"*Stop*, Hentzau, or the next one shall not miss!"

Hentzau slowly turned around to see Michael standing with Lauengram on the stairs leading to the second floor, his pistol leveled at him. Michael's face was livid with fury. He lisped slightly from missing the teeth that Falcon had knocked out.

"This does not seem to be my night," said Hentzau, to himself. He thought that he could probably make a dive and manage to release the drawbridge, but he would certainly be killed in the attempt, and that was not his plan at all. His one chance was to stall and hope for rescue by the play-actor.

"Don't be too eager to finish me off, Your Lordship," he said to Michael. "You have enemies without. You'll need help. Perhaps we can come to terms."

"I do not deal with traitors!" Michael said. "I should have

had you and Sophia killed when I first suspected your affair! Where is that treacherous slut?''

"Right here," said Falcon, standing in the archway that led to the old section of the castle. She fired her laser and the beam struck Michael in the chest. His gun went off, but the shot was wild and he was already dead when he fell headlong down the stairs. Her second shot dropped a stunned and disbelieving Lauengram, who tumbled down the stairs to land in a heap on top of Michael.

Hentzau stared at her in astonishment, the drawbridge momentarily forgotten. "The devil!" he said, awestruck. "How did you do that? What manner of weapon . . ." he stopped in mid-phrase as she turned toward him and aimed the laser at his chest.

Lucas held the warp grenade in his right hand, hesitating. He had never actually used one before. He was fully briefed on them and had trained with simulators, but the thought of setting off a pinpoint nuclear explosion gave him pause. Still, he had no other choice. He was badly hurt, he had only one eye left and the plasma burns were throbbing, causing him terrific pain. He wasn't sure just how much radiation he would catch. Supposedly, it would not be lethal. Supposedly.

The grenade, a miniature bomb really, was preset. All it took was for him to arm it, then either place it manually or throw it just like a hand grenade. It ws the latest in 27th-century weapons technology, a diabolical combination of nuclear device and time machine. It scared the hell out of him.

At the moment of detonation, the miniaturized chronocircuits created a Einstein-Rosen Bridge, or warp, with the result that the major force of the explosion was instantaneously clocked through time and space to the Orion Nebula, where such events were naturally commonplace. What would remain in his own immediate time and space would effectively constitute a pinpoint nuclear explosion, intensely concentrated, creating total devastation in a confined area that, theoretically, could be as small as a fingernail. Theoretically. In practice, they had not refined them that far yet. This one would be larger. Considerably larger.

Lucas swallowed hard and armed the device. He set it for air burst, then set the timer. His tongue licked at his cracked and blistered lips. He wondered if this was what it felt like for the bombadier on the *Enola Gay*. He shut his one remaining eye, counted to three, lobbed the grenade around the corner and dropped down onto the floor, covering his head with his arms and praying to God it worked just like the boys in Ordnance said it would. There was a blinding flash of white light, followed by a devastating roar.

"You always were too damned unpredictable, Rupert," Falcon said, pointing her laser at him. "It really is unfortunate. I thought you were rather nice and I was going to let you live."

"Wait," said Hentzau. "I can still help you. I can—"

"You can only interfere. You've become expendable. I'm sorry."

"Before you kill me," Hentzau said, stalling desperately, "at least tell me what that is. I've never seen such—"

"It doesn't matter, Rupert. It wouldn't make any difference to you, anyway. Say goodbye."

The explosion rocked the castle. Startled, Falcon jerked her head in its direction and Hentzau *moved*. She fired, missing him narrowly as he leaped aside and in that moment, Rudolf hit with an awkward tackle and she fell, the laser skittering across the floor. Hentzau quickly snatched it up. Finn stood with his own laser leveled at Falcon and Rudolf as they thrashed upon the floor, but refrained from firing for fear of hitting the king.

"*Rudolf, get away!*" he shouted.

Falcon rolled over on her back, dragging the king on top of her, holding him with one arm around his neck, the other locked behind his head.

"Drop the laser, Delaney, or I'll break his neck!" she said.

Finn fairly vibrated from the nitro hammering through him, but his shirt was soaked with blood and his vision was beginning to blur. "Break his neck and where does that leave you?" he said.

"Who the devil is Delaney?" Hentzau said. He glanced

down at the laser. "Where the deuce is the trigger on this thing?"

"Kill him, Rupert!"

"Really?" Hentzau said, insouciantly. "How? Besides, if I kill him, you'll kill the king and where would that leave me? I'd be left with one dead play-actor, one dead king, one dead duke and what must be a small army just outside. No, that would never do. I must come out of this ahead somehow."

"I can make you rich, Rupert," she said. "Richer than you could ever imagine! There's a small stud that fires—"

"Don't do it, Hentzau," Finn said. "I'd have to kill you."

Hentzau examined the weapon with curiosity. "Strange-looking contraption. You mean this stud here?"

"Hentzau, if I don't kill you, you can be sure she will. She doesn't need you," Finn said. "Don't be a fool."

"Shoot him, Rupert! Shoot!"

Hentzau held the laser the way he had seen her hold it, with his finger on the stud, then he came up to her and bent over, putting the weapon up against the side of her head.

"I'm sorry, my dear, but since the play-actor's thrown in with the king, I think that I'd best do the same. The odds seem better to me. Be so kind as to release His Majesty."

"Good man, Hentzau!" Finn said. "Now we—" his knees buckled and he sank down to the floor. "Oh, no!" he said. "Not now!"

He fell over on his side, unconscious.

Lucas huddled on the floor, holding his head from the concussion of the explosion. Fine dust filled the air with swirling fog and there was crumbled stone all around him. He sat up slowly, his ears ringing, to see if he was still in one piece. He was lacerated and bruised and burned in more places than he could count and he had no idea how much radiation he had received. His entire body hurt and he could barely see straight.

The corridor where the auto-pulser had been was gone. Completely gone. The cool night breeze that came in through the gaping, massive hole where the wall had been was a welcome relief from the musty atmosphere of the ancient castle corridors. Lucas got to his feet unsteadily and lurched over to the opening. The moat was directly beneath him. He took a deep breath and fell forward into space.

They heard the explosion at the opposite end of the castle.

"What in heaven's name was *that*?" said Drakov, his eyes never leaving Forrester, despite his being startled by the sound. His whole body stiffened.

"A warp grenade," said Forrester. "It seems that Priest isn't out of it yet."

Drakov shook his head, having no idea what a warp grenade was. It sounded as if it had blown half the castle away. "Your people certainly possess a dogged persistence," he said. "Very resourceful. My compliments. You've trained them well. I admire such determination."

"Then give it its due," said Forrester. "You have the upper hand. Let Andre go. She's no threat to you now. I'm the one you really want."

"True," said Drakov, "but Falcon wants you all."

"Assuming that she's still alive," said Forrester. "If she's managed to kill the king, then chances are that it's all over anyway. You've won. You've got what you wanted."

"Why should I release her?"

"Colonel—" Andre said.

"Shut up, Corporal. That's an order," Forrester said sharply. "Your quarrel is with me, Nikolai. Everything that's happened here in one way or another is my responsibility. This is a private matter between the two of us. Leave her out of it. You have nothing to gain by killing her now and nothing to lose by letting her go."

"Moses, don't—"

"*I said shut up!*" snapped Forrester. "Nikolai, please. I'm begging you. You want me to get down on my knees?"

"Enough," said Drakov. "I have no stomach to see you beg."

"Do you have the stomach to see what Falcon will probably do to her?" said Forrester. "You really think that she'll be satisfied with a quick kill? Look at her. She's already weak from loss of blood. She probably couldn't even stand up. But Falcon is a trained agent, a skilled assassin. She'll be able to keep her alive for a long time before she's finished."

"Yes, I believe she would," said Drakov, quietly.

"I'm not asking you for myself," said Forrester. "Remember how your mother died. Remember how you tried to help and couldn't."

Drakov turned pale. "How did you know that?"

"Falcon told me all about it in a letter," said Forrester, heavily. "She didn't spare me much. She seemed to take a lot of pleasure in reconstructing the graphic details of the scene from what you must have told her. Undoubtedly, she embellished a great deal. Somehow, I can't imagine you describing her being raped in quite that manner."

Drakov gritted his teeth. His eyes narrowed to slits. "Turn around," he said.

Forrester hesitated for a moment, then complied, slowly turning his back to him, facing the stone wall. He heard a muffled sob.

"The chronoplate is beneath her cot," he said. "I will give you the sequence code for its failsafe device. Set the coordinates for your time and send her home."

"No!" said Andre. "Moses, you can't—"

Forrester reached out quickly and rendered her unconscious with a nerve pinch. Then, under his son's direction, he deactivated the failsafe device on the chronoplate, assembled the border circuits, programmed the transition coordinates, and clocked her to Plus Time, to Pendleton Base. Then he turned to face his son.

"Here," said Drakov, tossing him the control unit. "If Major Priest is still alive, then perhaps this will give him a fighting chance."

Forrester turned off the defense systems, then tossed the unit onto the cot. It would end here and now, one way or another. Perhaps they had failed and it was all pointless, anyway. But his son was his responsibility. He would have liked to take out Falcon, but if she did not return in the next moment, he would be forced to leave her to Priest and Delaney, assuming they were still alive. He could wait no longer. At least Andre was clear.

Drakov lowered the laser and, to Forrester's astonishment, dropped it on the floor.

"We shall settle this like gentlemen," he said, as Forrester stared at him uncomprehendingly. "You have dishonored my mother, sir. I demand satisfaction. The choice of weapons is yours."

Forrester closed his eyes. He was seized by a sudden, irrational impulse to laugh. A duel. His son was challenging him to a duel.

"I fear that we have no sabres here," said Drakov, "but we have the lasers and a number of revolvers. Or, if you prefer, we can use knives."

Forrester smiled, ruefully. "What would you suggest?"

"Under the circumstances, I would favor knives," said Drakov. "The room is quite small and would provide for no proper test of marksmanship."

Forrester sighed and shook his head. "I can't," he said, softly. "God damn it, I just can't."

"You refuse me?" said Drakov, frowning.

"No. No, I don't have that right, Son," he said. "You misunderstood. I have a small device strapped to my chest, beneath my shirt. It contains a nerve gas, very quick and very lethal."

"I see," said Drakov. "That is why you were so concerned about Corporal Cross."

"Give me a moment," said Forrester, "and I'll remove it."

Drakov nodded and started taking off his own shirt as Forrester removed his. As Forrester disarmed the device and took it off, Drakov tossed aside his shirt, revealing a massive, muscular chest, powerful arms and rock-hard abdominals. He took two knives, both daggers with ten inch blades, and offered Forrester his choice.

It was almost dawn.

13

Lucas hit the moat feet first and thrashed his way to the surface. He was barely able to tread water. He knew that he was functioning on adrenalin and he wondered how long it would be before he collapsed. It was some thirty or forty yards to the drawbridge, a bit less to the bank. He struck out laboriously for the bank. He managed to pull himself out and he lay there for a moment on the ground, trying to get his breath back. The plasma burns were throbbing and he was shivering. With an effort, he picked himself up and began walking along the bank towards the chateau. He wasn't sure what he was going to do when he got there. He merely tried to concentrate on one step at a time. That was effort enough. He moved from tree to tree, using the trunks for support, resting as briefly as he could when it seemed that his energy had completely given out and then forcing himself to go on. He tried not to think about the mission. Apparently, it had failed. He tried not to think about Forrester or Finn or Andre. He tried not to think about the Timekeepers or about the pain and he tried not to imagine what he must look like with half his face burned away. He had seen what the plasma had done to his leg and the sight of it alone, much less the smell, was enough to make him gag. He concentrated all his will on getting to the castle somehow. All

193

he could do was to go on. He was still alive and so long as he was alive, he still had a job to do.

"It's over," Falcon said. "He's dead!"

"Perhaps," said Hentzau, "but there's still the king. Release him or I will fire this mysterious weapon of yours."

"If I release him, you'll kill me," she said.

"Perhaps," said Hentzau. "Perhaps I'll turn you over to Colonel Sapt and give you to him as a present. Or perhaps I'll take advantage of the opportunity to see how good you really are with a sabre. There should be no interruptions now."

She looked at him for a moment, then released the king. Coughing, Rudolf crawled away from her. Hentzau took the laser away from her head and allowed her to stand. He backed off a space, then tossed the weapon aside.

"I've always preferred steel, anyway," he said.

Falcon smiled and drew her own sabre. "You're a fool, Rupert. You should have killed me."

"You're probably right," said Hentzau, grinning at her. "But where would be the sport in that?"

"If it's sport you want," she said, "you're about to get more than you can handle."

Hentzau threw back his head and laughed. "*En garde!*"

The hall began to echo with the sound of clanging steel.

Father and son circled each other warily, knives held ready, each looking for an opening. Forrester quickly saw that his son was an experienced knife fighter. Drakov had assumed a slightly bent over stance with his balance on the balls of his feet, one hand held out before him with the arm bent a little, held slightly crossways of the body. Unlike the amateur, who knew no better, he held his knife not out before him, but in close to the body so that he could stab out or slash without leaving his knife hand out where it might be grasped or cut or where the knife could be kicked away. His eyes were on Forrester's, that being the only sure method to be constantly alert for any sign of movement. He carried a lot of muscle, but he moved nimbly, like a dancer, darting in for a quick feint, pulling back at once when he saw that Forrester had read the move, skipping lightly out of the way when Forrester attempted a move of his own.

There was no flurry of knife blades, no tricky motions with the hands to distract the opponent. Both men knew what they were doing and this was very serious business. Each used utter economy of motion. Each watched the other with a fierce intensity, knowing that with two skilled knife fighters, it was a war of nerves more than anything else. It was not like a duel with swords; one did not thrust and slash and parry. One waited for the other to make a mistake in judgment. Good knife fighters did not cut each other up, at least not very much. Forrester realized that he could not resort to any of the usual tricks, such as doing something totally unexpected—barking loudly and suddenly like a dog or spitting in his opponent's face, then taking advantage of the one instant in which he was startled to move in and gut him. Nikolai would not be fooled like that. It would take a great deal of concentration to avoid being caught off guard or off balance. The first one of them to make a mistake would lose and it would be over in an instant.

The only problem was that Forrester was losing his concentration. He kept staring into Drakov's eyes, trying to put all thoughts out of his mind, but it was like staring into his own eyes in a mirror. In combat, especially close combat, the mind had to be empty, free of any thoughts of winning or losing. The idea was to get into the rhythm of the deadly ballet, to flow with it without thinking. To think about winning was to admit the possibility of losing. To think about surviving was to dwell upon the spectre of death. Yet, try hard as he might to focus himself on the pure interplay of motion, Forrester's mind kept drifting, like a boat with a sleepy captain that kept wandering off course, then lurching back as the captain caught himself and seized the wheel.

Drakov's eyes were *his* eyes. It was like locking gazes with himself. His face echoed Vanna's face so strongly that Forrester kept seeing her. He kept pushing the vision away, but the thought resurfaced again and again in his mind—*I'm in deadly combat with my son, with my own flesh and blood.*

Don't think about it, he thought to himself, you'll slip,

you'll make a mistake! And, having thought about it, he made one.

He recovered in the very nick of time, blocking madly, and Drakov's blade opened up his forearm from wrist to elbow. The daggers were sharp, both at the points and on both sides of their narrow blades and the knife bit deeply. The blood flowed freely, dribbling down onto the stone floor. Forrester began to move more quickly, never staying for more than a second or two in the same spot, so that the blood would not puddle and create the danger of his slipping in it. For a brief instant, Drakov's eyes left his and glanced quickly at his wound. Forrester lunged. Too late, he saw that he had been taken in. Drakov had done it on purpose.

Already committed, Forrester tried to recover and, for a second, he was caught off balance. Drakov dropped to the floor instantly. Using his leg as a scythe, he swept Forrester's legs out from under him. As Forrester went down, Drakov rolled and in an instant he was on him, pinning him to the floor and grasping Forrester's knife hand with his own free hand while his other hand holding the knife flashed in on Forrester's throat. Forrester felt the point of the dagger penetrate the skin at the hollow of his throat ever so slightly and in that moment, a great calm swept over him and he ceased to struggle. But the white heat of the killing thrust never came.

Instead, Forrester looked up into his son's eyes and saw that they were wet with tears.

He saw the tremendous inner struggle going on as Drakov tried to will himself to finish it and found that he was unable to. He saw his son's lips begin to tremble, whether from rage, sorrow or frustration, he did not know. Perhaps it was all three.

"It's all right, Son," he said. "It's all right. I thought that I could do it, too, but now I know I never could. She never would have let us."

He let his hand go limp, opened it and the dagger rolled off his palm and onto the stone floor with a gentle clink. Slowly, Drakov got up and backed away from him, saying nothing, his tears speaking more eloquently than any words he could have said.

"Come back with me, Son," said Forrester. "You don't belong here."

Drakov shook his head violently, then turned and bolted out the door and down the stairs.

They fought fast and furiously, their sabres flashing almost quicker than the eye could follow. Hentzau was exultant, filled with seemingly boundless energy. He was in his element, fighting without the slightest care for his survival, reveling in the sheer joy of the swordplay. It was, Falcon realized, what made him such a deadly swordsman. It was one thing to train for hours, days, weeks and years on end, refining one's skill in constant practice until it was second nature, but it was something else entirely to put that skill to the test in earnest, deadly combat, where one would live and one would die. Hentzau was one of those rare people to whom it made no difference. Some people walked the razor's edge, but Hentzau fairly danced upon it. He felt himself to be almost immortal, admitting the possibility of death in only the vaguest sort of way, with supreme indifference. His life would have meant nothing to him without the chance of casually tossing it away with the same abandon with which a gambler risked all on one turn of the wheel. He quite literally did not know fear and *that* frightened her. He was better than she thought he was, far better. The better his opponent was, the better he became, rising to the occasion. It suddenly occurred to her that she could lose.

She thrust and Hentzau parried, turning her blade. She beat and riposted, using the flèche attack to drive at his face, then shifted at the last instant to his chest, but he had anticipated her. He caught her blade in a circular parry and almost hooked it out of her grasp with skillful fingerplay and easy motion of the wrist. He engaged, she disengaged, he engaged again and had her on the retreat, cutting and slashing at her while she parried madly, the sabres singing their steel song as they danced. He was laughing now, *laughing*, like a small boy balanced precariously on a rooftop, oblivious of the danger, his eyes sparkling, his teeth flashing and if this were merely practice, she would be incredibly excited by him, but the sud-

den, cold emotion of fear drove out all else. He was a primi-
tive, a damned 19th-century male and little more than a child,
at that, and he was better than she was and they both knew it.
She knew that he had staked everything on this, that he would
always put greed and ambition way above all else. He would
be merciless, just as she had been with Bersonin. In her entire
life, she had only met three men whom she could not control,
utterly and completely; Forrester was one, Drakov was another and now the third, Hentzau, whom she most belatedly
realized to be the most dangerous of them, would kill her
unless she could get away from him. One moment. One moment was all it would take to grab her remote out of her
pocket and clock herself to the chronoplate she had hidden in
the dungeon, then to safety. Only he would not give her a moment. He would not give her even so much as a second. He
was on her constantly, driving, driving, that lethal blade buzz-
ing around her like an angry hornet trying to sting. She was
beginning to grow tired and he was indefatigable.

She had only one chance, she abruptly realized. Out of the
corner of her eye, she saw Rudolf crawling towards the entrance, intent upon lowering the drawbridge. She willed him to
move faster. In his weakened condition, he seemed to be moving in slow motion, though she knew that it was only an illu-
sion created by the adrenalin coursing through her. She
wanted to shout at him to get up and run. If she could only
keep Hentzau at bay for a moment or two more, the king
would release the drawbridge, the very thing she had intended
to prevent, only now it was her only chance.

The hornet stung.

The sabre slashed her shoulder and Hentzau gave a triumphant cry at having scored the first touch. It was not a deep
wound, but it bled profusely. He was back at her again; the
clashing of the sabres reverberated through the hall. She was
no longer even trying to attack. Her one concern was to keep
him at bay just a moment or two longer. She could not let it
end like this. She could not allow herself to be killed by a mere
boy to whom this was no more than a game.

"Hah hah!" he cried, sensing victory near at hand. "I've
broken you, my dear! Where is that indomitable spirit now,

eh? Come on, come on, don't run away, have at me!''

She almost sobbed with relief when she heard the clanking of the drawbridge coming down. Almost immediately, shots were fired and she heard shouts, followed by the sound of rapidly approaching hoofbeats. Hentzau's reaction was extremely brief, just a quick glance toward the drawbridge, but it gave her time to bolt. She fumbled for her pocket as she ran, but she would have to break stride, if only for an instant, to get out the remote and Hentzau was already running after her. She swore and ran with all the speed that she could muster, through the archway to the old part of the castle, down the long main corridor with Hentzau hot on her heels. Her only chance was Drakov now. She had to reach him.

Sprinting hard, she reached the open courtyard and ran across it towards the keep, failing to increase the distance between Hentzau and herself. She kept trying to pull the remote free and she almost had it. If he would only trip, just for a moment. . . .

She ran at full speed, gasping, bolting through the entrance to the keep with Hentzau only yards behind her. She had managed to pull the remote out of her pocket finally and—the force of the impact stopped her cold for a nanosecond, then she rebounded and fell. She heard a deep grunt and realized that she had run right into Drakov. The remote was gone from her hand. She had fallen in the entrance, in clear sight of Hentzau. Drakov was on the stairs, out of his view. Hentzau stopped. As Drakov stood, she saw that he had her dropped remote held in his hand.

''Give me that!'' she said.

He held it up and looked at it, knowing it for what it was, her escape, the unit slaved to the chronoplate that she had hidden from him.

''There's no hiding in there, Sophia,'' Hentzau called. ''Come now, I thought that you were going to give me more sport than I could handle!''

''There's one man that I don't think you can walk out on,'' Drakov said.

''Nikolai, please, he'll kill me! *Please!*''

''I told you that I would see this through with you to the

end," said Drakov and she noticed for the first time that he was weeping. "I have kept my bargain. Besides, you said you didn't need me."

His thumb hit the switch.

"*Drakov, no!*"

He disappeared.

"Come on, Sophia!" Hentzau called. "Let's finish it!"

She heard shouts and the sound of hooves on stone and several horsemen galloped through the corridor into the court- yard. Sapt sat astride the lead horse, with the king holding on behind him.

"You! Hentzau!" Sapt shouted.

She shut her eyes. *Thank God*, she thought.

"No," said the king. "Let them finish. Do not interfere."

His words chilled her to the marrow. She turned and fled up the stairway to the turret. The chronoplate! There was still the plate up in the turret. If she could only reach it in time. Sud- denly she recalled that she still had the other remote. She stopped at the first landing and clawed it from her pocket.

"There's no escape, Sophia," Hentzau said.

He sounded so close that she jerked involuntarily and the remote slipped from her sweaty fingers and went bouncing down the stairs.

"*No!*" she whispered.

She looked up and he was there, mere feet away, coming up the stairs towards her and grinning a vulpine grin.

"It seems we have an audience now," he said. "I'm afraid we mustn't disappoint them."

She screamed and threw her sabre at him, then, when he flinched away from it, she leaped forward and kicked him in the chest, sending him tumbling down the stairs. She turned and flew up the stairs, taking them three at a time in a mad dash for the turret. She burst in and confronted Forrester, who was sitting on the cot with his head held in his hands.

"*Moses!*"

He looked up at her.

"Moses, *help me!* Hentzau, don't let him kill me!"

He stood up and came towards her.

"Please, Moses, I beg of you, don't let Hentzau get me!"

"All right," he said. "I won't."

He hit her with a bridgehand strike to the throat, collapsing her trachea.

Rats! The rats were everywhere! Drakov kicked out in total darkness, his boots connecting with small furry bodies that snarled and squealed and bit. Where was the plate? He had to get out! There were hundreds of them, their chittering deafening, they swarmed all over him. It had to be somewhere close by, it had to be! Filled with mindless fear, he dropped down to all fours, groping madly, tearing the rats off him, making small whimpering noises, trying to keep from screaming.

He found it! He didn't even bother to check the programmed setting. Nothing mattered more than escaping those loathesome creatures before they devoured him alive. The glow of the border circuits lit up the cell, revealing all the slithering tails, all the feral eyes and snarling mouths. He leaped into the circle screaming, beating at the beasts in an effort to dislodge them.

The circle flared. Drakov and the chronoplate clocked out to an unknown time and place. Transition was complete.

Hentzau came into the turret, sabre held ready. Falcon, the woman he had known as Countess Sophia, lay dead on the floor. He frowned and prodded her with the toe of his boot, then turned her over. He grimaced with distaste. He looked around him. The turret was empty, save for a couple of cots and several blankets and a few other odds and ends that suggested that someone had lived here for a time. Forrester had taken advantage of the chronoplate's being already set for Pendleton Base to hurriedly clock out all the weapons and equipment, leaving only seconds to spare to reset the plate for coordinates outside the castle. He had heard Hentzau's boots upon the stairs and had clocked out an instant before he came into the turret. Hentzau had been in no great hurry. He had known that there was no place she could run.

How had she died? He wondered, looking down at her, what had happened. Perhaps she had fallen on the stairs and struck her throat upon the edge of one of the steps, then managed to crawl this far. . . . He heard the sound of several pairs of footsteps coming up after him. He had helped to save the king, after all, but he wasn't certain that he could count on royal charity. The stairs led up for a short distance to the tower's summit and it was the only way left for him to go. He ran to the top of the tower and came out high atop the battlement, into the early morning sunshine. Dawn was breaking. There was nowhere to go.

"Hentzau," said a voice behind him. He turned to see Colonel Sapt standing with several of the king's men. "You're under arrest."

"What? After I saved your king?"

"If His Majesty chooses to have mercy on you, you will have to take that up with him," said Sapt. "Now come with us."

"I think not," said Hentzau. He threw his sabre at them and leaped off the tower in a graceful swan dive. Sapt and the soldiers ran to the edge and looked over in time to see him hit the moat.

"The fool," one of the soldiers said. "He's killed himself."

A moment later, they saw Hentzau surface. From far below, he looked up at them and gave them a cheery wave, then struck out for the bank. One of the soldiers aimed his rifle.

"No," said Colonel Sapt. "Let him go. It's finished now. Let the devil take his due."

EPILOGUE

It took an hour of searching, but Forrester finally found Lucas. He had collapsed some thirty feet short of the chateau at the base of a large oak. For a moment, he thought that Priest was dead, and it was with enormous relief that he saw that he was breathing. The sight of him made Forrester shut his eyes, but he knew that the injuries, the visible ones, at least, were not serious enough to be permanent. If he lived long enough to receive medical attention in Plus Time, he would be as good as before. As Forrester bent over him, Lucas opened his one eye.

" 'Lo, Moses. You're okay?"

"Yeah. I'm okay."

"Finn? Andre?"

"They took Finn back to the palace. He had a scarf tied around his face, but that may have been only to prevent the soldiers from seeing what he looked like. He seemed hurt, but he looked all right. I think he'll make it. Andre's back in Plus Time. I'll check up on Finn later. Right now, we've got to take care of you."

"The king's alive, then?"

"Yes," said Forrester. "The king's alive and well."

"The Timekeepers?"

"Falcon's dead. My son got away."

Lucas nodded. "Good. At least we didn't blow it."

"Just rest easy, kid. I'll assemble the border circuits and slide them underneath you."

Lucas nodded again. He swallowed hard. "God, I'm tired," he said. "Just want to get some sleep."

"Go ahead," said Forrester. "Lord knows, you've earned more than that."

But Lucas was already fast asleep. Forrester smiled. "Sweet dreams, soldier," he said. "You're going home. Until the next time."

Finn woke up in Rudolf's bed. His shoulder was heavily bandaged. Sapt and von Tarlenheim were standing by the bed, looking down at him anxiously. He smiled.

"Good morning," he said.

Sapt grinned. "Morning it is," he said. "You've slept through all the day and through the night. You had nightmares, but last night you broke your fever. The doctor says you will be well. The king has had him sworn to secrecy. You've done it, Cousin Rudolf. You have saved the king and you have saved the nation. We are forever in your debt."

"Think nothing of it," Finn said. "It was fun to be a king, if only for a little while."

"Heaven doesn't always make the right men kings," von Tarlenheim said, softly. Sapt glanced up at him quickly, as if he were about to reproach him, then he pursed his lips, looked down at the floor, and nodded.

"There's someone waiting to see you," Sapt said. With that, both he and Fritz turned and left the room. A moment later, Flavia came in.

"Thank God you are all right!" she said, rushing over to the bed and taking his hands in hers. "I've simply been beside myself with worry."

Finn smiled at her. "Never fear," he said. "The short stay in Michael's dungeon did little more than dampen my spirits."

"There is no point in going on with the pretense, Rudolf Rassendyll," she said. "You see, I know."

"How—"

"Rudolf and I talked all through the night. He told me everything. And I told him that you are the only man that I have ever loved. The only man that I will *ever* love."

"Flavia—"

"No, please, let me finish what I have to say and do not speak. I know that what you did, you did for Rudolf and for Ruritania. It was a very noble thing. I know that you made love to me for Rudolf, in his name and for his sake and I do not blame you for it. Rudolf, also, understands. He knows that I do not love him and he, in turn, does not love me, but perhaps, with time, we will learn to like each other; royal marriages have been made upon much less. He says that you have shown him how to be a king and he will not forget you for it. You cannot stay in Ruritania, otherwise we would both beg you to remain, but know that if you ever have need of anything, you have but to call on us and we will move heaven and earth for you. There, I have finished."

Finn took his hand away from her and touched her cheek. "Since we're being so honest with each other," he said, "I will tell you that I may have made love to you in the king's name, but I did it for my own sake."

She took his hand, turning her face into it and kissing his palm. "We will probably never see each other again," she said. "What might have been with us can never be. I will always think of you, Rudolf Rassendyll. And I wish that you would take this in remembrance of me."

She handed him a ring with the crest of her family upon it.

"Goodbye, my love," she said. "They told me I was to have only a few moments with you. They would even have denied me that, but I insisted. Time was ever our enemy."

She leaned forward, her eyes wet, kissed him briefly on the lips, then ran out of the room.

"You're right, love," Finn said to himself, feeling miserable. "Time is the enemy. Always was, always will be."

Behind a door, in a small room with no windows high atop the Headquarters Building of the Temporal Army Command, there was a collection of artifacts the like of which could not be found in any museum anywhere. Upon one wall hung a shield emblazoned with an uprooted oak. Upon another hung a surplice with the gold cross of the king's musketeers embroidered on it. In a small frame on a bookshelf, there was a lorgnette and a star-shaped red flower called a pimpernel mounted against a dark blue background. And beside this frame with the lorgnette and the flower, there was a small glass box inside which, resting on a bed of purple velvet, were two rings. One was a signet ring that had been removed from the finger of a woman who had led many lives until she had run out of lives to live. The other was a ring with the crest of an old, noble family upon it. A princess had removed it from her finger, to give to a man who cherished it, yet felt he had no right to wear it, having gained it under false pretenses.

During the quiet times, when a great wistfulness would come upon the Time Commandos, they would meet in this small room, which had once admitted only one of them. They would take their seats in the crammed quarters and Forrester would pour their wine for them while they would sit in silence, gazing at the collected artifacts. Sometimes they would smile as the memories flooded back to them.

SIMON HAWKE

THE IVANHOE GAMBIT

FIRST IN THE EXCITING NEW TIME TRAVEL ADVENTURE SERIES

TIME WARS BOOK ONE

Lucas Priest is a Sergeant Major in the US Army Temporal Corps. But fighting the Time Wars isn't an easy way to make a living – not when you have to sail with Lord Nelson, battle Custer at Little Big Horn and spend a year pillaging with Attila and his infamous Huns.

Now a demented scheme to impersonate the King of England in the twelfth century is threatening to change the course of history. Two army teams have already failed to intercept the madman.

So Lucas and his band of men clock back to try and prevent an irreversible split in time. They are the last hope for the future of the world. . .

0 7472 3059 5   £2.50

SIMON HAWKE

THE PIMPERNEL PLOT

Third in the bestselling time travel adventure series

TIME WARS BOOK THREE

Major Lucas Priest, veteran of the Time Wars, is well aware that time travel isn't simply an adventure and that one false move could change the course of history — with disastrous consequences.

The Time Commandos face the greatest challenge of their career — to readjust the events of the French Revolution and correct a blunder made by a soldier of the Temporal Corps. That error caused the death of Sir Percy Blakeney, code-name The Scarlet Pimpernel, a brave English aristocrat who rescued innocent victims from the kiss of the guillotine. Now someone must impersonate him and carry out his task.

But a double agent from the twenty-seventh century has his own diabolical ideas about how history should proceed.

Science Fiction   0 7472 3086 2   £2.50

Headline books are available at your book-shop or newsagent, or can be ordered from the following address:

Headline Book Publishing PLC
Cash Sales Department
PO Box 11
Falmouth
Cornwall
TR10 9EN
England

UK customers please send cheque or postal order (no currency), allowing 60p for postage and packing for the first book, plus 25p for the second book and 15p for each additional book ordered up to a maximum charge of £1.90 in UK.

BFPO customers please allow 60p for postage and packing for the first book, plus 25p for the second book and 15p per copy for the next seven books, thereafter 9p per book.

Overseas and Eire customers please allow £1.25 for postage and packing for the first book, plus 75p for the second book and 28p for each subsequent book.